A GATHERING OF REBELS

VOLUME 1

(Published in 2 Volumes)

By D. L. Keur, writing under the pen name E. J. Ruek:

Old Hickory Lane

To Inherit a Murderer
Book I: The Ward

Available in both print and eBook

A GATHERING OF REBELS

VOLUME 1

SPACE FICTION

BY AEROS

D. L. Keur &/or F. W. Lineberry

Sandpoint, ID

FIRST ELECTRONIC EDITION, Published on the web in monthly installments starting in 2005 at www.thedeepening.com

FIRST PRINT EDITION, Published 2014 in trade paperback

VOLUME I— ISBN-13   978-0692255698 (D. L. Keur)

ISBN-10   0692255699

VOLUME II—ISBN-13   978-0692255681 (D. L. Keur)

ISBN-10   0692255680

Artwork copyright © 2014 D. L. Keur

Cover art & design by D. L. Keur, artist, www.zentao.com

For Cheyenne Wind Ryder, who believed.

A GATHERING OF REBELS

VOLUME 1

SPACE FICTION

BY AEROS

Before…

I

SOUND….

EVEN THE MOST INFINITESIMAL VIBRATION can be detected, given the right technology. Still, silent, invisible to sensor, they wait—giant, black, funnel-ended cylinders. Just beyond is the focus of their listening: a small, haze-occluded planet.

It is a planet of fog—interminable fog—and echoes. The echoes are the lifesong of the planet's biosphere, the fog its sustenance. This is a place of knowledge, a place of peace. It is also a place of high-minded politics, its residents, the Hoy, active, interested participants in Omniversal governance.

The Hoy are very unimportant. Except now. Except for precedent. It is the politics that draws the secret listeners. And they have their answer. They have their orders.

A small, flattened diamond of a ship departs the haze. It carries the blazing emblem of a solitary, silver-white flame. As it clears the envelope of the planet's gravity to enter free space, a warble forms directly before it, and, purposely, the small ship drives for it to vanish.

Purposely, the cylinders have let the small ship go. Their focus is the planet.

From each cylinder two columns form, one of chemical, one of light. Now the planet's haze begins to roil. It condenses suddenly, shrinking inward as if consolidating, then ignites.

The echoes fail; all lifesong stops. The planet becomes a glorious burning brilliance that momentarily illuminates the horde of cylinders. Those cylinders turn and move away.

Flames fade. Fine, bright, sparkling serpentines of orange light dance across the planet's now bald surface, then slowly gutter out.

o   o   o

II

THE SEAMS OF THE NETTITE SPHERE are clearly visible in the three-dimensional semblance that hangs suspended in the flagship's holomorphic stage. Around the Sphere, station-keeping, are others of their fleet, each one black, cylindrical, funnel-ended…invisible to sensor.

The fleet's listening is complete, the decision rendered.

The crew is nervous. The regulus stands near, a member of the High Consul with him. Though he is high commander of their battle fleet, the crew is not used to the presence of the regulus on-bridge. Neither are they accustomed to presence of one of the highest ranking diplomats in the Omniverse. But this target is more serious than was the planet of the Hoy.

A tiny bright spot forms upon the sphere in the center of one of the multitudes of plates that form it. That spot looks like an eruption of molten light, but isn't. A gate is opening, and through it comes a diamond-shaped ship, a brilliant, silver-white flame emblazoned on it.

The command is given by the regulus himself. Three pulses, each a different frequency, initialize. The sphere bursts, light, debris, and atmosphere its deadly blow-out.

o   o   o

III

SILENCE.

THE MEMBERS OF THE AUDIENCE HALL JUST STARE. Some seem regretful, others thankful, that their visitor is going. Many wince at the percussive footfalls of his angry leave-taking, footsteps punctuated by the screeching of the small, winged creature that rides his shoulder ridge.

All would have voted 'yea' to the proposal their visitor had brought. Yet, they couldn't. Not after what had happened to the Hoy and to the Nettites. Freedom means nothing without life.

The chancellor stands suddenly. "Commander Pryr," she calls out to the retreating figure. "Secure Andromedan endorsement. Gain their support. Then come back. We'll join you, then."

There are agreeing murmurs all around the chamber. "We'll help you if the Altans do," the eldest member of the governmental council says. His words are spoken quietly, but carry easily to the deepest recesses of the hall.

The visitor turns, the silver-white of the flame crest on his uniform blazing in the low light at chamber's end. His yellow eyes watch them. Then, he's gone.

TWO HUNDRED TURNS HAVE PASSED since first the Omniversal League was formed. Founded on three fundamental principles—the right for all species to exist, the right to self-determination, and the right to non-interference—a consular government was empowered to administer this league. But corruption is now rampant throughout Omniversal government, an elite and lustful few beginning to own the institutions of force necessary to control many. Only the Cadre, a small, but influential group whose membership includes some of the greatest minds in the cosmos stands between oppression and preserving freedom for all kind. And the Cadre is losing.

They were a gathering of rebels
Thrown together, not by happenstance,
But by design and intrigue—
The Ben-Drom's design
And the Cadre's intrigue—
Except for one wild radical,
One unpredictable element,
Who threatened to undermine
The efforts of all sides involved,
And all because of one small minor—
A Syrene who belonged to
None other than the Ben-Drom.

They were a gathering of rebels,
Fighting one another and themselves
In a clash of titans.

o   o   o

Part I

Design & Intrigue

1

'AUDIENCE DENIED.'

THE FLATNESS OF THE TWO-D IMAGE suspended in the full-scale holomorphic conference stage only enhanced the cold finality of the message. Superimposed was the crest of the house of the Zharkahn K'har, supreme and revered leader of the ancient and powerful Altan Andromedan Empire. Moments later, the holo stage went blank.

Leon Belamy began whispering curses to the sender behind the now vanquished message. They were Andromedan curses, expertly articulated, but Belamy was completely oblivious that he so spoke. Slowly, purposefully, he removed the silver-white, flame badge that identified him Cadre. Deactivating it, he dropped it, clattering, to the surface of his console.

"What do we do, now?" Quiloc asked.

With a muttered command, Belamy turned off the com stage. "Damn K'har. *Damn* him," he said, turning to the Xentaurian High Consular who'd spoken. But his sight strayed back to the now dead stage. "Damn them *all*. Them and their elitist isolationism!"

Despite his words, Omniversal High Fleet Director Leon Belamy felt defeated. Utterly. There was nothing else that he could do. There was nowhere else to turn. The Altans had been the last hope for the Cadre, and the Cadre was the only thing standing in the way of complete capitulation of the Consul.

"I repeat: What do we do, now?" High Consul Quiloc asked again, his quiet voice firming until his soft speech became clipped and keen.

Belamy had no answer.

"Tellurian?!" Quiloc snarled, his triangular, tufted ears pinning.

Closing sore, tired eyes, Leon Belamy rubbed his brow, the retainer field that encased his body buzzing its objection to the field-on-field violation. "I don't know. I just don't know. …Pryr?" Belamy asked, raising eyes to the military end of things.

High Commander Pryr paused mid-stroke in his habitual petting of the small, lizard-like creature that was his pet, a creature that looked, except for wings and tail, exactly like him. He pulled his booted feet down from where they had been thrown up on Belamy's most expensive Naxian sculpt.

Belamy flinched as the fragile art-piece wobbled, but the Draconian steadied it with a touch of heel as he drew a hissing breath. "Without Andromedan support and endorsement, no other government will brave the potential repercussions that collusion with the Cadre could precipitate. Remember the Hoy and the Nettites. Remember the words of the Chellendites, the

Faras, and the Temz: 'Secure Andromedan endorsement. Then we can help you.'"

Shifting his pet from sinewy forelimb to rucked shoulder ridge, Pryr touched the comboard before him. Snips of recordings of his meetings began to play in quick briefs on the main stage. "You can taste their fear, even in holo," he said. "All worlds know the result to the Hoy and to the Nettites upon alliance to the Cadre. Death of one's species is too high a price to pay. Yet, without the Cadre, that is the future we all face. That, or slavery."

Turning his strange eyes toward, Pryr focused his sight on Belamy, and Belamy, who hated that gaze, felt his eyes begin to burn. "All governments have so indicated," Pryr said. "They are terrified. With cause."

Pryr's gaze compelled. Belamy found he couldn't break away.

"It is fact that, without Andromedan support, our Cadre dies," the Draco said, then pointed to the holo stage. "It is fact that the Andromedans refuse to hear us."

Finally, Pryr dropped his eye lock, his voice turning sly. "If we cannot *force* Altan listening, is it not obvious that there is little we may do except let the Cadre die a natural death?"

Then, reaching dactyls to his tunic, Pryr's horn-tipped digits closed upon his Cadre badge to tear the active flame crest from it. Belamy watched, startled as the Draco's strong, strange dactyls crumbled that badge as easily as if it were dry mud.

Agitated, Pryr's pet rustled its leathery wings and hissed into the room's sudden silence. Shushing the pet quiet, Pryr said, "We have done our best. It is over."

Quiloc flicked both ears in strong acknowledgment to Pryr's judgment. Lurad, the other member of their group, said nothing. Belamy himself felt rare anger rise in him and saw the Draconian smile—the creature actually smiled!—and Belamy realized that he'd been manipulated by the strange, hypnotically gifted alien. They all had. But the Draco's words had stirred something Belamy needed reaffirmed. He rose, locking his attention on each of his confederates in turn.

Each so different from, so alien to, the next, all of them in that room were steadfast to the Cadre cause— the black-furred felid, Quiloc, senior consul to the small but influential Xentauri system; Draconian Pryr, an arch commander in the Omniversal High Fleet of which Belamy himself was the civilian director; lastly, giant, amoeba-like Lurad, so reticent, so brilliant—Lurad whose strategies had given the Omniverse its only fighting chance in the Tornigan Wars, and who had helped bring the latest short, but fierce, civil war to a swift and successful resolution. The enlistment of each of them had been a victory for Belamy in his battle against oppression and corruption in the Omniverse. Each brought certain resources and power along with an undeniable respectability to the Cadre. All were Belamy's most trusted, even the shifty Pryr. Now Belamy stood watching them, knowing what he had there in that room, knowing what he had in the Cadre, to be valuable—a confederacy of disparate aliens genuinely committed to each other and to one cause. And he knew that, should the Cadre die, odds were that such a confederacy could never again be formed, so violent were the differences of ideology among the species in its membership.

Striding to center room, a silent Belamy let his eyes speak for him in simultaneous demand and entreaty. He hoped to force some movement, some idea, from these, his most potent advisors. Receiving none, he settled for the obvious: "Since the Cadre's inception, our ranks have swollen to include some of the highest placed diplomats, militarists, and strategists in the Omniverse."

Belamy said this to them, *of* them, and watched them all avoid his meaning. Stubbornly, he persisted. "To give it all up now just because we don't have the necessary predatory clout and buy-out credits—"

"Leon!" Quiloc interrupted, his ears flicking impatiently. "It isn't a matter of buy-out credits. The Cadre's impoverished. We have few reserves and no resources. We can't continue. Not without the Andromedans. Not without help. And the Andromedans won't hear us. It is, as Pryr says, *over.*"

Pacing now, Belamy snapped, "We have to continue. Two million independent governments depend on us. More. What *about* the Hoy and the Nettites? We owe them, their deaths, *something.* What about the very right for any of us to exist, regardless of our politics or ideologies or cultural idiosyncrasies? What about the Ideal? The Standard!?"

Belamy paused, his voice quieting. "What about all that?" he said.

Purposely, Belamy had spoken of the one thing all of them within the secret Cadre organization fought for—the right to exist, as a species and as an individual, self-determined, without interference. Purposely, Belamy chose to speak of the Standard and the Ideal—principles upon which the Omniversal League had been founded and which proved basis for all Omniversal law. Those were the principles that were being flagrantly ignored, abused, and bypassed by a corrupt and degenerative core of rich and powerful magnates, all supported by unscrupulous government mandarin, this to the affliction of the weaker, poorer, or less-influential.

The Ideal—it was a good thing to fight for, and the Cadre's roster had filled to millions in the short four ita since the alliance had first been conceived by Belamy himself, a roster that was still growing. To Belamy's words, though, once more, only silence answered.

His sight again traveling from one to the next, Belamy settled finally on the Yulandan's ambiguous form. "Lurad? Nothing to say?" he challenged.

The Yulandan's surface constricted in a squelching spasm, its jellied interior briefly turning from clear amber to a pale shade of embarrassed lavender. But the being, Lurad, remained mute.

Returning to his conference console, Belamy sat and averted his face from them. He couldn't let go of it. Equally, he couldn't hold the Cadre together by himself. No one of them could. "The scymied Droms won't even *hear* us!" Belamy snapped, erupting suddenly and savagely, his voice still low, but seething, now. He slapped a hand down on the console, the sound explosive.

All bodies, except Pryr's, jumped. All biofields flared, coloring violently. …Except Pryr's.

"Not so much as a preliminary audience!" Belamy erupted, again. "Damn them! *DAMN* them! It's not like they don't hold the very same convictions we—"

"Tellurian Leon Belamy."

The words resonated, their peculiar timbre sending a thrill of hope through Belamy. He looked to the Yulandan, surprised that it had finally deigned to speak. "Lurad," Belamy acknowledged. But Belamy's initial eagerness was tempered now with more than a trace of anxiety. Lurad's counsel was consequent, and the Yulandan's insides had shifted to a transparent indigo that did not bode well.

"There is another way to gain audience with the Altan Andromedans." That was all Lurad said, its vocal construct contracting to meld into its wet-looking, slippery surface as spontaneously as it had appeared. And, though all sight in the room was focused on it, waiting, the Yulandan did not immediately speak again. Instead, Lurad seemed to turn inward as if deciding, as if weighing, something, its various bubbled internal paraphernalia retreating to its center.

It was Pryr who broke the silence. "Explanation, Lurad?" he requested.

The Yulandan's construct formed again. "It would be very risky."

"How risky?"—Quiloc.

"Perhaps deadly to all involved," the Yulandan replied. "To the Cadre itself. Andromedans deal remorselessly with those who threaten…." Lurad paused, seemed to reconsider, then said, "Altan Andromedans deal remorselessly with those who *assault* their own."

Draconian Pryr cocked an eye-ridge, the diamond forecrease between his brows sharpening as a small, calculating smile began to form around his so thin mouth. "*Assault*, Lurad?" he hissed softly. "What *do* you contemplate?"

"A moment, please," the Yulandan said. And its vocal construct again vanished, this time permanently, as extensions of itself began to spread themselves across the face of a large, round object the Yulandan readily extruded from somewhere inside its languid, lambent body. When it had finally finished, it shared.

Belamy whistled. Pryr grinned wickedly. Quiloc shook his head, ears flattening in consternation. "The Ben-Drom," Belamy whispered. "The Andromedan Bjen Dvorkahn."

It would be dangerous. Andromedans were ruthless. But the plan made sense. The idea touched something deep inside of Belamy, and he smiled. Abruptly, he began to laugh. The Cadre had asked K'har, the Zharkahn of Andromeda, for audience. Now it would demand.

o o o

2

REPEATEDLY, PERSISTENTLY, one large, multi-cambered dactyl reached. Each time that dactyl reached, the hint of something dark and shiny protruded a little more from its long, thick, terminal segment until a saber-like length of hard, sharpened curve was bared.

Now it was the tip of that blade-like curve that reached repeatedly, insistently—reached to touch clear an invasive image that kept superimposing itself over the names, ranks, and service classifications of the High Fleet personnel listed on the comstage before it.

Annoyingly, the invasive image kept returning.

With a bellowed oath, Regulus Primus Ben-Drom canceled power to the comstage, terminating all possible access to it and to the mainframe computer that controlled it. Then, he engaged a special high-security lock-out to all com access ports within his residence.

Waiting the few itat necessary to satisfy himself that the lock-out was complete, the Ben-Drom again extruded a talon to touch the maincom's liquid input plate and reinitiate his construct. Instantly, that comstage exploded, shattering into a million nano-bits of morpholumenotropic holo medium, the cold, opalescent shards spraying across the Ben-Drom's face and torso.

Sprung to standing with every talon fully extruded, the Ben-Drom barely managed to smother the roar of outrage that had risen from his gut to his throat as he recognized the formidable and intimidating visage that began to form before him. Shaking himself clear of the once more liquid holo slag, the Ben-Drom let his talons retract to half as was respectful before his sire...before the Zharkahn K'har, omnipotent leader of his kind.

"K'har," the Ben-Drom said, his deeply basso voice subdued. "Kr'eiheit mo'ob."

"K'heirisat, Bjen Dvorkahn," the Zharkahn answered, calling the Ben-Drom by his formal title. Then, K'har began to speak. He brought warning.

THE BEN-DROM SAT STARING at the solid icon of the Zharkahn's personal crest. It hovered in the exact place that K'har's stern and uncompromising face had been but moments before. The light from that bright, self-illuminated morph reflected off the various globed and rod-like surfaces of library data-base that formed the interior of the Ben-Drom's large, working office. It reflected off the Ben-Drom's bronze-brown hide.

The Ben-Drom rarely paid heed to any warnings of conspiracy against him as the Zharkahn's heir. He rarely paid heed to anything politically provoked, except as it affected his purposes in fulfilling his own objectives, objectives which had nothing to do with becoming zharkahn. But, this time, the Ben-Drom paused from immediately dismissing K'har's warning.

The Ben-Drom knew his sire to be always reasonable, his rationales sound, his concerns never idle. That this warning had not been as every other, a cursory notification, that K'har had personally delivered it utilizing overburden transponders to breach the Ben-Drom's heavy security lock-out, showed the Ben-Drom that K'har was genuinely worried. Andromedans especially respected another's—any other's— privacy. Only extreme urgency could justify such trespass as K'har had effected. Therefore, the warning had merit.

Yet, K'har had told the Ben-Drom little, just that there could be danger to him and to his fleet from some clandestine organization called the Cadre whose aim was ostensibly like all others: to free the Omniverse of all oppression. This Cadre had sought an audience of K'har and had been denied it, and it was K'har's opinion that they were desperate enough to attempt forced persuasion or retaliation.

Of whom and where—the identities of its most powerful members and its operations bases—K'har claimed to know little, dismissing all of the Ben-Drom's questions with a cursory wave of heavily taloned mitt. "It matters not," K'har had said. "You would but scoff." One thing was certain, though: K'har seemed to think that this Cadre was authentic in its goals.

The Ben-Drom *had* scoffed at that. Liberation was the tired battle cry used to legitimate every bigoted or self-serving purpose in the cosmos, from imperialistic expansion to outright genocide. He had said as much to K'har.

"Be that as it may," K'har had answered. "That is my judgment, and, as well you know, the authentic is often powerful. Protect yourself. Protect your fleet." K'har had said that, showing the direction he deemed the attack could take, which was all the Ben-Drom really needed to know. His fleet he could and would protect against any and all who coveted it and its extraordinary technology.

"They will take neither I, nor my fleet," the Ben-Drom muttered. "This I swear, K'har." And the Ben-Drom's fisted mitt crashed against the console of his maincom, the action startling the silent Syrene who played nearby as the blow shattered the still extant, solid icon of K'har's personal crest. With that oath, the Ben-Drom dismissed the warning and the Zharkahn's visit from his thoughts to return, once more, to his lists.

The Ben-Drom was driven—driven by a memory and a promise—and, because he was the Bjen Dvorkahn, he knew he had to fulfill his own goals before the Zharkahn K'har succumbed to final metamorphosis. The Ben-Drom didn't have time to dwell upon the constant stream of threats to him and his. He had his own worries, his own agenda, and, presently, that was finishing the crew rosters for his new battle fleet, a task to which he had been assiduously applying himself when the Zharkahn's visit had interrupted him. And he was almost done, the final lists ready and only awaiting transfer from maincom to datasphere.

Touching in a command, the Ben-Drom initiated that transfer, and, instants later, the last of his work was appended to Fleet-appropriate record, the small, archaic dataspheres that contained the culmination ejecting from the maincom's synthesizing mechanism. Now, all that remained necessary for launch was to validate that record and collect his personnel.

o   o   o

3

THE CADRE CONFERENCE was showing signs of ending, and, still, High Consul Quiloc was not convinced. Though Lurad had completely and thoroughly explained the plan, and it seemed solid, Xentauri Quiloc didn't like the feel of it. He said as much, and the other Cadre members, even Pryr, listened respectfully to his objections.

"What about just asking the Ben-Drom for his help in gaining audience with the Zharkahn?" Quiloc asked finally. "K'har is, after all, his base progenitor."

Belamy nodded, a distinctly patronizing look descending his naked face. It was a face Tellurians adopted when, perceiving themselves superior, they were "practicing" patience. Though Quiloc didn't like it, he squelched his urge to swat the insolence away— useless in virtual and decidedly against all protocol.

"I asked the Ben-Drom to get me an audience with K'har," Belamy said, "long before formally presenting the petition to the Altans. You can guess the outcome." Belamy dropped his voice down a register in imitation of the Ben-Drom's guttural rumble. "'Well do you know that I concern myself not with your petty maneuvering and politics, Fleet Director Belamy.'"

Belamy began to chuckle, his mimicry turning satirical. "Actually, he said 'Fleet Director *Tellurian* Leon Belamy.' And that should show you, Quiloc, knowing him as well as you do, just how testy he got to the suggestion."

What he considered to be Belamy's second bit of insolence—the mocking of the Ben-Drom—Quiloc also ignored. "Kidnapping the Andromedan crown prince, its 'bjen dvorkahn', is no different than attacking the Zharkahn himself," Quiloc said. "…Which is no different than attacking the Empire itself. And, as you well know, Altan Droms don't negotiate with what they consider to be terrorists."

Quiloc addressed the whole group, rising to take virtual center floor. "On principle alone, the Andromedans will come after us. And not to talk. With no consideration whatsoever for the consequences to the Ben-Drom. That's the way they are."

Quiloc was expert in Altan Andromedan culture and ethos, and it was this knowledge he used to push his objections. "They won't try to rescue the Ben-Drom," he said. "They won't negotiate. They will attack us, though—immediately—and the Ben-Drom will welcome their death strikes, glorifying in them, if he hasn't succumbed to suicide by then."

"That is one thing," Pryr said, nodding. "We will have to pinion the Ben-Drom and immobilize his talons to prevent such self-kill."

Quiloc scrowled at the Draconian, but before he could snap reply, Lurad swelled, formed, and spoke in one spontaneous action. "We recognize all that you say, High Consul Quiloc.   But, please remember, Altan

Andromedans are tactical and strategic geniuses. Their logic is impeccable. Only once all reasonable avenues are negated do they resort to violence. With Altan Andromedans, emotion always comes as enhancement to, rather than cause of, action."

"Lurad's right, Quiloc," Belamy broke in. "There's nothing—"

"...And," Lurad continued, interrupting Belamy's interruption, "we give them perfect and reasonable solution. We do not demand their support. We simply ask them but to listen to us in return for the release of their bjen dvorkahn and his fleet."

Lurad paused, reduced both his size and his vocalization to normal, then spoke again. "It is the fleet and its many personnel the Zharkahn will think of before loosing his shierka hordes upon us. Altans do not lightly take the lives of the innocent bystander, especially when such innocents are out-kind species."

Ears flicking back and forth in surprise at Lurad's uncharacteristic forcefulness, then, making note of the discrepancy for future analysis, Quiloc accepted both the "unnatural" dominance and the "normal" timidity as being, either one, just more of the Yulandan's tactics. "And what about the Ben-Drom fleet, Lurad?" Quiloc asked.

Quiloc greatly respected the Yulandan's strategies, but hijacking a fleet of battle translights—cardinal to the plan—would, to Quiloc's thinking, be nearly impossible, especially since the Ben-Drom's new fleet was fitted, at least in part, with superior Andromedan technology. He mentioned this, listing the precautions in place aboard standard High Fleet translights to prevent just such a possibility. "You would have had difficulty hijacking the fleet I commanded during the Tornigan Wars, even one ship. I don't see how we can bypass what's rumored as fitted to this Drom-designed fleet."

"This has been explained, High Consul Quiloc," Pryr hissed.

Quiloc bristled, and Belamy, unofficial keeper-of-the-peace, visually warned Pryr silent, then leaned toward where Quiloc's holomorph stood. "With Pryr established as fleetmaster and the Cadre liege we plant in the Ben-Drom's crews, there should be no problem. Lurad's plan covers every contingency. If we follow it, our complete control of both the fleet and its personnel is ensured."

At home on Xentauri, Quiloc moved to the lone window of his office suite to look out at the night. In the conference room at Iban, his holomorph followed suit, the computer adjusting and compensating for all disparity. Quiloc was not convinced. Quiloc was worried. He had a bad feeling in his gut about the whole thing, but it was a feeling that he had no logical basis for. The plan was solid.

Looking back to the group, Quiloc saw that all of them watched him. They were waiting for his verdict. Each of them had to approve the plan. Each one was to be assigned his part and tasks, and, of them, Quiloc's were the most critical, the most involved. His part was crucial. And not only because he was to be the Cadre's chief negotiator with the Zharkahn K'har, but because he had been, both, a well-respected High Fleet battle commander as well as Belamy's immediate predecessor as High Fleet Director. It would be his influence that would convince the High Command Crew Requisition Board to substitute Cadre personnel in the Ben-Drom's crews.

"What is your true objection, Xentauri Consul Quiloc?" Lurad asked.

Quiloc turned away again, shaking his head, ears pinned flat. He had finally isolated what disturbed him. He was afraid for himself and his kind. Of all of them, he, because of his lofty political position, had the most to lose by the plan's failure. Presently, his home system held good position. Should he be prematurely identified as part of the conspiracy to destroy the power brokers who were steadily and surely gaining control of the Omniverse, there was the potential that Xentauri could be attacked before it could get its defenses up. Yet the Cadre was the only hope to save the Omniverse, and the reality was that the Cadre, which cause Quiloc wholly believed in and supported, was dying. In fact, at the beginning of this conference, once the Altans had denied audience, Quiloc had thought it irrevocably dead. This was, truly, the Cadre's only chance.

Taking a breath of clear Xentauri air, Quiloc savored the taste of it in his pre-lungs before assimilating it. He alone was afraid to risk. He alone held back this last effort to save the Cadre. And there was a way to preserve Xentauri, though not his own life, nor his family's exalted position in Xentauri society. …He could protect his family's lives, though.

Hissing to himself in anger born of his disgust at circumstances, High Consul Quiloc stepped back amongst his compatriots. Reseating himself, he flicked an ear, then smiled his crooked smile, one canine glinting rakishly. "Damn the doubts," he snarled.

o   o   o

4

HIS LONG TALONS CAREFULLY RETRACTED, the Regulus Primus
Omega Ben-Drom, highest ranking active field officer in
the Omniversal High Fleet, picked up the archaic
datasphere that contained his final crew roster and began
to place his seal upon it, the stiff, calloused tips of his
dactyls clumsy in the effort. Dataspheres were not well-
designed for Andromedan manipulations, and the Ben-
Drom grumbled in himself in his frustration, irritated at
the necessity of using quaint and inadequate Fleet
technology. He persevered, however, until the seal was
finally set on the absorption relic. Done, he placed that
datasphere alongside two others, both similarly sealed,
shut down the maincom, then sat back, his body
slumping with fatigue.

His head was throbbing painfully, his eyes burning
beneath their shields with the intense strain of having
spent the last quintitar selecting personnel for his new
battle fleet. The work had taken full toll: the Ben-Drom
was exhausted.

Snarling a command, the Ben-Drom ordered the
environmental controls to darken the already dim
chamber to almost void blackness. His sight safe from
light, he stripped off his eyeshields to scratch at all the
itchy places where the eyeshields adhered beneath his
knurled browplate, then began to rub the groove of

sulcus that ran between the two lobes of his immense, bi-hemisphered cranium.

He was stiff, and he was sore—so sore that, when he moved to stand, the vesicles that covered his bronze-brown body from head to plantars began to turn from rust to orange with the beginnings of a pain-induced venom flow. And the Ben-Drom realized that he had sat too long, that the lubricants within the iridescent, pearl-white stringing that overlay every moveable portion of his body had gelled.

Beginning to rub that stringing, he tried to work the fluids within the stringings' sheaths to normal viscosity again. He rubbed the cam joints that underlay that stringing, too, the edges of his talons working deep into the seams. And, all the while, the Ben-Drom yearned for Ka and his blissful ministrations. He carefully masked that wish, however, for fear the super-sensed magus would ken his wish and respond.

To the Ben-Drom's mind, he depended upon his friend too much…beside the fact that, upon seeing his fatigue, Ka would insist upon his swallowing of one those horrible elixirs the magus was always forcing down him whenever Ka deemed him physically distressed. And the Ben-Drom was always physically distressed in one way or another, mainly because of his size.

Huge of body—bigger and more heavily armor-plated than any Altan ever to have metamorphosed—the Ben-Drom was the pride of his species. He was that now, though it had not always been so. In pre-petrilarval, he had been subject to every ridicule and cruelty the more normal of his stage of species could invent. Because of that, the Ben-Drom had long ago spurned his kind and sought a life beyond Altan Andromedan society. It was a course which had led him, for various reasons, to become entrapped, conscripted to the Omniversal High Fleet through a betrayal by one who had once been closest friend—a friend who was now a Fleet superior, the High Fleet Director, Leon Belamy. Presently locked into completing his service, the Ben-Drom endured, instead of Andromedan rancor and prohibitions, a Fleet bureaucracy of regulation and policy that constrained him and his private purposes at every turn.

Fighting against what he considered to be mindless and, in many cases, destructive, the Ben-Drom had set himself against that huge Fleet bureaucracy and had won—won, at least, small victories, one of which included convincing Fleet hierarchs to allow him to use a personally-owned, Andromedan-built fleet of seventy-five ships for the remaining tenure of his service obligation—a fleet only contracted to, not owned by, the Omniverse.

Having managed that, and with his fleet's construction almost done, the Ben-Drom had engaged in personally selecting every one of the personnel he needed to staff it. That was finished now, the requisitions, in the form of those black, sealed dataspheres, ready for delivery to FleetCom, the Omniversal High Fleet Central

Command Complex—personal delivery. The Ben-Drom would deliver them himself.

Turning to his two silent companions, the Ben-Drom waited for a natural pause in their game-playing. The Syrene were peaceful and absorbed, their softly photoluminescent bodies beautiful against the chamber's darkness. Always intrigued by them, the Ben-Drom watched as the elder one's long, fine, strand-like tactiles seemed to dance as it directed in intricate patterns the glowing globes that were game-pieces, made by its own forming, for the contest. The smaller Syrene, still a minor and in natural form, bobbed in and out, avoiding globes of certain colors while catching others of different hue to send them back against its opponent.

The Ben-Drom watched them thus for fully one-fifth decitar, but there seemed to be no imminent pause, and, while the Ben-Drom didn't want to disturb them, disturb them he must. "Sitad," the Ben-Drom grumbled softly to the eldest.

The Syrene significant paused the game. The mobile globes momentarily became suspended as it turned huge, matte, grey-black orbitals to the Ben-Drom, silver lights inside those orbs still sparkling its pleasure. Those silver lights were a rare thing for the Ben-Drom to see, and he felt privileged.

The lights in the Syrene's orbitals immediately vanished, though, and Sitad's affected, obovate face with its false nasal ridge and useless slit of mouth became staid and serious. "Master," it said, its speaking a deeply sonorous emanation that seemed to vibrate the very room itself, even its darkness, as it resonated forth from the Syrene's whole being.

Inside himself, the Ben-Drom withered as the Syrene's orbitals dulled. Sitad never shared itself with him as it did with Ka, and the Ben-Drom knew not why. But it hurt him—desperately. "Do not so call me your master, Sitad," the Ben-Drom said, his voice catching at the phrase in his unhappiness.

"Yes, Ben-Drom."

Syrene Sitad was so stoic with him…. The Ben-Drom drew a heavy breath, then forced himself to the blank neutrality he'd been taught. "Prepare the Sheeta, Sitad," the Ben-Drom said. "We fly to Ivalan, the planet Iban."

"As you wish," Sitad replied, ending the game of floating lights with a dispersing flick of its tactiles, then rising, its long, informal pale-green robe rustling faintly with its so smooth movements. The minor Syrene, still shapelessly natural as Sitad was not, presently withdrew, blinking out to elsewhere—to the Syrene habitat built beneath his residence, the Ben-Drom guessed. "Do you wish Ka?" Sitad queried.

The Ben-Drom reared his head to negative. "No. We need not trouble him. We will to Ivalan alone."

But, even as the Ben-Drom spoke, the being, Ka, appeared, accompanied by the Sier, a hovering, expansive, flowing gilt of warping energy. "No, Lord. You do not to Ivalan without me," said Ka, his gaunt, sallow, anthropoidal face a study of moving shadows as he fixed still, fully void-black eyes critically upon the Ben-Drom.

The Ben-Drom scowled, trying desperately to hide his pleasure as he squinted against the Sier's light. Then, retrieving his cast-off eyeshields, he gave up the farce and let his face draw down into a grin. "Do you use your magus ways against me, Ka, harkening to my very thoughts? ...Or does this, my trusted Sitad, alert you to my intent?"

The magus-warrior, Ka, friend and self-appointed guardian to the Ben-Drom, cast his eyes aside for just an instant before replying, "No, Lord. It was the minor's return that warned me."

Acknowledging the explanation, the Ben-Drom sideslipped his big head just a little in acceptance, but, beneath his shields, his chatoyant red eyes glimmered with suspicion. "Hmrr," he muttered, and, again, a smile drew down his lipless mouth.

"My leave, Ben-Drom," Sitad said, bowing its large head, the fake shackle that encircled its neck-like lumenals shimmering with reflections of the golden glow of the Sier's presence.

The Ben-Drom cast his head again, this time in assent to the Syrene, and Sitad vanished. Once the Syrene had gone, the Ben-Drom rose to face his closest friend and only trusted confidante. "Ka, I would have you convince Sitad that it need not seek permission of me for its every move."

Ka's angled brows rose. "It must maintain the semblance, Lord. Else would bring it notice and, therefore, danger. What would come of it…what would then become of any of your Syrene were they discovered to be entires, whole and of complete intelligence?"

A grumble was the Ben-Drom's irked response to that. "As you say, Ka. But it vexes me, as does the shackling."

"The shackling is forged and fraudulent."

"It still angers me."

The Ceoheician nodded patiently. "Laws of the domain, Lord—laws which even you cannot evade. Circumstances exist as they must—the shackling and the affectations of servility. Why do we to Ivalan?"

"I go to see that scoundrel Belamy and other offices of Fleet. It is Fleet business, Ka. There is no need that you accompany."

"No need, perhaps, but what of choice, Lord? My choosing." And, here, the Ceoheician let his horn-like head-crests rise just momentarily in emphasis. It was a mild and teasing warning.

"Do not so call me, Ka. I am neither yours, nor any's lord," the Ben-Drom growled, then purposefully sighted the beautiful, if dangerous, raptorial energy sentient that hovered beside the magus. "What of the Sier?"

Ka bowed his head just slightly. "It, likewise, will accompany, if such is acceptable. It misses its own realm and has need of our companionship."

Instantly, the Ben-Drom's head reared to negative, then stopped short. "Well enough," he agreed, feigning a reluctance that he did not feel as he let his sight drift over the marvelous creature. "But it cannot accompany within that form."

In truth, it was not safe for the Sier to accompany at all. It would not do for others to know of it—not yet. It was the Ben-Drom's secret, its existence not to be exposed until time was ripe to shatter the ancient prejudices that enslaved such species as the Syrene.

Immediately, the entity in question consolidated itself, collapsing in and on itself until just the smallest gleam of intense golden sparkle remained visible. Once stable, the glimmer shot a ray out toward the Ben-Drom, momentarily engulfing him. And the tittering question: *"Is this more to your mega-highness's liking, Bjen Dvorkahn?"* echoed through the Ben-Drom's being.

The ray dispersed as quickly as it had formed, and the Ben-Drom chuckled. "It is sufficient, Sier…provided that you do not likewise bathe some unsuspecting in similar manner."

The gilt glint twinkled; then, subsiding, retreated toward Ka where it buried itself within the fabric of the magus' coarse, black, woven robing.

Sitad appeared beside just then, blinking into being just long enough to advise ship readiness, only to immediately disappear once more. The Ben-Drom frowned. Sitad was his finest, most cherished Syrene, and he was fortunate it had decided to accompany him (though the act of removing it from its home nebula had been, in principle—at least to Altan thinking—theft). But for all Sitad's superb skills, talents, and intellect, it was no Raganth, and it was a Syrene of Raganth's rare type that the Ben-Drom coveted. It was a Syrene identical to Raganth that the Ben-Drom needed, in conjunction with the Sier, to fulfill his life's ambition, to fulfill the vow he'd made to himself and to the dead Raganth so long ago as he'd knelt beside Raganth's shattered husk.

He would free them all—all Syrene—and never again see them stripped, their brains destroyed for fear, their remnant bodies shackled and conformed for mere utility's sake, "safe," mindless tools for interspacial travel between universes. The Ben-Drom would see the Syrene free, and, to do it, he needed, not only his fleet and the Sier, but a Syrene as powerful, as evolved, as Raganth had been. To find one, though….

The Ben-Drom had spent ita looking for a Syrene of Raganth's rare subtype, both in the Fleet's Syrene auction complexes and within the poacher markets, but never again had one been captured. He had looked, and he'd had others looking. He hadn't looked lately, though. Not lately. He'd been too busy fighting Fleet bureaucracy.

He really didn't have the credits to spend on one, not with the costs of building his new fleet. But, then, he couldn't afford not to spend if a minor of Raganth's rare type did surface. And the Ben-Drom had a feeling, though he knew his feelings rarely bore good fruit without a heavy price.

"Ka," the Ben-Drom said. "Fetch a containment pod."

Again Ka's angled brows rose, this time steeply. "Lord?"

"I am of a mind to visit the auctions, Ka. …Perchance a minor of Raganth's variety."

And Ka, a magus, sensitive and sighted, felt foreboding rise in him.

o   o   o

5

THE BEN-DROM'S UNANNOUNCED ARRIVAL at FleetCom did, in fact, rattle High Command bureaucrats. It especially rattled Leon Belamy who was just emerging, Lurad and Pryr with him, from the failed conference with the Zharkahn K'har and subsequent Cadre planning session. Hearing the Ben-Drom's distinctive booming bellow reverberating through the maze that was the upper level of the FleetCom edifice, Belamy visibly blanched. He hurried into Lurad's lift which whisked them both away to some harbored elsewhere.

While Belamy chose to hide, high commander Megan Primus Kathon Pryr strolled down-corridor to find the source of those bellows. Following the percussion waves the Ben-Drom's eruptions were causing in the universal respiratory medium, Pryr rounded a curve, then settled to lean against the corridor's wall. Thus comfortable, he watched the Andromedan who was to be the Cadre's target, unaware that he himself was being watched by the Ben-Drom's Ceoheician paladin.

The Ben-Drom was beleaguering a quint of varied-species High Fleet administrative regulus commanders who had been luckless enough to be caught loitering by the big Altan. Chuckling to himself, Pryr watched those regulus shrink and shuffle, each in their own unique way, as the Ben-Drom verbally flagellated them for their shiftlessness.

The fact that the Drom was center-target in his censure made Pryr's pleasure all the more. If the Ben-Drom wasn't destined to become Cadre bait to trap the Andromedan Zharkahn, Pryr could easily have persuaded himself to pledge himself and his loyalty to the bestial Altan and his new fleet.

That the Ben-Drom was notorious for his audacity and daring in combat, that the Ben-Drom never backed away from conflict—not ever—Pryr admired. Had it not been for the Cadre, Pryr, who relished action, who savored risk, and who deeply appreciated efficiency, would have gladly cast his destiny with that of the Omega Ben-Drom's whose commands were conspicuously the most operationally excellent and always seemed in the pivotal midst of the most perilous situational encounters in the Omniverse. That luxury, however, would not be Pryr's with the Cadre operation now planned. Even were the Andromedans to agree to support the Cadre, the Ben-Drom would not suffer him a post—not after Pryr had deceived him. Pryr would have to be satisfied with this one ride only under the Altan's command.

And, in that moment, watching the formidable Drom, Pryr vowed to enjoy the coming contest to the outermost limits. He would have to, because, regardless the outcome of this ride, the Ben-Drom would ensure that Pryr's career in Fleet was finished.

Again, a quiet chuckle escaped Pryr's thin mouth. Yes, he would enjoy matching wits against such a heady opponent, even if it meant his premature retirement to some private service.

"Your laughter at those regulus' misfortune under the Ben-Drom's rage is unbecoming of such a handsome Draconian, Megan Primus Pryr."

Pryr leisurely reached to stroke his dragonet as he cast an eye to his censor. He said nothing.

"…But it is typical of you and *your* kind."

Pryr bowed his head ingratiatingly. "Thank you, Metan Matac. You, likewise, hold a tongue that is truly representative of your Xentauri kind—a rasp to everything it touches."

"Crrr," the Xentaurian she-queen responded, her amber eyes smiling at him.

Unlike Quiloc who was Verdajan, Matac was of the little-known Nadejan sub-type of Xentauri—a slightly less civilized, slightly more archaic, and definitively wilder variety of the species. Pryr liked her.

Matac flicked an ear toward the disturbance. "What holds your interest in this?" she asked. "…Besides your obvious pleasure at others' agony."

Pryr laughed outright. Then, tasting opportunity, he eyed the golden, cat-like she. Matac was High Fleet Special Operations—one of its top agents. Some even dared say she was better than the illustrious Draconian Gor had been before he'd been so grievously wounded that he'd had to take a posting in the regular forces.

Pryr doubted that Matac was better than Gor, either because of Draconian pride or because of his innate skepticism, but he did admire Matac's abilities. Best, Matac was a Cadre insider. Gor was also Cadre, but he was completely and understandably loyal to the Ben-Drom.

Casually brushing his weapons-harness, Pryr touched on a device there, setting off an interference wave that would disrupt building security within the corridor enough to mask his words and fields, yet not disrupt it enough to be taken for anything more than simple technical difficulties in the system. He watched, then, as Matac dropped her head in understanding and reinforced the effect with a touch to a similar device she wore. "Are you between assignments?" Pryr asked once Matac signed them safe from sensor.

The Xenti arched a brow, the long follicle cresting that brow quivering just slightly. "Why do you ask?"

Pryr grinned. "Do you see that Andromedan?" At Matac's ear twitch, he said, "It would be good for the Cadre cause were he watched for opportunity."

"And should opportunity present itself?" Matac answered softly.

"Delivery to safe-holding."

The furry nodded.

"Knowledge of his new fleet's security codes would be fortuitous," Pryr added.

"What you suggest will not be easy," Matac replied. "That Drom is shrewd, his security the best."

Pryr knew that. He knew what he asked of her to be nearly impossible. He kept watching her.

Presently, Matac inclined her head. "I will do my best," she said, then cocked an ear, this time toward where the Ben-Drom, finished finally with the regulus bureaucrats, was entering a farther office. "He is prone to stress illness. It brings him to more carelessness."

It was Matac's hint to him. "I trust your judgment in such matters," Pryr said, smiling. "Take all license."

Matac's brows rose. Her ears came stiffly upright. "You wish him alive?"

Startled, Pryr stared at her. "He is to remain alive and unharmed," Pryr said, realizing he had erred in his use of the term 'all license' to one of Matac's training.

"Currur, Megan Primus Pryr," Matac replied, almost purring. "Then so it shall be done. It will make the game so much more interesting."

◦   ◦   ◦

6

JUST AS THE BEN-DROM'S SURPRISE VISIT had disrupted FleetCom, so did it disrupt Fleet Academy's Syrene Auction Complex. Altan Andromedans were rare visitors to Galaxy Ita, central administrative and geopolitical core of the Omniverse. Even those few like the Ben-Drom who called Ita temporary home were reclusive to an excess. Therefore, the appearance of one, especially one of the Ben-Drom's notorious stature, caused much stir.

Upon the Ben-Drom's arrival at the auction center, unctuous attendants immediately surrounded, all of them anxious to serve the Ben-Drom's every need, not so much because the Ben-Drom was feared—which he was—but because he was thought to be scandalously rich—which he was—though the Ben-Drom never thought himself as such.

With an eye for the Ben-Drom's safety as well as comfort, the Ceoheician, Ka, stepped between the Ben-Drom and the sycophants, letting his black, shiny, sheethair-covered crests rise to their steepest until they looked to be fused, curl-back horns. Immediately, most of the would-be attendants retreated, Ka's mere presence enough discouragement. The obstinate few who remained dispersed soon after when the ever-silent Ka faced them down, his pale-skinned hands beginning to emanate a cold, green fire.

"You need not frighten them of their very wits, Ka," the Ben-Drom remonstrated. "They only do what is natural to them at the bidding of their overseers." But, despite his protest, the big Drom chuckled. Before Ka, he had always had to suffer the persistent pestering that Ka's presence now discouraged. For that, he was unceasingly grateful to the magus. Sad as it was, it was useful to him that Ka's kind were despised and feared by most, considered to be evil ones of daimon nature and origin.

Clear of the scavengers now, the Ben-Drom easily made his way to the sale registrar's office, there to identify himself as potential buyer. A young, multi-limbed Durav, who was too obviously an out-cross misconception, labored there. The Ben-Drom waited until the mule-female clerk finally completed what was to her an arduous task—ordering a phonic sequence of identification tags.

Finally she looked up, her artificial sight enhancements apprehending him. She also apprehended Syrene Sitad who was standing near. The clerk's biofields flashed excitement. Every ownership transfer of Syrene netted profit, and all auction personnel were urged to push for them. New to her post and, therefore, ignorant of the Ben-Drom, she asked if he wished to consign Sitad as she handed him a quota of magnetic tokens with which to identify Syrene he wished to bid upon. "You should get a good price for such a fine specimen," she said.

Glowering, the Ben-Drom said, "*No.*"

The registrar flinched, and, stammering, tried to redeem herself, but the Ben-Drom pivoted, derisively turning his back upon her, and strode off.

Barely able to tolerate the manner of handling of Syrene within the auction complex, the Ben-Drom could less tolerate the attitude that abounded here. Legitimate Syrene auctions were supposedly civilized affairs, but, to Altan sensibilities, especially the Ben-Drom's, they were barbaric. Treated like commodities, the Syrene to be auctioned were categorized according to development and, while entire, according to type, then closely confined to individual cylinders that lined the auction center's many isles. There was no chance to commune with them, or for the individualities to be discerned of what few entires there were. Hence, it was rare for the Ben-Drom to visit the auctions, preferring, instead, to buy from his favorite dealers on the raider's market and one or two hunters.

But the dealers' stock had been lacking, and the hunters had been notably absent or idling as was their wont when they had profited overmuch and hunting was slow. Therefore had it been fully three-quints of a turn since last the Ben-Drom had added to his Syrene inventory, an inventory of growing natural minors and unadulterated significants kept more as a preserve than for utility. With a mind to both ends, the Ben-Drom began to examine the Academy's offerings.

There were, of course, thousands of Syrene encasements within the sterile aisles of the auction center's massive lower level, but most all of them were filled with devoids being sold for one reason or another by their owners. Devoids, however, were not the Syrene the Ben-Drom pursued. He sought newly captured minors—entire minors—those that had not yet been stripped of their base encephalon. Finding the section devoted to them, the Ben-Drom walked amongst their tiny cylinders.

Most were already undergoing conforming by the fine filamentary latticework of techtronic mesh designed to permanently alter their natural configuration once they were stripped devoid. There were some Syrene minors, however, that retained their natural amorphous shapes—mostly the common and less evolved Beta types that were considered to be next to harmless, even when entire. While all of them caught at the Ben-Drom's sympathy, he was only looking for particular varieties, and so tried to inure himself against thinking of the minors' plight.

Coming upon several that, though not of Raganth's rare type, were, nevertheless, of the scarce and gifted Xi type like Sitad, the Ben-Drom placed tokens upon their capsules. Reaching the end of the section, the Ben-Drom turned to Ka, his despair at not finding anything more, clearly evident. "I was so sure, Ka," he said. Then, scanning all nearby surroundings, he frowned. "Where is Sitad?"

"*Sitad requested sanction to independently move, and I permitted,*" replied Ka. He answered telepathically for he verbally communed not with his lord in public unless absolutely necessary.

"Find it," was the Ben-Drom's growled response. He was, at once, worried for the entire.

Inclining his head, Ka backed away before turning to comply with his lord's fiat. Then, with the Ben-Drom close upon his heels, the Ceoheician moved through the crowds, mentally summoning the significant.

Ka himself grew worried when Sitad did not respond to his call. His pace quickened, leaving the agile but slower, heavier Altan behind.

Ka rarely left the Ben-Drom for any reason, especially when he felt such latent threat to his lord as he did now. But, directed to, he did so without anxiety. The Ben-Drom was well capable of defending himself, else Ka would not have so left him.

Weaving his way back and forth through the maze of containment aisles, Ka ceased his useless summoning and, spreading his perceptive senses outward, followed what he thought to be Sitad's essence to its source. Rounding a column of empty minor's travel encasements, Ka finally found the significant in a darkened, seemingly vacant corridor. The entire was deeply concentrating upon one faintly glowing capsule, its tactiles lengthened and extended to commune with whatever lay inside.

"*Sitad*," Ka charged. But, still, the Syrene remained oblivious.

Ka moved to the significant's side and touched the being.

A ripple coursed Sitad's long, lithe form in recoil, its tactiles immediately shrinking and curling back from the encasement. *"Trainer,"* it answered, its large orbs blackening in intensity in its alarm. *"I did not apprehend you. Is there crisis?"*

Ka disavowed any crisis, easing Sitad's anxiety even as he telepathically communicated to the Ben-Drom the Syrene's safety and their combined whereabouts. *"The master worries,"* Ka told Sitad, feeling the significant's unsated question. *"It is dangerous for you here."*

The Syrene bowed its large obovate head in a gesture as much acknowledgment as it was shame, but Ka ignored it, casting his sight, instead, to what had so captivated the Syrene.

It was a minor—a tiny minor—in an unlighted containment, and it was different. Ka had never known Raganth, but he had seen and known the characteristic of many Syrene of different type. This sort, though, with its oddly charan photo-luminescence, was unknown to him. *"Ben-Drom,"* Ka petitioned. *"There is something here of interest."*

"Where in shift's void *ARE* you?" came the Drom's return bellow, the sheer force and volume causing the numerous empty casements surrounding the odd minor to rattle, though the Altan was, at minimum, a full six corridors beyond.

Ka cocked just one angled brow and, with a small shake of his head, blinked out to appear just beside the still bellowing Drom. Uncomfortably aware of the stares of curious onlookers the Drom's outburst had precipitated, Ka said, "Here, Lord," breaking silence and startling his oversized friend.

"Hmrr," the Ben-Drom grumbled, then allowed himself to be led through to where Sitad again communed with the minor floating in its small capture case. Seeing it, the Ben-Drom exhaled suddenly—forcibly—and, kneeling down, he placed his mitt against the vitriform shielding. "She'har't," he whispered, recognizing its type as that for which he had so long and assiduously searched.

Looking to Sitad, the Ben-Drom asked, "Did you find it?"

The Syrene tipped its head, neither acknowledging nor denying, but, at the question, a tiny mote of gleaming glint disengaged itself from within the minor's containment to return to Ka's robes.

Scowling at the Ceoheician who was gently touching those robes with obvious bewilderment, the Ben-Drom barked out a demand for the services of an attendant, four of whom were immediately beside him. A fifth appeared moments after, this one the Academy's chief administrator. She dismissed the rest.

"I wish purchase of this minor," the Ben-Drom said, still kneeling.

The administrator, a tall Regellian female of rank equal to that of the Ben-Drom's, looked at the darkened cylinder, then down to where the Ben-Drom squatted. "This one," she said, "just arrived a few itar ago and hasn't even been cataloged or branded yet." Her attitude was haughty, and so was her speech.

"I wish its purchase," the Ben-Drom said again, rising.

"All right," said the administrator, backing off in the face of the Ben-Drom's looming presence that, when standing, was more than a third again her own substantial height, though she was taller than most. "Place a token on its encasement, and I'll arrange it."

By this time, a crowd had gathered round. Disruptions were rare in the auction center, except during bidding, and, even then, such disruptions were temperate affairs. Therefore, even the smallest disturbance brought onlookers.

A few of the gathered pressed close to peer at what had brought on the excitement and hollering. One in particular—a yellow and brown, striped Xentauri youth— took particular interest in the encased minor. His furred hand reached out and, as was legal, placed a token of his own upon the capsule. Now there would be at least two bidders for the strange and tiny minor.

○   ○   ○

7

SITAD WITH HIM, KA RETREATED to an open space beyond the crowd, there to scan and keep watch upon the Ben-Drom. Beneath his robe, Ka's hands stroked his jian, the touch of their latent, deadly lightning a comfort.

Ka felt strong intent against his lord. It was the same danger of which his prescient senses had warned when first the Ben-Drom had chosen to visit Ivalan and its auction center. But, for all Ka's native skills and training, he could not isolate source. Though he probed deeply and carefully, the enemy remained unrevealed, its intent masked and still unfocused. Yet menace existed, and it lay within the auction center.

It worried Ka that he could not identify the threat's origin. It meant that whoever held scheme against the Ben-Drom employed either a magus like he, or others of similar surreptitious skill. That would make their plot difficult to evade or neutralize. Therefore did Ka worry. The Ben-Drom had told Ka of K'har's visit, of the Cadre, and of the warning K'har had delivered. That the Draco at FleetCom who had watched the Ben-Drom was a part of whatever scheme of which K'har cautioned, Ka had no doubt. But Ka had felt no real threat at K'har's admonition; he'd felt none from the Draco—not this aching feel in his senses, their incessant warnings.

Within the fabric of his robe, the condensed form of the Sier sent a small sparkle of energy to burst against

Ka's skin, the burn of it gently potent. *"Does not Master Ghiza say that worry gets in the way of sensing, Ka?"* the Sier asked, forming the communication, not telepathically as Ka did, but as conceptualization and ideative.

Ka ignored the communication, though it was markedly an exact echo of his training master's teachings. Ka ignored the Sier, concentrating all his awareness upon protecting the Ben-Drom who had presently begun bidding upon his more common selections. And still Ka probed, trying to reveal the enemy and its intent, all the while reviewing contingent strategies of defense should an attack come. Ka's warrior-way was now as heightened as his magus-way, the two combining to form a unique integrity that alone was Ka's. But, for all of Ka's abilities, no perceivable menace was exposed. All was quiet, except for that same persistent internal warning: *DANGER. DANGER.*

The Sier had since become exceedingly subdued, and, with its earlier undetected leave-taking still memory-fresh, Ka reached with mental question to assure himself of its continued presence. It would not do to lose the Ben-Drom's prize, regardless his worry. *"Sier?"*

"I am here," the Sier responded, its thought images tasting of misgiving to Ka's mind. *"Move closer?"* it asked to Ka's surprise when the odd minor's lot came up for bid.

Reluctantly, Ka complied, though he was loath to leave his open vantage point.

Sitad still shadowing, Ka entered the crowd to ease himself into a position immediately beside the Ben-Drom.

The Ben-Drom frowned at their arrival. "Do you feel threat against me, Ka?" he hissed.

Ka avoided the question, responding only with a slight inclination of brow out of courtesy to his lord. He then lifted his head toward the stage where the minor's encasement was being placed for view, the mechanical porter that moved it floating gently just above the floor.

When the Ben-Drom's first lots had come up, the Andromedan had easily bought his two chosen Xi minors without event for less than seventy credits each against the other bidders who had also shown interest in them. Now that the odd minor's lot was open, however, Ka felt an aggressive shift in the atmosphere of the room. Several other of the more sensitive variety of entity also seemed to feel the change. Some of them retreated; others became restlessly wary. Ka went to deeper stillness, all his senses tuned, his crests raised to full as overt warning to those around them. But, though his instincts continued to tell him that true danger lurked, what he felt was just the same unfocused latency, not some physically imminent threat. Nevertheless, Ka palmed both his jian.

The Ben-Drom began the bidding for the charan-colored minor, and the young Xentauri whom had also claimed right to bid immediately countered. As the bids climbed, the Xenti swaggered forward, shouldering his way through to stand between Ka and the Ben-Drom.

The furred he-creature's scent was strongly pungent. It reflected the haughty insolence the Xenti wore like a badge of privilege, all of it hiding what Ka knew to be a weak, sniveling, and skulking character. Here was no threat to the Ben-Drom, at all, so Ka let the Xenti stand where he was. The furry wouldn't be there long. The young he-felidae would prove no contest for ownership of the minor that Ka's lord coveted.

Surprisingly though, the Xentauri proved an obstinate opponent to the Ben-Drom. The bidding soon broke all records ever paid for an unformed minor.

"Ten-thousand credits is the standing bid," the auctioneer said, signing for a break. She took the moment to touch something into her console, then asked of the Xentauri whose present turn it was, "Do you counter?"

The Xenti curled a lip to the Ben-Drom, then sneered, "Fifty-thousand!"

The crowd's gasp was audible. It was an extravagant, even incredulous, amount to offer for a minor. But the Ben-Drom only chuckled. Five-hundred-thousand paltry Omniversal credits, equivalent to less than twenty Dromedan shaagl was nothing to him, so fifty was laughable. And the Xenti had shown his hand.

Though it was usual for a bidder to jump the price, making an offer so much higher than the last that the opposing bidder was warned to the extremes the other was willing pay, to jump a price by such large percentage only gave the contender an idea of the credit limits to the other's purse. The Ben-Drom immediately and nonchalantly bid eighty-thousand to equally astonished gasps from the onlookers.

The auctioneer looked to the Xentauri for another offer, and the Xenti bid another five-hundred higher, then another, in answer to the Ben-Dom's repeated counters. But when the Ben-Drom jumped the price to one-hundred-thousand, the Xenti dropped his head in defeat.

"Sold to the Ben-Drom for one-hundred-thousand credits," said the auctioneer, sealing the sale with a touch to her com-board.

Pushing his way off the floor, the Xentauri glanced briefly back toward the Ben-Drom, exposed his fangs in ill-humor, then disappeared through the crowd. The Ben-Drom lowered his head, curling his own lipless mouth and whispered, "He is a sour loser, Ka. Unlike most his kind. His youth, I would wager…. But he does accept his loss."

Ka, whose sight and senses had followed the Xentaurian's movements until the furry, joining with a companion, exited the building completely, did not agree with his lord. Now the Xenti had somehow become part of the source of real menace Ka yet felt directed against the Ben-Drom.

It was in following the retreating path of the Xenti that Ka's perceptions fell across yet another Xentauri, this one a golden female very similar in characteristic to the one with whom the Draco at FleetCom had spoken. And if the Draco were involved in some conspiracy, so perhaps was this she-queen. That this female was, indeed, the same Xentauri with whom the Draco had spoken, Ka could not be sure. The height and breadth of body—her total mass—were different. And her fields read differently than those of the other Xentauri queen. That she had been and was surreptitiously watching them, however, Ka was sure, though how she had masked from him her spying all this time he could not fathom. He had an uncomfortable feeling about her. Ka memorized her characteristics, just as he had those of the Draco and the other Xenti she-queen. He memorized what he could, that is—everything this one overtly let him read.

Deepening his probe of her, Ka tried to penetrate her very nature with his magus ways. But Ka's senses failed that penetration, and, with a jolt, he realized that all that could be discerned was a lie. Whatever the watcher was—and the entity was not magus—it was skilled in the deceptive arts. He would not recognize it—not the species, for there was no guarantee that what he saw was surely Xenti; not the body, eyes, nor fields; not the nature, nor the thought peculiarities—were he to meet it again. The watcher was canny and well-versed. This, therefore, did Ka know—the conspiracy against the Ben-Drom, whatever its goals, was dangerous if it employed so competent a spy, and this particular creature was the quarter from which true danger did come. It held the potent intent he felt building against his lord. It was Destiny—Ka's idea of destiny—that surrounded it.

THE BIDDING WAS CLOSED AND FINALIZED, and the Ben-Drom was purchasing two additional containment pods in which to transport his new minors. Ka kept watch. Though the spy had disappeared, misgivings still flooded him. Those misgivings increased when the sub-administrator who had functioned as auctioneer refused to release the strange, charan-colored minor to the Ben-Drom. "You may collect it next itar," the sub-administrator said.

"Why this delay?" the Ben-Drom demanded.

"It must have its Academy brand laid before leaving premises."

"Lay it now."

"Yes," she said, "but it must also finish its quarantine period of which there remains a full nine decitar. You may collect it then."

Grumbling, the Ben-Drom demanded audience with her superior, the administrative head of Fleet Academy's Syrene Operations—the same one who had originally arranged the auction of the minor for the Ben-Drom. Likewise, however, the Regellian claimed to be constrained by Academy regulation. Ultimately, the Ben-Drom had to agree to the terms or forfeit the sale, and no amount of threatening or bribery could get the chief administrator to change her decision.

"Lord," Ka said, purposely speaking to jar the Ben-Drom. "I would not leave the minor," he said, knowing that the Ben-Drom knew he would never warn unless there truly was impending danger. And there was strong danger with this development. Every one of Ka's magus instincts whispered it. Similarly, the Sier also burned against Ka with repeated warning for the minor not to stay.

The Ben-Drom frowned. "What do you sense, Ka?" he asked tersely.

"Just an uncertainty," Ka answered. "I would not leave the small one. I believe it is endangered. ...I believe there is threat to you should it remain."

Vexed, the Ben-Drom looked from Ka to the head administrator, then back. "What would you have me do, Ka?" he whispered. "They will not permit me to remove it." The Ben-Drom directed another glare to Ka, then readdressed the administrator. "Would you allow me or my companion to remain with it?"

A look of horror descended the Regellian's countenance. "No! Absolutely not! No one but Academy personnel are allowed in the confinement areas. Security regulations."

"What danger pose I to such security?" the Ben-Drom retorted.

He had a point. He was a top, the very top, ranked regulus.   The administrator hesitated, then said stiffly...lamely, "If something were to happen.... I'm sorry, but what you suggest is impossible."

And the Ben-Drom, well used to Fleet bureaucracy, knew what constraints did bind her. She could not legitimate denying him, yet she could not give sanction to what he suggested. It would be her record, not his, that would suffer for it should she. She was crossed. If she allowed it, she would receive reprimand. If she did not allow it, and should he register complaint, she would also receive reprimand.

"I'll take its containment and personally have it ready for you next itar," she offered.

The Sier, who had been unobtrusive during the discussion, wriggled another small energy surge against Ka's skin, singeing him, and, Ka, sensitive to it, apprehended its thinking. *"Lord,"* Ka communicated, reverting to telepathy. *"Allow the Sier to remain."*

Casting his head hard up, the Ben-Drom glowered at the Ceoheician.

"The Sier will stay, Lord," Ka repeated. *"It cannot be detected."*

"No," came the exasperated answer. "I cannot approve such an arrangement. It is too valuable to me," the Ben-Drom said to Ka, ignoring the look of incredulity that flooded the administrator's fields and countenance as she misunderstood him to be refuting her. He allayed the Regellian's confusion moments later by bowing toward her and saying, "We will trust this regulus who is my ranking equal to keep her word."

Understanding the meaning in the Ben-Drom's choice of words, relief flooded the administrator's biofields. "And I will do that," she said, taking the containment. "I will personally ensure its safety, securing it myself to confinement for the duration of its quarantine."

"Hmr," the Ben-Drom muttered, then backed away an appropriately polite Andromedan distance before turning to exit the office.

Following, Ka was, meanwhile, steadfastly resisting the increasingly uncomfortable scalds of the Sier. He resisted until finally the Sier's scourging stopped.

Suspicious, Ka probed—first with his mind, then with his hands—searching for a peculiar point of warmth. But there was no point of warmth. The Sier was gone.

o   o   o

8

STILL ANGRY AT HAVING LOST his bidding war against the Ben-Drom for possession of the strange and valuable Syrene minor, Xentauri Riloc muttered irritable grumblings into the flask that held his drink. He had wanted that minor—wanted it badly. As soon as he had seen it, he had known it was the perfect gift to soften his sire's anger toward him.

"Oh, quit your mewling, Ril," said one of two other Xentis present at-table. The speaker, Greroc of the Losts, tossed back the contents of his drink, gulping the potent liquor in one swallow. "It was just a minor. You bid too much for it, anyway," he spat, slamming his flask back to table. "You were lucky the Drom was stupid enough to outbid you."

Riloc shifted in his seat, his eyes angry. "Damn filthy rich Andromedans. It should have easily been mine at a tenth the price…at most. No minor should go that high."

The she Xentauri sitting next to Riloc tipped an ear toward him. "Why was that minor so important to you?"

With directed insolence, Riloc turned his head just so and snarled, "Because it was the same type as the one called Raganth that my father owned and always talks about, that's why! It has been his dream to own another just like it for turns."

Unaffected by Riloc's manner, Xentauri Matac nodded in seeming sympathy. Within her fields, though, another sentiment was manifest, masked from any's view by a special cloaking mechanism. Matac was calculating. She knew Riloc well. She had known him when they were both kits, and, though they weren't exactly friends, they were Xentauri, which had been enough to permit her to join them when she had seemed to just happen by into the same bar Riloc always frequented when at Ivalan.

Eyeing the two at table with her, especially Riloc, Matac measured them closely. She wasn't sure. The turn of events she had come upon at the auction in her surveillance of the Ben-Drom was too perfect. Though Riloc was not Cadre, his sire was none other than High Consul Quiloc. Therefore, that Riloc should have just happened to be at the auction the exact same itar as the Ben-Drom, that Riloc, ever one to pad his credit account, even to the point of jeopardizing his own family, to have just happened to bid against the Ben-Drom for ownership of the same minor, was too coincidental to Matac's taste. She couldn't have better orchestrated it herself had she planned it. And that was why Matac hesitated. The Drom was wily. He was almost Sighted in his cunning, especially now in his association with the magus-warrior, Ka. To Matac's mind, it was entirely too possible that Riloc was the hired agent of the Drom, bait to catch the Cadre at its work.

It was too possible that the Zharkahn K'har had somehow discovered the identities of the Cadre leaders and divulged them to the Ben-Drom in that impregnable communication that Security had tracked from the to the

Ben-Drom's Ita residence. That K'har's transmission had come just itat after the Cadre's scheduled meeting with K'har, brought Matac deep suspicion. It would be typical to Andromedan irony for the Ben-Drom to utilize Quiloc's own son against him. There had been just time enough for the Ben-Drom to have set up this fine scenario— everything from his surprise arrival at FleetCom just moments after the Cadre meeting had ended to the scene at the auction center. ...It was all too coincidental, and coincidence, at least in Matac's business, was Not.

Although Matac had hidden the fact from Pryr, she had been privy to the attempted conference with the Zharkahn K'har and subsequent Cadre planning session earlier that itar, tapped into it, as usual, by Belamy, via special monitor. Then had come Pryr's request for her special efforts to be applied to securing the Ben-Drom and his fleet. And here was the ultimate chance to catch the Ben-Drom, but....

Matac smelled trap. Did the Ben-Drom know the Cadre's plans? Had he somehow overheard the Cadre planning session or Pryr's discussion with her within the FleetCom corridor? Andromedan technological ability was legendary; Andromedan informants—well-paid informants—were everywhere.

Watching Riloc and his friend, Matac could see no hint of deception in or manipulation of them. That meant nothing, though, so well programmed could they be by Andromedan implants. But, the way both of them were downing drinks, if she didn't act now, they would soon be too incoherent to talk.

Matac toyed with her own still untasted drink. Then, deciding to chance it, she pointedly looked to Riloc. "Just how important is your father's good favor to you, Riloc?" she asked.

Both males looked to her, their eyes as startled as hers were purposely calculating. "What d'you mean, Mat-?" Riloc asked, his eyes squinty with a mixture of suspicion and rancor.

"I mean what I ask," she replied.

Riloc and his friend exchanged glances, their uncertainty and confusion so grossly evident in their body language that Matac didn't need the validation that came to her by sensor implant. She wouldn't have trusted those field-reads, anyway. "I mean," she said, "would you be willing to chance your own freedom to get that minor?"

Riloc glanced nervously around the small, dark bar in which they drank. Then, with a guilty look toward Greroc, he muttered, "I don't know."

Matac nodded, almost positive now that Riloc was, in fact, the Drom's agent. Else he would not have hesitated. Riloc had often chanced his freedom for much less valuable prizes in his various illicit activities. And she knew he needed his father to help him cover his present gambling debts. For that, he needed his father's renewed good favor. Therefore, his hesitation was her clue to his duplicity. "Mmm. Well," she said, rising, "should you decide, you know where to find me."

Reaching to stop her, Riloc caught Matac in a grasp that locked her arm vice-like between the four long digits and opposing brace of thumbs of one strong hand.

Matac let him so grab, smiling haughtily. "Then it is that valuable to you?" she asked sweetly, distrusting him completely.

"Curr, it is," Riloc said tersely.

It was a judgment call. Matac couldn't be sure. Still, she could play it through safely enough without jeopardizing the Cadre, without jeopardizing even herself…except, perhaps, in the sight of the Ben-Drom, for using his minor. If caught, she could take the line that she, as an agent of military law, was within her right of jurisdiction entrapping a thief, especially considering that Riloc could potentially destroy the credibility of Xentauri's chief representative, High Consul Quiloc.

Matac slipped Riloc's grip off in one quick, easy turn of wrist. "Very well," she said, reseating herself. "The minor is still in the Academy holding. The Altan will not collect it until next itar. I overheard him yelling at the Academy Head when he discovered he could not immediately remove it."

Acting out her part, Matac shook her head in feigned pity at Riloc's purported astonishment to her information. Then she nodded, her cynicism plain and very real as she wondered again if she were the duped instead of the dupe. Yet, despite her doubts—perhaps, because of them—Matac plunged on: "I just happened to be at that auction. I saw you bidding."

Matac paused, waited for Riloc to digest that, then said, "You should not let your emotions overcome your need for knowledge."

Eyes pinning, searching Riloc's, Matac said, "The Drom was so angry, he almost forfeited the sale. You could hear him all over the complex, even when he closeted himself with the Academy's highest. Had he forfeited and had you been there, you could have owned the minor on a technicality."

Riloc scrowled. "Get to the point, Matac."

Matac almost stopped, almost succumbed to her suspicions of Riloc. Then, deliberately, she committed herself. "The Academy's Syrene Holding is a high security area, but, if you have the right tools, breaching it is easy."

Riloc immediately looked interested, but he didn't bite…just stared at her. If he were the Drom's agent, it would be here that Riloc's program would engage. "…I cannot go with you," she said, "but I can give you the means to accomplish the operation safely. It will be your responsibility to follow my instructions exactly if you wish to succeed."

Riloc's fields brightened, his ears pricking stiffly upright, and, at that, Matac's eyes became black and glittery as her pupils dilated to full. It was a warning—a Xenti warning in kindway body language. She reinforced that warning verbally. "If you fail, do not try to implicate me, because, I assure you, it will not work. If you try to implicate me, I will ensure your stay in Detention to be terminal. Am I understood?"

Matac saw Riloc hesitate as if to weigh her warning. Then his fields flared with a specific pointed rouge—his male ego rising. "Perfectly," he snarled. "But we won't get caught if your plan's decent."

"Hold on, Riloc," Greroc said, his body coming stiffly upright, his fields suspicious. Greroc's sight caught Matac's. "What's in this for you?" he asked.

"Partial payment of a debt," Matac replied.

"What debt?"

Riloc laughed. "She owes me for helping her escape a whore's life in my father's house," he said.

Matac felt her anger rise, but checked it, even as Greroc chuckled, a leering look descending to the slit on Matac's belly beneath which lay her genitalia. "She would have made a good whore, though," he said.

"She did," Riloc replied. "The one time she agreed to have me…. But my father caught us."

Matac forced a smile. "Actually, Greroc, I owe Riloc's sire, since he's the one who freed me."

"Oh?" Greroc asked, his tone inviting explanation.

"It was the price for what Riloc forced—"

"Never mind!" Riloc snarled. "She just owes the Q Dynasty. In general. …For big favors. …For her freedom and her education."

Greroc's countenance grew thoughtful. He slid a nasty glance toward Riloc, then looked to Matac, a new respect for her displayed within his fields. By those fields, Matac saw that Greroc realized that she'd tricked Riloc into being caught by his sire for indiscretions with her. He nodded to her. "So it's Quiloc you're paying," he said. "Currur!" And he seemed satisfied.

"Let's get back to grabbing this minor for my father!" Riloc growled.

"Fine with me," Greroc said, relaxing into a slouch.

Matac could have purred. She was very sure now that Riloc was no agent for the Ben-Drom. Riloc was what he had always been—just a dumb, self-centered scrap, no partner, unwitting or otherwise, to any Andromedan scheme of discovery—for what she offered would serve no purpose set by the Drom to trap the Cadre. The right questions had not been asked, the wrong questions had been answered, and the correct scenarios had not been drawn.

Both Riloc and Greroc were leaning forward eagerly, and Matac realized that this turn of events would fulfill the Cadre's purpose perfectly. With it, they could easily penetrate the Drom's heavy security. All Matac had to do once Riloc got it out of the Academy Holding, was implant the minor with a special sub-enceph program. After that, it was simply a matter of letting it return to the Drom's possession until the time was ripe to engage that programming. The minor would then become an agent for the Cadre.

Her plans formulated, Matac herself leaned forward, genuinely joining Riloc and his friend in their enthusiasm. "All right," she said. "Here is what you must do to steal the minor."

o   o   o

9

THE MINOR WAS IN PAIN—grievous pain—and the Sier felt that pain in all its blistering intensity throughout her being. And, although pain was not something the Sier completely understood, it was something that she did, now, begin to recognize "consequences-of."

Empathizing, the Sier could feel the burning, the confusion. She could feel the minor's agony as if the brands that had been seared into the minor's plasma had been laid upon her own being. The echoed keening of the minor's torment coursed her stuff and substance until, knowing herself one with the small Syrene, she reached to salve, to mute, that pain, that horror, done so callously to its fragile, plasmic body.

It, the minor...he, she discovered at the instant of their joining, reached his consciousness out to her, and, in that moment, the Sier realized that she knew, had always known, this one. Somehow, someway, this one was also come from beyond the Gateway. Its...his...being drew at her.

At their fusion, the minor's writhing stopped, as did his keening. But the pain of body was too much for him. He could not transmute it as she could, no matter how she showed him. And, seeking in her depths some solace, some escape, the minor's consciousness moved upon her foundless core and vanished.

The Sier, imbued within the small Syrene's body, waited, still and silent, even when they who had done the branding moved the minor's limp and devastated form, her within, to another chamber, this one filled with countless cells. Encasing her chosen charge's body within one of the empty cells, those who had so carried, withdrew. They left all of them—all Syrene locked within those numerous small cells, and the Sier—in peace.

Alone, now, the Sier separated from the minor's body and returned to her own pseudo-natural form, her golden energy folding and fountaining out in warping, fluid veils. Quietly, she began to call to the departed minor.

At first, she called just lightly. When that failed to summon him, she reverted to the deeply penetrating harmonies that transcended the actualizing temporal— resonants that pervaded even to the essence of pure being. She called thus, resonating to the very depths, urging his return. Then, she waited, contemplating.

It was very dark and still within the Syrene Holding, the faint, pastel glow from the minors' catalyzing cells gentle to the Sier's sensibilities and essence. Likewise, the minors' consciousnesses were equally gentle. Unlike so many and, in fact, most entities within this realm that the Sier's host, Ben-Drom, called the cosmos, Syrene of all type and kind were as close as the Sier could find to entities likened to herself. All Syrene, excepting those called devoid that were distinctly not, were as purely at-one with what the Sier knew to be core essence as were her own kind, those existent so far beyond the Gateway.

Syrene were clear of all disturbance, all decisions, all split and fractured perception that created the limitations of this realm...and its strife.

No, the Sier corrected. It was the interactivity of the realm coupled with the rest that caused the strife. Were it not an interactive realm, there could be limitation, but not, necessarily, strife. She had learned that. She had become used to that, in a way. And becoming used-to worried her. She hoped she wasn't so used-to, wasn't changed so much by this realm, that she could never more come to be among her own again.

Banishing those disturbing thoughts, the Sier watched her charge's body. The minor was still retreated, despite her repeated and continuous calling, though the plasma-like, homogeneous, liquid-crystal radiancy that formed his body had congealed, sealing over the burned-in symbol wounds that had been laid upon him opposite the huge, singular perceptor that was his exposed core. The pain, the trauma to his body, was gone, but, still, the minor did not return.

The Sier watched the minor's body, so tiny, so vital, so alive. There was strong bond between them—more bond between them than she'd felt with any other in this realm. It was almost as if the minor were a temporal precipitate of the Sier's own kind. That brought her joy and comfort, just as her presence in his agony had seemed to bring him ease. The minor needed her, and, perhaps, the Sier mused, she needed him, though need was also not normal to her being. But, then, again, perhaps it was…now.

The Sier had felt a longing since she'd come into this reality. It was a longing that nothing slaked—not her host, the Ben-Drom; not her host's paladin, Ka; not her tutor-friend, the Bota Ghiza. However, this small minor seemed to satisfy some echoed melancholy that lay within her, and, for the first time since the Sier had come to understand the existence of a temporal reality, she felt a sense of kindred spirit.

A small one in a chamber two rows over began keening, breaking the Sier's musing with its cries of loneliness and terror. Moving to comfort it, the Sier spread herself to touch it, all the while maintaining vigilance of her own charge. Then, she spread herself to touch them all—all Syrene within the place—for she felt empathy for all of them in their plight. They were lonely—lonely for their own domain. And it struck the Sier that, perhaps, this was the affinity they shared—she and they, all so far from their own respective realms.

The Sier knew their realm. She had come through it, summoned by the minors' elder kind in answer to the dreaming of her host, the Ben-Drom. And, even as she knew what had brought those ancient Syrene elders to so summon her for one not of their kind, she comprehended why those ancients with their formidable, even awesome, powers of manipulation of this realm they called the planal would permit that taking of these, their new-formed kind, as slaves. She knew the why, but she did not like it, though dislike was something alien to her and to all her kind. Dislike was a contradiction of the Sier's very being—her sense of we, not I, self. It was as contrary to her as was loneliness, as was perceiving right and wrong, good and evil.

Abruptly, the Sier stopped herself. So she was changed. She knew, understood, these contradictions.

No. There is no change, came the long away and echoed answer from her core—from her we-self—that did itself still remain at-one.

But I am changed, she answered.

Of ourself, we are. There is no change of being, only an acknowledgment of ways that are, though our ways they are not.

And the Sier took comfort in that knowledge.

A movement, a ripple, in the quiet consciousness of the minors' chamber alerted the Sier. Sinking into herself, she rejoined the body of her charge, embedding herself once more within the minor's photo-luminescent plasma, a golden gleam amidst his body's mercurial charan blackened gilded silvering. There, she waited, hoping what she felt to be an error in perception.

But the perception wasn't flawed. What the Sier perceived was actual: It was a being, stealthy in his movement, naming himself, to himself, as guilty of some evil, even as he claimed self-righteous purpose. He moved among the Syrene catalytic chambers as if searching for something. Coming close, a furred one the

Sier recognized as the one who had proven challenge to the Ben-Drom's possession of the minor at the auction laid his hands upon her charge's cell. Those hands opened the chamber.

The Sier reared, flaring, but, immediately, the voice that was her core said, *Stop. It is the dreaming's destiny. It is the Ben-Drom's destiny, and the minor's.*

Confused, the Sier hesitated, then obeyed, consolidating herself within the minor once again. *Do I accompany?* she asked self.

We do accompany, her deeply moving center said.

And the Sier felt split between herself, wanting to remain with her small, chosen charge, yet unwilling to be permanently separated from the Ben-Drom. She had promised. She had promised both the Ben-Drom and the minor, the first promise long before the last, but both vows equally binding.

Alternatives—the Sier sought within herself for them. To split, perhaps. All was possible, even in this realm of seeming limitations, especially for such that was unlimited. And she began to think herself between time into two.

Yet, again, her inner core responded, *No. Remain unto ourself one whole, not two.*

The hands that reached had momentarily hesitated as she'd flared. Presently, those hands grasped the body of the minor. The Sier, now inured within, yet, simultaneously, extended, watched everything. She observed those hands lift the minor's body wherein she dwelled to place it into another, smaller, chamber. Then, darkness completed itself upon the senses of the minor's body, and the Sier knew movement.

DEEP IN SOMNOLENCE, BUT YET AWARE, Ka opened sleep-blind eyes, unseeing. In that moment, he knew that it...that both, Sier and minor, were gone.

o   o   o

10

MATAC SMILED. THE TECHTRONICS were holding, and Riloc was tight to schedule, well inside the "safe" window created by the device she'd given him to produce the single loop permissible before the Academy's security-net signaled alert. Right now, Riloc was coming down a service corridor, the minor safely stowed in a containment pod he carried. In a short few itan, Riloc should be exiting the service entrance closest to her. That would be her time to act.

Matac shut off everything but the audio transmission from the mote-sized bug she had planted in Riloc's fur, and, easing herself back to lean deeper into shadow, she picked a tiny, needle-like sheath from a slip grafted in her palm pad. Inside that sheath lay a jacul, a carrier so small as to be all but intangible. Hence, the sheath as coating.

The most advanced self-propelled penetration carrier ever designed, jacul were correspondingly expensive and highly illegal, even for use by High Fleet Special Operations personnel. That didn't stop Matac and every other agent from using them. Almost every high tech piece of equipment that Special Operations used was illegal, a thing widely known, even approved of, by highest-ups...unofficially approved, that is. "Don't get caught" was the only rule. The difficulty was that jacul were not designed for manual use, but the device designed to handle them, itself illegal, was just too noticeable in the field.   So other methods were employed—dangerous methods—and those methods included the insertion of special implants in the agent's brain. Matac had those implants.

The jacul pinched securely between the thumbs of one hand, Matac blinked, thinking the code that engaged the lens implants that augmented her already keen sight as well as those which locked the jacul's movements to her thoughts.   Then she busied herself activating the program she had pre-loaded into the jacul, fine-tuning the time sequence between release, penetration, program dump, and carrier disintegration.   She worked intently, easy in her schedule.

It would have been far superior if Matac had been able to use one of her subagents rather than Riloc for the minor's theft, but she refused to put them at risk. Special Operations personnel had no jurisdiction within the Academy. All High Fleet Academy grounds were strictly off-limits to their operations, the penalty being a choice of death or permanent incarceration, this by order of the Omniversal High Consul after an operation had cost the lives of some cadets. Likewise, Cadre personnel would have served, or, better still, Matac herself could have undertaken the task (which she was more than willing to risk), but for the fact that, were any of them caught, they would be put under BT and the Cadre discovered. So, despite the risks, using Riloc was the best course...especially since Riloc would immediately take the minor out-universe and, unknowingly, straight into

Cadre hands. The plus was that Riloc's travel time would give the program time to do its work of making the minor her…the Cadre's…agent, which was the only safe and sure way Matac saw to infiltrate the Ben-Drom's fields of circumstance to thereby broach his fleet's security.

Unable to use a viral programmer or any similar device upon the Ben-Drom without harming and possibly killing him, Matac had originally decided to try to infiltrate one of those nearest the Drom and in his confidence. She had thought to implant one of the Drom's ever-present Syrene significants…until she had learned that they were full entires, immune once grown from minorhood to such control. She had even toyed with setting a virus into the Drom's paladin, Ka, who was the only other being besides the Syrene who had access to the innermost workings of the Ben-Drom's various realms—his fleet, his fortress-like residence, his private warships—and the mainframe biocoms that controlled them all. But, if the virus failed, either by killing the magus or by simply being overpowered by Ka's will, the Cadre's purposes would be forfeit and probably discovered. The Ben-Drom would be warned.

Matac had all but abandoned Pryr's suggested course…until Riloc had happened into things. And in the instant of her surety of Riloc's usefulness, Matac had seen advantage. A minor entire, as opposed to a full-core, entire significant, was programmable, and, by the way the Ben-Drom had acted when he'd seen the charan-colored minor, Matac knew the Altan would keep it quite near him.

Matac knew the Raganth incident. She also knew about the Drom's crusade to try to find a Syrene of similar subtype. That had been part of her suspicion of what had seemed a set-up at the auction. Now that she had discovered that all of it was indeed happenstance, everything seemed to easily fall into place.

A noise beyond the normal...! Warned, Matac stopped her any movement.

Careful tread. Coming close. Matac remained frozen—stilled to seemingly inert. A body—a tall Xenti body—was approaching, coming dead for her. He was wearing badge, which ID she recognized. It was none other than the Megan Quroc, and rumor had it that he was fitted with implant sensors as delicate as any agent's. If the rumor held truth, and Matac figured that it did, then the implants he wore could easily detect her, though she was heavily cloaked. A primus commander, now, and as prickly about regulations as his sire had been, if he noticed her, Quroc would have had no qualms in alerting Academy guards to her presence, even though she had every right to be exactly where she was, so long as she remained out-building. Quroc would report her, the guards would check it out, noting the time. The time of her sighting and the time of the minor's disappearance would be found to coincide.

Mentally, the immobile Matac shuddered. If Quroc happened to notice the jacul sheath.... She closed everything down. …Even stopped her sight and breathing. And she prayed, prayed to Xenac that the Megan Quroc's feet be guided elsewhere rather than where they aimed to tread—right on top of her.

The Xenti passed close by—so close, almost stepping on her—she felt his presence tangibly. But his path had deviated. Slightly. Just enough.

Matac cracked a sensor, the silhouette of a Syrene significant just behind the Megan Quroc was immediately beside her now. But it too failed to notice her, and, mentally, Matac thanked her luck and Xenac, for either one or both was all that saved her from discovery. But now she had a new worry, and that was Riloc's potential discovery by the Megan Quroc.

Unlike Quroc, Riloc was civilian and had no right, at all, to enter the Academy's Syrene Hold after hours. If Quroc saw him, no matter that they were half-brothers— perhaps more so because they were—Quroc would have Riloc arrested on the spot.

Matac could monitor Riloc's steady padfalls from the bug. She could hear his breathing. *Slow down, Riloc. Stay where you are*, Matac prayed. But Riloc's movement remained steady. He was still on time and traveling, his track almost sure to bring him face to face with Quroc. And Matac could do nothing, not without exposing herself.

Tensely, Matac marked Quroc's progress. Mentally, she urged him, willed him, to move faster, but, his progress remained steady, his paced, sure, never-deviating stride biting at her nerves as he made his way across the sandsea park to the main entrance of the holding.

Matac's anger rose. Why ever Quroc had decided to pick the middle of deepest shadowfall to appear! Then, unwittingly, she remembered, her eidetic memory flashing recall of a Fleet personnel update she had, of habit, scanned that very itar. Quroc was scheduled for a mandatory leave-of-absence. Psycho-therapeutic had been the reason given, which, translated, meant career-threatening mental instability. The fact of it had caught Matac's attention since it had seemed so strange. The Megan Quroc was so Fleet appropriate, so correct. He did absolutely no wrong, which, on its own, was a sign of psychological imbalance. But, in Fleet—or anywhere—as long as the problem enhanced your job performance, there was no problem. Quroc's perfectionism and career correctness was renowned. It was why he had climbed the ranks so fast. It was also why he was subject to the most ridicule by other fleets, the biggest joke within the upper echelon.

Riloc had stopped. Matac breathed a small thanks to Xenac for twice answering her prayers. Through the bug she could hear Riloc adjusting the minor's carrying capsule. Be quiet, you fool, she mentally cursed as she watched the Megan Quroc approach the front entrance instead of the usual side one used after hours—more luck. Matac relaxed now, and a new idea of a more mortal, perhaps even pitiful, Quroc came to her as she watched him finally disappear inside the Academy Syrene Holding. He did so just itat before Riloc emerged from the side entrance.

Quroc forgotten, Matac concentrated on the task of moment, and, with a flick, she engaged the jacul, the device coming alive inside its coating in her hand. Now, it tracked exactly what her sight traced—exactly—and Matac's sight was glued to the small Syrene travel containment Riloc carried. Letting the jacul free to hover in front of her, Matac waited for Riloc to get clear of the sandpark's floating stones, chuckling as she watched the young male. Riloc actually sauntered away from the Academy Holding, trying his best to feign a nonchalance that was obviously contrived. Riloc was scared witless.

Matac grimaced. It was a good thing she had notified the Cadre-infiltrated Iban Security and Perimeter-Net to disregard anything happening in her area of operations, else Riloc would already have been caught, the heavy overhead computer surveillance alerted because of his antics, despite him protected by best camouflage.

Now. The time was now. With a thought, Matac honed her sight implant's magnification, the jacul becoming stationary in its hover as she herself stilled. Riloc was out on the landing platforms, stupidly sprinting the last short distance between the Academy and the small shuttle that waited for him there, the ship's outer disc-like structure barely spinning as it hovered, humming faintly, just off-paving. "Stupid," Matac muttered absently, her focus on the containment capsule.

With a thought, Matac loosed the jacul. It fled to target. A whispered "crr" passed Matac's lips millitat later as the jacul penetrated, the device already disintegrating, its potent programming virus impregnated and beginning to work itself into the minor's encephalon.

◦   ◦   ◦

11

CASPIN WATCHED THE LITTLE SHUTTLE spin spaceward. His computers told him that the Special Operations super-code he had imposed on it was fixed and holding on monitors throughout the tracking system. He was pleased with that. It had been done quickly, and things done quickly did not always stay done.

The shuttle was out of Iban's atmosphere and securely within his jurisdiction, now. Sitting back, Caspin idled, flipping a keying stud over and over with a free palp as he waited for the alarm.

Caspin knew the shuttle's destination exactly. The Xentauri private transport had been obvious in its too normal movements for it not to be noted. Without hesitation, Caspin had marked that ship under Matac's operational super-code, as well, never needing authorization. Caspin was authorization. Fleet Perimeter-Net was his jurisdiction, and, when Matac had called requesting special clearance, Caspin himself had taken the duty-station, dismissing the regular fleets who usually attended such things.

Matac was friend, and a good one to have. Therefore, it paid well to keep her happy. Whether or not she was Cadre like he was, Caspin didn't know…though, in himself, he doubted that she was. But that didn't really matter to him. Matac was tops in Caspin's estimation, and, if she was working, it was for the good of the Omniverse, just like was the Cadre's work.

Right on cue, the alarm began. Fleet Academy Security was on alert. It was only a matter of moments, now. Caspin caught the key he'd been flipping and held it suspended over its lock, two of his other palps working the intricate lightboard to keep the monitors happily busy in redundant checks of every ship in the vicinity except the shuttle and the Xentauri privateer's transport.

Soon, too soon, the computers would notice the two, consistent scan-aborts and target them anyway unless Caspin was very good. And he was good, but no one could fool the numbers indefinitely. Fleet Academy had priority-overrides that only Caspin and a select few others could overrule, but to overrule would immediately pinpoint the very ships Caspin was trying to cover for Matac. His key-override wouldn't be challenged, but there would be questions for Matac, and those questions would be very difficult for Matac to answer without jeopardizing whatever operation in which she was engaged. Caspin wanted to spare Matac that questioning, knowing that it was imperative for her success.

Matac never worked a mission that was simple or less than critical to Omniversal security. But every operation she worked usually wound up exposing a corrupted influential somebody's genitals and lopping them off. To say that she was not popular with debauched potentates was understatement. She was hated; she was marked for death by many of the most powerful. But she also had many friends—key friends, powerful in their own way—and Caspin was one of them.

Random—the scanner misses had to seem random, yet logical. Caspin worked the board, hoping that he wouldn't have to use his key. "Come on," he whispered to the computers. "Miss it. Miss it." And they did. They kept missing it, so well did Caspin work the lightboard. Then, something happened that shouldn't have happened, and Caspin swore. The mach patrol had picked up the alarm signal and was moving in, homing on just what Caspin was trying to cover. Somehow, they had unerringly picked the one target Caspin was hiding, and, if they persisted, the computers were bound to notice the scan-misses, too, and he would have to key.

Initializing query, query answered, Caspin knew. He now knew how the machon had come to cover the exact target he was hiding. The leader of the flight was none other than a prescient-sensed Ghirran by name of Rajan.

Freeing another of his palpi, Caspin touched open a link, coding it to a specific scramble. Lucky that he knew Rajan. Cadre just like him, Rajan would listen and comply. The Ghirran would comply, because he, unlike most other machon leads, wasn't after the glory that could come with winning a capture. Instead, Rajan was like every other Cadre member—dedicated to winning the war to maintain individual rights and freedom in the Omniverse.

Caspin spoke calmly and softly, explaining the situation to the machon wing-lead. When he'd finished, Caspin touched out the link without waiting for reply. He received acknowledgment moments later, though. From his monitors came a seemingly normal arc of a steepening vector adjustment as the warbirds under Rajan's command aimed toward another potential.

His palps never slackening their movement over the lightboard, Caspin smiled. Now, Rajan was giving double effort. His mach flight was beginning to run a course over a bevy of civilian craft that were also leaving Iban.

Communication traffic told Caspin that the mach were doing sweeps just like the Academy was demanding, flooding sensor input into the computer system that would make the computers take more time-consuming, careful looks at what was there. That helped Caspin and his slippery task. Computers had their limits, and, if one knew how to work the numbers right, it was an easy thing to stymie them.

The shuttle had boarded the transport, now. Soon, the transport itself would be running outbound. Just a little more time. Just a little more skill. And the codes were holding. Caspin watched, playing the lightboard, his override key still held over its lock in case of need.

The transport's engines flared, then seemed to die in an unnatural blink. Finally, the ship was gone, slipped unchallenged into interspace. Matac and her operation, whatever it was, were safe.

o   o   o

12

THE BEN-DROM'S MITT DROPPED heavily to his lap upon termination of the sublink communication with the Academy head, the talons on that thickened member working in and out in his distress. Ka had been only too accurate in his instincts, once again.

It was taken, the Sier with it, stolen from him before he'd even touched or been touched by it. The rarest of all Syrene, the charan minor had been identical in every way to Raganth, and the Ben-Drom had thrilled to finding it. Now, it was gone, and there was nothing he could do except to wait and hope—wait and hope that the Sier would protect the minor and itself from any harm and, somehow, find safe passage back to him.

A deep, steady rumble of discontent rose of its own accord from the Ben-Drom's gut, the quiet, massive sound vibrating at such a low frequency that it actually seemed to fall to roll about the floor of the quiet room that was a personal sanctuary. The Ben-Drom was unaccustomed to quiescence, to being powerless against those who moved against him and his own. He was, after all, the bjen dvorkahn, voted heir-apparent leader to all his kind and more. Yet, for all the wealth and might and power that title meant, he was helpless to do more than was already being done to find his property by the Academy and by Fleet itself.

How long the Ben-Drom sat there, mindlessly staring out at Regar's landscape, he was unaware. He wasn't even cognizant when the night's darkness gave way to light on the planetform of rugged, craggy mountains and contorted bionts that proved poor substitute for the real Rhegar, the Ben-Drom's home world.

Regar suited neither species for which it had been manufactured—not the Altan, not the Low. It was a product of compromise, and the Ben-Drom despised the safety-minded engineers who had designed it. Though it provided a tolerably light gravity and a bearable atmosphere, that was all it did. Here, there was no real semblance of home.

A riskless place, this Regar, there were no insurmountable jagged peaks, no endless desert plains, no static storms against which to test oneself. There were no crystal labyrinths for the wind to moan a melancholy echo through. Not even murk-filled, moss-encrusted forests were to be found anywhere within the landscape. Here, there was nothing, nothing of the real Rhegar—not one wild thing that could pose threat to life, that could pose challenge. All of it was so blandly safe, so unpleasantly controlled, the design molded by minds that preferred their own environments that way. The Ben-Drom missed the risks of home. For the first time in his life, the Ben-Drom missed Rhegar.

It was Ka who broke the Ben-Drom's miserable reverie some long while after first light. "Lord," the Ceoheician said quietly. "It is time. The meeting?"

The Ben-Drom turned, and, remembering his obligations, he tossed his head aside in curt acknowledgment, though he was in no mood for a meeting with the High Fleet Requisition Board.

"Do you robe, Lord?" Ka asked.

"No. Let them see me as I am," the Ben-Drom replied, rising heavily.

Ka's head tilted just a fraction, his sclera-less eyes seeming to darken beyond their void-like blackness. "Lord," he said. "There are none who can ever see you as you truly are. None can ever know you."

Stung by the words, the Ben-Drom sank into himself. What Ka said condemned him forever to the loneliness he'd always suffered and sought remedy. *None can ever know you*—the verdict whispered its lifelong sentence deep inside him.

The Ben-Drom looked to Ka, his eyes pleading beneath his shields. "Not even you, Ka?" he asked, his voice husky in his anguish.

"Not even I, Lord," Ka said softly. Then, again: "Not even I, good friend. You are that which is unfathomable—The Deepening."

Recoiling from the potency of the Ceoheician's intent, the Ben-Drom began to anger. "Then I am a lonely deepening, Ka," he said. "…And powerless—powerless to thwart even common thieves, powerless to defend that which I most cherish."

Ka's eyes kindled at the Ben-Drom's words, beginning, at once, to glint hints of deep green fire. "The minor's fate is its own, and even you, Lord, cannot oppose such."

The Ben-Drom's rumble turned to a full-blown growl, his talons snapping out to full extrusion. "The minor's fate is not its own," he snarled. "It is slave to the greed and oppressive manipulations of its possessors!"

Headcrests swelling, the magus-warrior's already gaunt face tightened even more, his thin lips compressing to a harshened line. "Even you, Lord?" he asked severely, chastening.

Jerking his head hard by, his eyeshields glare harshly reflective upon the magus-warrior who dared reprove him, the Ben-Drom took a menacing step toward, then stopped himself. "Yes," he said, finally, meanly. "Yes," he said, again, this time more calmly. "Even I. It would have been slave even to my possessing," he said bitterly, turning his back to Ka, not in insult in the Andromedan way, but in uncharacteristic shame.

So it is beginning, Ka thought to himself. *The sickness is come, again.* The dusky fire in his eyes receded, and, with a shadow of cynicism just touching his drawn features, the Ceoheician bowed unseen to his mighty, chosen lord, knowing what the Ben-Drom spoke as false, even as he knew there was design—destiny's design— behind the tiny minor's strange abduction.

o   o   o

13

OMNIVERSAL HIGH FLEET DIRECTOR Leon Belamy laughed outright at the holomorphic scene and turned to the Yulandan strategist. "He's formidable, isn't he, Lurad?" Belamy said, pointing at the Ben-Drom's semblance. "Imagine having that subject to Cadre control, vulnerable to our every whim." And Belamy laughed again.

To Belamy's words, the Yulandan's surface seemed to crawl across itself. Then, two bubbles that Belamy recognized as Lurad's endeavor to simulate eyes formed on an upper curve of the being's surface. A vocal construct formed, too. "The Bjen Dvorkahn is formidable, Tellurian Leon Belamy," Lurad said. "Do not become so enraptured with an idea of domination that you lose all good caution and sense. Any Andromedan, especially the Altan, is not lightly trifled with. Particularly this is true in present instance. This Altan may very well prove indomitable, and not only because he is the bjen dvorkahn. …Or, perhaps, because he is."

Lurad's surface rippled, then became mirror-like, and Belamy found himself watching a distorted version of himself. It was a Yulandan's method of warning. "The Bjen Dvorkahn is of nature that exemplifies all that is Altan Andromedan, from his strict sense of what is honorable to his unfaltering will, the very fact of his selection to leader status by his kind proving his nature as redoubtable," Lurad said.

Belamy's laughter had long since dried to a sterile silence at Lurad's words, and he took a new perspective to the Andromedan beast he had known so long—a beast who was presently storming up and down in front of the assembled Requisition Board, alternately berating them, then demanding remedy. The Ben-Drom would get no remedy, though. Belamy himself, along with Quiloc, had ensured as much.

It had taken a good deal of convincing and, in some cases, outright blackmail, to induce the high commanders serving on the Requisition Board to approve the changes to the Ben-Drom's crew rosters necessary to carry out the Cadre plan, but, in the end, Quiloc and Belamy had done it, thanks in part to Quiloc's reputation and influence both as a retired Fleet commander and regulus. As Belamy's immediate predecessor to the office of Fleet Director, Quiloc was liked and trusted whereas Belamy, who was new to the post, was not, especially with the more Protocol-oriented of the High Fleet archon. It was Quiloc who had finally persuaded the most obdurate. Now, all that was needed was to convince the Ben-Drom that the changes to his crew rosters were unavoidable. …And get him to accept Pryr as navarchon. That was something the Requisition Board was presently endeavoring to do. But the Ben-Drom, angry at the amendments, was having none of it. He was, instead, still trying to get the Board to recant its decision.

Leon Belamy shut off the monitor that secretly tapped the meeting. Then he spoke the worry that ate most at him. "I don't really think we are planting enough Cadre liege within the Ben-Drom's crews to secure control of his fleet," he said, visibly flinching as he said it.

Belamy had never doubted Lurad's strategies before, and he didn't like doing it now, but he did have his doubts—strong doubts—in this present operation. The future of the Cadre was at stake as it had never been. To succeed was not only necessary, but vital. To lose all by failing to seize the Ben-Drom and his fleet because of lack of operatives…. Belamy shook his head, trying to banish the disastrous images that rose at that scenario.

Lurad's double-bubbled "eyes" slid together, and it turned yellow—patient, gentle condescension. "The number aboard each ship is more than sufficient, if any number can be successful," the Yulandan said. "Allay your fears, Tellurian. The very strength of our strategy resides in its meagerness. Only those of your ilk and kind could fail to see this."

Belamy began to object, but the Yulandan's body swelled to silence him. "I will again remind you: the Bjen Dvorkahn is a tactical genius, as are all his kind. If too many of our own were to be substituted into his crews, he would become suspicious, quickly discover the likelihood of plot, and move to neutralize us."

The sack-like body decreased.

"You think he's that good? That our plan is that transparent?" Belamy argued. He shook his head. "I've known the Ben-Drom for a long time, Lurad. I was at the 'Cad with him, then friends with him for turns."

"You think him dull, do you?"

Belamy shrugged. "Not dull, but…."

"This is my sentiment: I believe that, were we to increase the number of our operatives involved, we surely would be undone. The adjustments—both the implanting of Cadre operatives and the removal of the Bjen Dvorkahn's most potent loyalists—will prove sufficient."

And that brought up another problem in Belamy's mind. "The Ben-Drom's definitely not happy about losing Dra as navarch. I'm not sure we can successfully keep him from finding the Orconian and installing him anyway."

"We must." And Lurad's body darkened to inky indigo. "The removal of the Ben-Drom's most loyal machon and his core elite commanders, especially Dra, is crucial. 'Control the mega-command and the machon fighters, and one controls the fleet," Lurad quoted. "This you know."

Belamy mentally went through the list of personnel they had deleted, then shook his head. Those personally known to him—Dra, Gor, Jastoc, Milan, Rajan, and Kahn— were the Ben-Drom's most steadfast. The moment news spread of his fleet's readiness to launch, they would themselves seek out the Ben-Drom, and Belamy had no doubt that what was true for them would be true for the others he didn't know. The Ben-Drom had a way of cultivating loyalty that was almost eerie. They would, all of them, flock to him once his fleet was spacebound, abandoning their present assignments, and, by law, if the Ben Drom wanted them, there was nothing that the High Fleet, much less the Cadre, could do to stop them.

Overwhelmed, it was frustration that made Belamy erupt then. "My God, Lurad, we're trying to hijack a fleet of battle translights here! And not just any translights. These are Drom-built ships. Prototypes. Ships with such advanced technology, such tight security, that none of us, not even the engineers who are helping build them, understand them! And you expect to successfully break that security and gain control of them with so few liege?! Without casualties?!"

"It can be done," the Yulandan said again.

Belamy didn't see how. Quiloc had been right in his objection. Quiloc had been only too right, once again. But Belamy hadn't listened.

As if in answer to Belamy's thoughts, Lurad again repeated itself: "It can be done."

"How?!"

"Meticulously careful manipulation, Leon Belamy."

"And you tell me how we stop his loyalists from joining him, too!" Belamy demanded.

"I will do that," Lurad said, its construct vanishing as its jellied surface rippled in what Belamy now recognized as a Yulandan's peculiar humor.

That humor angered Belamy. He tipped his head, one brow raised in skepticism. "Then, tell me," he said. "The whole strategy. All the details."

And, to that, the Yulandan's vocal construct formed again. But the Yulandan strategist never got the chance to use that forming organ for the Ben-Drom himself burst through the office access just then, Belamy's secretary, Kiel, flailing beneath after what had been an obviously unsuccessful attempt to block such ingress. The Ben-Drom actually strode right over the top of Kiel…though, notably, the Altan never stepped upon the toppled secretary. *"DIRECTOR OF FLEET, TELLURIAN LEON BELAMY. WE HAVE NEEDS SPEAK. IMMEDIATELY. THERE IS CONSPIRACY AGAINST ME."*

o   o   o

14

LURAD HAD EXCUSED HIMSELF, leaving Belamy to handle the angry Ben-Drom. And Belamy was afraid—afraid that the Cadre and its plan were discovered.

"Do you want Security, Sir," asked Kiel, who had since picked himself off the floor. "I'll be glad to call for it," he said, glowering up at the giant Altan as he straightened some of his ruffled plates.

A rumble of exasperation and contempt arose from the Ben-Drom to that suggestion. Ka, ever-present shadow of the Drom, cast what Belamy could only interpret as a humorous glance toward Kiel—*that* in a being who seemed to have no humor. Even Belamy had to smile at Kiel's simplicity, however. The secretary, a civilian new to working at FleetCom, had not yet realized that, had he wanted to, the Regulus Primus Omega Ben-Drom, or any reg-prime, for that matter, could affect entrance to Belamy's office at anytime with little to no effort and even less nay-say. No Security, not technological, not sentient, would stop a reg-prime. The reg-prime *were* Fleet.

"No, Kiel," Belamy said gently. "No Security. It's all right." And, with a wave, Belamy dismissed him.

Once Kiel was gone, Belamy addressed his visitor. "Regulus Ben-Drom," Belamy said. And he was surprised at his own calm. "Won't you sit?"

The Drom grunted, then squatted himself into what was a typically Andromedan confrontational parleying position. That squat brought the Drom down to a height just higher than Belamy's own two meter frame had Belamy been standing, and, as usual, when present before this particularly huge alien, Belamy felt the weak, impotent midget.

The gilded shimmer of the Ben-Drom's eyeshields had leveled themselves on Belamy. That was in itself a sign. It was mostly by the brilliant, wet-orange hue of the Altan's venom vesicles, though—vesicles that were usually rust colored—that Belamy knew that the Ben-Drom was incensed. Gone from Belamy now was any of the heady feeling of power and control over this creature that he had confidently wallowed in moments ago with Lurad.

…Silence, and the Drom's lifeless, shielded gaze. Belamy drew his eyes away from their mesmerizing effect, then checked a hidden monitor to try to analyze the Drom's extensive fields. He looked for clues to the cause of the Ben-Drom's state, but the only thing that showed within those biofields was an odd neutrality that Belamy knew was forced. Belamy again looked to the Drom. He could only guess what character the eyes beneath the shields held, and that made Belamy vulnerable.

Belamy took a conscious breath, trying to staunch his fear that the Ben-Drom had discovered the Cadre's operation. He tried to quiet his fear of the creature, his fear of its violent hatred of him.

It hadn't always been this way. The Ben-Drom hadn't always hated him. There had been a time when the Drom would expose his fields, would even remove his eyeshields. But that time was long ago.

That the Ben-Drom's fields had once been open to him, that the eyes behind the shielding had once been those of friend, that loss—the loss of the Ben-Drom as comrade and confidante—troubled Belamy. The Ben-Drom's presence always brought the guilt, the remorse. But what Belamy had done that had ultimately spoiled their long-term friendship, he'd do again if he had to in order to secure the Ben-Drom to regulus in Fleet. It had needed to be done, just as this present labor for the life of the Cadre needed to succeed.

What manipulation Belamy was guilty for in the past with the Ben-Drom, Belamy wasn't necessarily proud of, but neither did he regret. The Ben-Drom conscripted to Fleet as regulus was best for Fleet, best for the Omniverse, and best for the Ben-Drom and his purpose of freeing the Syrene, though the Ben-Drom didn't see it quite that way. And now that Belamy had founded the Cadre, its purpose that of fighting the rampant corruption that threatened everything for which the long historic wars over Omniversal control and destiny had been fought, he'd be damned if he'd see everything forfeit—not for the sake of Altan Andromedan policies of isolationism and non-interference, and certainly not because of the Ben-Drom's priggishness when it came to the matter of his crews. And Belamy was, with his guilt washed clean and his conscience finally quieted so that he could again think clearly, beginning to guess that the matter of crews, rather than some inkling of Cadre conspiracy, was the reason for the Ben-Drom's visit.

Belamy shifted his position and tapped a finger to his console. He did it purposely to show impatience. His long silence had been fruitful. The Drom was definitely testy, but calm now overlay that irritability, a calm that Belamy, with no empirical evidence other than his instincts, sensed at some gut level. "Well?" he asked.

A low rumble—some guttural Dromedan remark, Belamy supposed—rose from somewhere deep within the Ben-Drom's torso. Then the giant finally spoke. "My crew requisition," the Ben-Drom snarled. "It has been delayed, amended, and delayed once more. I demand intercession by your office." A fisted mitt, dark, shiny talon tips clearly exposed and digging into the heel of that mitt, slammed onto Belamy's desk. "NOW!"

Belamy nodded at the confirmation that the Cadre's operation was undiscovered. Relief mingled oddly with a queer nervousness. Here it came, he thought, and he took an audible breath. He was as ready as he'd ever be. Time to broach the Dromedan head-to-head. "There is good reason for the Requisition Board's decision, Ben-Drom," Belamy said. "As usual, you selected mostly malcontents, and, because of the prestige of your new fleet being the most unique and advanced ever built, there's talk of making it the flag-head of Fleet."

The eyeshields just stared.

"…That's the highest honor, Ben-Drom."

The eyeshields stared.

Giving up any hope of softening the creature, Belamy sighed and plunged on. "Because of that, Command thinks that your rosters should be populated with…ah, shall we say, more regular personnel." Belamy said that, then paused to wait for some response.

What Belamy had told the Ben-Drom was a lie—a half lie. While some of the Requisition Board's membership did think that way, most of its members were only too pleased to dump the fleets the Ben-Drom had selected into his command. Most of the Ben-Drom's selections were independents who didn't take either the Dictates or the Protocol well, and more than a few were close to being mustered out under charges of Disgrace, that in a service where securing enough personnel to fill its ranks was difficult. None of the Ben-Drom's selections were very biddable. None respected rank for rank's sake. That was why Belamy and Quiloc's manipulations had been necessary.

While Belamy, and Quiloc, for that matter, didn't condone the Protocol or the Dictates, and, in fact, the Cadre fought against their continued employment in both government and Fleet, for this operation, the Cadre needed the Ben-Drom's crews submissive to those institutions. And that meant purging most of the Ben-Drom's selected mega-commanders, as well as the most indomitable personalities from the lower rankings. It was especially necessary to purge those who had already served under the Ben-Drom and knew his predilection for the Standard and Ideal.

It was the hard-liners Quiloc and Belamy had replaced on the Ben-Drom's crew rosters—the ones who were Ben-Drom loyalists, more allegiant to him than to Fleet itself. They were the ones capable of carrying the crews in opposition to Cadre machinations. They were the ones who, even though many of the same were numbered as Cadre liege, could and would oppose the Cadre in this, so loyal were they to the Ben-Drom.

The silence between Belamy and the Ben-Drom suddenly became oppressive. Belamy shifted uncomfortably. "Well?" he asked.

The eyeshields stared. Then, finally, a grumbled growl and: "I care not a whit for an honor of naming to flag-head. I will not abide it. I care only for my crews, crews personally selected, each one, by my hand." The giant paused. "And I will have them, Director of Fleet Tellurian Leon Belamy!"

"Most of your choices were approved," Belamy replied, ignoring the intended insult of his species naming. He touched up the requisition on the office's huge central mainscreen. Data accessed, Belamy set the list to scroll, having the machine highlight those of the Ben-Drom's selections that had been approved. Through the list finally, the computer projected a tally of results. Belamy pointed and said, "Only six-hundred-thirty-one were rejected, Ben-Drom. Out of seven-hundred-fifty-thousand. That's a very good percentage of approvals."

And it was. And keeping the Ben-Drom's favorites from him was only a temporary situation—only temporary. Once the Cadre mission was complete, despite the outcome, the Ben-Drom would be free to assign any being he liked to any position he chose…within Fleet parameters, of course.

Canceling the listing, Belamy said, "The only problem I can see is your own stubborn refusal to approve the Requisition Board's revised roster."

Again, the eyeshields just stared; still, the biofields held to neutral. But the twitching of the external cordage that worked the jaw—that, and the fact that the vesicles on the dark-brown skin were now streaming minuscule amounts of venom betrayed the Drom. "Most were approved, Tellurian," the Altan sneered.

Belamy flinched at the Ben-Drom's continued caustic manner of address.

"MOST." And, again, the fisted mitt slammed down. "I will have those six-hundred-thirty-one—six-hundred-thirty-one which notably include some of my most crucial operations officers. Six-hundred thirty-one which include my chosen navarch, the Megan Primus Kathon Orcan Dra!"

Despite his best efforts not to, Belamy flinched again, his retainer-field buzzing. "Yes, Ben-Drom," Belamy said, his voice mollifying. Then, softly: "But Dra wasn't rejected. He's a no-show."

"The stink of political maneuvering is highly evident, Director," the Drom shot back. "This is the conspiracy I speak of. Dra would never refuse me. The Command is against me. Well do they ken Dra key to my fleet's military successes."

Belamy shifted, more uncomfortable than ever. "I know nothing of any political maneuvering, Ben-Drom. Dra never responded to summons. Neither did some of the others." And that also was a lie, a lie that Belamy, watching his own fields on monitor, was thankful that he hid well.

"And Gor?! And Bixum?! *AND RAJAN AND KAHN?!*"

The volume of the Drom's deeply basso voicing was thunderous, the waves of it tangible. Sympathetic vibrations hummed and rattled through everything. Belamy's favorite sculpt crashed to the floor, shattering. Even the monitor screens blinked wildly until damping was effected.

Belamy was, at once, angry. That sculpt had been valuable—irreplaceable. And he was tired of the Ben-Drom's petulance. Steel ice inside now, Belamy said: "Ben-Drom, I know how much you depend upon all your personnel, but I can't force them to respond. Not Dra. Not any of them. The notices were sent out to all names on your roster, just like they were supposed to be, before ever the Requisition Board saw those listings." Belamy said it quietly, the hush of his voice his own warning. And, this time, he didn't need to lie. The notices had been sent out before the Requisition Board had seen the Ben-

Drom's roster. Though not before Belamy and Quiloc had supplanted some of the names there. "Now, either you accept the roster, or you can fight the High Command from now until forever and never launch your fleet. I don't care."

It was a bluff. But it was also truth. One way or the other, fleet or no fleet launch, the Ben-Drom would be taken.

"I must have Dra," was the Ben-Drom's only response.

And Belamy could sympathize. He knew how much a regulus depended on his fleetmaster—in the Ben-Drom's case, even more so, since the Altan, as regulus, really did only act as judiciary as was the mandate by the Standard. Except in the most extreme and extenuating circumstances. In that, the Ben-Drom was unlike most regulus in Fleet who took advantage of their lofty positions to act as overlords—pompous kings, in fact. That's why Belamy had so long ago tricked the Drom, forcing him to accept a regulus posting. The Ben-Drom was the start of the Standard and Ideal being applied successfully throughout the Omniversal High Fleet where officers were supposed to act, not as superiors dictating to subordinates like they did under the Protocol, those subordinates treated almost as slaves, but rather as team coordinators for crews of highly trained specialists. It was the specialists, after all, who ran the ships and carried out the missions. Leaders were supposed to be the team coordinators responsible to those subordinates. But that wasn't what the reality was. Except upon the Ben-Drom's fleet. And the Ben-Drom's command was the most successful at winning its campaigns and battles of any in Fleet. Performance mattered, and the proof that the Standard worked was undeniable. So, in time, the Standard would become Fleet Operations Standard too. With the Ben-Drom used as model. If Belamy had his way. If the Cadre could succeed. So Belamy could sympathize with the Drom's plight, but he could only sympathize so much. Even without the Cadre's secret agenda and even though the Drom was lacking Dra and quite a few other favorites, the Ben-Drom still had numbered among his crew some of the most competent, if notoriously renegade officers ever to serve in Fleet…thanks to Lurad's conservatism. "As I said, Ben-Drom, I can't force Dra to respond," Belamy said. "Open your mind, Ben-Drom. Accept what you've got, and take the Requisition Board's suggestions for alternates."

"And what of navarch?"

Belamy punched up another list. Several meg prime candidates, including, of course, the Megan Pryr, came on-screen. Belamy pointed them out. Those are good officers," Belamy said. "Test them if you want. But stop being stubborn and surly. You're just defeating yourself."

"Hmgrr." And that was all the Ben-Drom answered as he rose to leave the office.

"Is our meeting adjourned?" Belamy said nicely, his own sarcasm clear.

"It is," the Ben-Drom snapped, and began to back from Belamy's office, giving in Dromedan way at least that much respect. Ka also backed away, immediately behind the Drom and pacing him exactly.

The Drom stopped, though, before reaching the access. "Director Belamy," he said.

"Yes, Ben-Drom?"

"You have heard of the theft of my minor from Fleet Academy Syrene Holding?"

"I have," Belamy replied. He had, in fact, heard just that morning.

"I expect search for it not only to bear positive result, but for such result to be brought quickly."

"Talk to the Academy, Ben-Drom, not to me." And Belamy was glad that the particular problem of finding the Drom's missing Syrene had nothing at all to do with him *or* the Cadre. He didn't need another headache.

o   o   o

15

CHE'EERT AND MODOC LOOKED TO ONE ANOTHER, both of them disbelieving their own senses. They had the robo-monitor check the civilian transport's holds, again, just to assure themselves that it was indeed empty.

"Where's your cargo, Captain?" Modoc sneered, turning from his viewer. "You seem to have lost something in transit."

"I have no cargo. I'm here to load. Not to deliver."

"That lie," Che'eert hissed, her silver saliva beginning to string between her striata with her rising distemper. "You cargo take—ship—before Ita leave. It be where?"

"I don't know what you're talking about," replied the captain.

And the captain stuck to his story, despite any evidence to the contrary Modoc showed him.

"That's not my ship," the captain said when shown hazy images of his transport as Riloc's shuttle boarded it. "I was never in that sector of Ita. Stick to the main civilian routes," he said. "Stay away from the military. Don't like them."

The captain was lying, but Modoc couldn't prove it. He couldn't force the issue, not without risking exposure of the Cadre op. It was risky even to waylay the privateer this much. Che'eert and he were employees of a civilian security net, not a military one. As that, their only responsibilities were to insure that nothing dangerous to the ecosystems or inhabitants of either of the twin planets of Verdaje and Nadeja passed into the Xentauri system. That included armaments, toxics, and a host of other potentially hazardous materials. That was all it included, though. Everything else—capturing illegal contraband and such—was beyond their jurisdiction. They really had no grounds to impede the privateer transport as much as they had.

"In got go," said Che'eert once they cleared the captain's ship for system penetration.

"Riloc was supposed to be right there," said Modoc.

"He not be," Che'eert said. "Privilege he take, maybe, like all you pretty pamper furline baby do." Laughing sarcastically, then, she said, "Rules, why bother?" She spread an offing web. "You no one challenge. E'en you get caught do thing awful, you daughter elite—"

"Son," Modoc corrected absently.

"Too you do. You I see."

Modoc snarled, "That's enough."

"Too true."

And it was. Modoc knew it just as well as Che'eert did. If you were Dynasty—any of them—even of the Losts like he was, you could do just about anything you wanted till you got to age. And even then.... "Riloc probably got off at Dejanoc's and flew in from there," Modoc said, playing probabilities on his board. "That means he's already inside Verdaj. Probably already home."

"That way I tell, too," Che'eert agreed, her tongue slipping out to rub itself across the brain bulge that was harbored in a cleft just below the torso of her spongy upper body. "Faster we in, get minor, get out, better. So, now we do."

"Do you have any idea of the kind of security Quiloc's bound to have?!"

"We both ex-SO. We can do."

"We don't have the technology to safely breach."

"So we lay? Not get?"

"No."

"Then?"

"We go in," Modoc said with a small sigh. At least if they were caught, ill-tempered Matac couldn't do anything to them. There would be proof that they had tried. Besides, there was half a chance that they could succeed, especially with Che'eert's infiltration skills, the benefits of a boneless, tube-like body that allowed her to slip into and through almost anything. But he had always handled the technology so that she could do it without getting stung by sensor—something to which she was very sensitive. And all that was before—before when he'd had access to top technology. All he had available now was archaic in comparison to the advancements since they had been Special Operations partners in the field. "If we get caught, Che'eert, you play dumb," Modoc said. "You know. Just following my orders, okay?"

"Tat," she agreed, as ever. "But caught no get."

Modoc scrowled. Che'eert, as ever the optimist to his natural pessimism. And, so far, she had always been right, no matter how great the odds against them. He just hoped she was right this time.

o   o   o

16

THE SYRENE HOLDING SEALS, set more than seven full ita past, had been broken, and, suspicious, High Consul Quiloc, in company with a small hosting of his household guard, went to investigate. What Quiloc expected to find was his daughter Surac's son, the most notoriously mischievous of his grandsons, playing infiltrator within the underground complex, especially since the young genius could not be found on monitor. What Quiloc discovered, instead, set his course black fur on end.

Quiloc dismissed the guards and stood staring at what lay upon the service table, its keening, writhing form eking luminous streams of evanescent plasma from wounds where its sheathing had been compromised.

"Do you like it, Father?"

Ears instantly pinned flat, Quiloc raised angry yellow eyes to his youngest son's smiling face and hissed, "What have you done, Riloc?!"

The younger eased back a pace, the smile fading from his face at once.

"What have you done?!" Quiloc hissed, again, as he quickly slipped on soft, protective gloves with which to handle the suffering Syrene minor.

"It's a gift for you, Father," Riloc said, his voice hesitant, his eyes wary. "It...it's just like Raganth."

"You maimed it. You—" And, here, having gently lifted the minor to examine it, Quiloc drew a harsh breath at its wounding, wounds inflicted, not only from Riloc's clumsy application of the Q dynasty brand and the conforming lattice that he had tried to fit around it, but from knife cuts—deliberate knife cuts intended to remove a newly laid Fleet Academy brand. Those knife cuts meant one thing only to Quiloc: heavy trouble. No one who legitimately purchased a minor need worry about its branding. Ownership transfers were common things. To cut out a brand, however....

Facing his youngster, Quiloc snarled, "You stole this from someone!"

"No, Sir!" Riloc protested. "I didn't."

But Riloc's fields showed otherwise to Quiloc. Carefully, he set the minor down, and, stripping off his gloves, he softly cuffed his miscreant son. "Kind does not lie to kind. Ever," he said. Quiloc then cuffed the younger, again. "And especially not in-family. You defame this house of the venerable Q Dynasty."

Riloc's head dropped away, as it should have, but, still, Quiloc saw no true penitence. He shook his head. "Riloc, you disgrace me."

Returning his attention to the minor, Quiloc saw that, truly, it was comparable in type to his long-terminated Raganth, and, except for the marring and one small glint of pure light gold within its charan-colored body at the internode beneath its base encephalon, it was perfect, if too small to be suffering the severity of the conforming lattice Riloc had inexpertly applied.

Slipping the gloves back on, Quiloc adjusted that lattice as best he could without further damaging the minor's plasma sheathing, then placed the tiny, squirming bio- within a charging cylinder, there to, hopefully, heal. Once done, Quiloc again snapped off the gloves. Then, turning back to his scoundrel son, he asked, "Whose was it?"

Riloc dropped his head away again, but said nothing.

Quiloc grasped his young male get by the shoulder, his claws sinking into the other's yellow and brown striped fur until their tips broke skin. "Answer me. I'll need to make them compensation."

Snarling, Riloc raised his head and sneered, "You would! After everything I went through to get it, too!"

"Whose was it?!" Quiloc hissed, his eyes glittering with barely checked anger, now. "You'd best answer me, Riloc," he warned.

Riloc spat, his own eyes angry. But, just as suddenly as he had fired, Riloc capitulated and mumbled something.

"What?" Quiloc demanded.

"I said, it was the Ben-Drom's," Riloc said, raising eyes that were brilliant and challenging.

Staggered by that disclosure, Quiloc released his grip on Riloc and turned away to stare at the minor's containment cylinder. He tried to find equilibrium, tried to calm himself enough to think. But, much as he tried, he couldn't calm the panic that was beginning to rage inside him.   Of all the multitudes of beings in the Omniverse from whom Riloc could have stolen the tiny minor....   Nightmare scenarios paraded themselves across Quiloc's inner vision, all of them disastrous—to him in his consulship, to Riloc, to the Cadre, to the Q Dynasty's reputation. And that brought up the subject of his greatest pride, his firstborn son, just home this itar. Quroc, the only of his get to walk in his padfalls and the only one suitable to lead the Q Dynasty at Quiloc's death—his future would be affected by this.

If Quiloc took the honorable course and notified the Ben-Drom of the minor's whereabouts, the Altan would want his minor back, and, despite anything that Quiloc did, once the Ben-Drom saw that minor, its condition, he would be incensed that Quiloc had allowed it to be so mutilated. To Andromedan thinking, the family leader was answerable for any trespass done by any familial member, and the Ben-Drom, having never forgiven Quiloc for the termination of Raganth, would be especially sagacious in his treatment in this affair. Fanatical about Syrene to an extreme, the Ben-Drom would systematically go about destroying every vestige of trust that had existed for generations between the Q Dynasty and the Altans. The Ben-Drom had the power, prestige, and influence to do that, and his position would be legitimate.

Raganth's termination had been legally justified. No Altan could deny that, but there was absolutely no excuse for the condition of the minor. Quiloc and, after him, Quroc, as well as every subsequent family head, would be condemned by Altan Andromedans everywhere. The Dynasty's greatest power—its prestigious heritage as Xentauri's and the Omniverse's chief ambassador and liaison with the Altans would be forever forfeit. This incident would taint the Q Dynasty, destroying its any future as a political power, and *that* Quiloc could not abide, especially if the Cadre operation was successful, which looked promising.

"Father?" Riloc queried.

Quiloc turned. He had forgotten Riloc. Seeing him, now, he snarled, his teeth vicious in their full exposure. "You've ruined me," he screamed. "You've ruined the family. Everything! Get *OUT!*"

Confusion flooded Riloc's fields. "Father?"

Quiloc took a threatening step forward. *"GET OUT!"* he screamed, pointing to the access. *"NOW! BEFORE I LOSE WHAT LITTLE PATIENCE WITH YOU I HAVE LEFT."*

Riloc fled, leaving Quiloc alone within the holding to stare at the valuable Syrene that now lay calmly in its encasement, at rest in the glow of catalyst, its newly conformed tactiles gently stirring as it fed itself from the flow of energizer. Quiloc knew what he had to do.

Fingers quivering, Quiloc touched the controls that fed the catalyst into the encasement, then paused, desperate to find another answer. There was no other answer, though—none that would put things right, yet save the family future. But this was the most dishonorable answer, and Quiloc had never done a dishonorable thing in his life.

He tried to justify it. Better that the minor just never be found, he told himself.

And he knew the truth of it, but he also knew the shame.

The minor opened its sight and watched him as if it were aware of what he planned. Quiloc shuddered, twitching in a guilt that was new to him. And, seeing the Syrene anew, he felt another thing—the sorrow.

Such a waste. Sick in himself, he spat. Such a terrible waste to kill it. But there was no other way.

He touched his pads across the cylinder's intricate controls. Having engaged the detention field, Quiloc then switched on the controls to the tiny shackling that had been set about the minor's newly conformed neck and appendages. The minor's body jerked. Then, the minor began to fight against the restriction.

Turning off the cylinder's feed, Quiloc watched in mesmerizing horror as the life-giving glow of catalyst beneath the domed vitriform faded to darkness, the minor's photo luminescent body stark in the gloomy interior of its berth.

And the tiny thing began to writhe.

Averting his head from the sight, Quiloc stole away, out the holding. His only hope was that the minor's termination would be short and peaceful, though he knew within himself with saddened certainty that it would not.

It was then the keening started.

○   ○   ○

17

THE SIER ROSE, URGENCY DRIVING HER. The minor was starving, he was suffocating—the two, one process in the creature, Syrene.

Unable to be manipulated, so also was the Sier unable to manipulate. She could know and know not things within any event horizon or set thereof—create and destroy, as Ka said—but she could not, or, perhaps, would not, alter or change what was without co-union and agreement from and with that which she would alter…not without some counter-action to her nature to spawn a catalyst. Therefore were the controls that initiated the catalyst flow beyond her influence, for they resisted knowledge-of.

Desperate to aid her chosen , the Sier tried to nourish the minor on her own energy body, but what was herself was not a tangible radiant. He could not utilize it. Despite her best efforts, she failed. The gateway of potentiality did not exist for that contingency.

In the end, all the Sier could do was try to soothe away the minor's perception of suffering.

But the minor would have none of that. He fought against his disbecoming in this specific temporal domain. He fought valiantly, audibly keening his objection until his energy was so depleted that he couldn't naturally sound more. And, even then, he keened, sounding a resonance that few other than the Sier could hear. It wasted him down quickly, quickening his approaching dissolution. And the Sier fought *with* him, screaming his objection through herself into the void.

o   o   o

18

IT WAS THE KEENING—a Syrene's keening—that drew Quroc from the depths of sleep. It was his Metaxi's keening—his ever screaming, ever dying Metaxi. The keening stopped as soon as Quroc opened up his eyes…just like it always did.

Quroc groaned and rolled over on his sleeping pallet. Burying his head beneath his arms, he cursed quietly to himself. It always happened when he came home—the haunting of Metaxi's memory-ghost. No matter how long a time passed, the soft orbs, they still lived within him in his memory, the soft keening still forever sounding in his mind. Metaxi would not die.

Knowing from experience that sleep was forever vanquished this rest cycle, Quroc reluctantly heaved himself upright, flinching as his bare pads met cold stone floor. He sought mental diversion from the memories. That alone would bring him peace.

He rose, creeping over to his castoff gear to touch the new rank insignia embedded in the crystalline fabric of his uniform. The golden wedge glittered in the low light of the grotto-like room, light that seeped around corners to show him that it was still midday—mid-sleep time.

Quroc looked about the room that had once been his when he'd been a youngling, but was now just impersonal guest quartering. The matriarch-surrogate, his sire's recently dead mate, had been thorough in destroying any vestige of his presence. Idly, Quroc wondered what had become of the possessions of his youth—his knives, his bone collections, the bits and pieces of techtronics with which he had liked to tinker. Not that it mattered. He'd taken everything he'd wanted when he'd left so long ago to enter Fleet Academy.

Quroc's sight dropped back to the insignia. He rubbed his interior thumb over it. Pride, he realized. He was proud of that insignia. He had worked hard for it and the responsibilities it represented.

Picking up the uniform, he opened the skinsuit's almost imperceptible front pressure seam, watching as the material separated cleanly where the molecules ceased to bond at his touch. He began to pull the uniform on, then hesitated.

His skinny blue-and-white striped fur was a disgrace. Thin and lank, it lay flat against his nearly translucent skin. He raked his claws through it, but that didn't help. Ten long ita of compression beneath High Fleet skinsuits had done their worst. The fur felt dead.

He was home. On leave. He didn't need to robe. And, leaving the fleetwear alongside ship codifier and weapons harness, Quroc slipped out to re-explore the home of his youth.

CAREFUL NOT TO WAKE THE SLEEPING HOUSEHOLD with his movements, Quroc wandered through the sprawling residence at will, nodding to the occasional guard. Never challenged, he was left alone.

The house was much as he remembered it—still home, despite his matriarch-surrogate's best efforts to change it to something less than Q Dynastic. It was still cold, still sparsely furnished, though the fixtures were the best. The ancient timbers of the vaulted ceilings were still hung with dusty strands of webbing.

A sigh escaped Quroc as images from kithood kindled—memories of climbing the towering timbers to reach the hiding places those huge ceiling stringers offered with their curtains of ancient web. He had always had to be careful in his climbing of them, so as not to disturb the webs' huge and irritable, poisonous owners, the life guardians, protectors against infiltration by the multitudes of insectivores intent upon devouring all meat, live or dead, including sleeping family. But they were also vicious in their own right and would bite if their webs became disturbed or if one discovered them out on hunting prowl.

Quroc carried his own share of scars from them, and, remembering, Quroc chuckled at how many times he'd used those webs high up in the ceiling timbers to provide sanctuary from his teaching masters. And to watch the nightly goings-on, him watching with Metaxi and his sister the visitors his father entertained when Quiloc was home on leave from war.

Immediately, a bitterness rose to crush the laughter in Quroc's throat. He spat, his ears pinning of their own volition. All his memories held Metaxi, even after all the turns away from home. Everywhere he looked, everything he touched, brought memories of time spent with his kithood chum. And those memories were destroying him.

Angry, now, Quroc purposely crossed the large front entry hall to find the hidden access in its farthest reach that led to the Syrene Hold two floors beneath. He would crush Metaxi from his memory somehow. Even if it meant destroying the entire holding to do it. He would do what the psychotherapists had ordered. He'd go back to where the sorrow had begun. And he'd relish doing it—destroying his eidetic memory of Metaxi—killing it, once and forever. But, as the access resolved to expose the dark, sloped corridor to the hold and to the catacombs beyond it, Quroc's anger faded, leaving only sorrow as its residue, not resolve. Stepping in, he began to descend.

Eyes not yet adjusted to the intense darkness of the old stone passageway, Quroc felt his way along until he gained the sealed threshold. He had not been here since Metaxi's death so many turns past. Now, standing before the access to the place, he wasn't sure he wanted to face it all again—all the memories. Even the smell of the cold, dry rock was enough to make his gall rise. Still, he reached to touch the access panel and key his code into the locking mechanism.

Quroc held his breath. There was good chance his access code had been deleted. He expected that. He was prepared for that. But, itat after, the ancient, hewn stone doorway slowly, silently rolled back.

IT WAS WARM INSIDE THE HOLDING—an odd thing. It shouldn't be. The chamber supposedly hadn't been in use since his sire's retirement from Fleet service.

Something touched his hearing. Quroc turned, and, for a moment, he swore he saw a flash of light. But, engaging scanners, there was nothing there except the memory-ghost. He turned his scanners off again. He needed natural mind, not watching artificial sensori.

Touching on the controls, his finger pads still sure even after so many turns of absence, Quroc turned them all on—all the cylinders—watching as each and all of the encasements slowly began to glow, their antique bubbled cylinders filling with the haze of catalyst.

He walked among them and let long buried memories rekindle just as the catalyst, so long denied, rekindled. This cylinder had been Raganth's. This one, Tegran's. He remembered when both Syrene had been newly captured.

Two series left, then one bank deeper…and Quroc stopped. After a moment's hesitation, he let the furred feathering at his pad-tips just brush the vitriform surface of the haze-filled cylinder. This one…this one had been Metaxi's.

Old sorrow, long constrained, rose within him— sorrow and guilt. His Metaxi.

Vivid, poignant memories engulfed him—of Metaxi's uncomprehending orbs asking…asking…as it lay dying. Memories of its pain-racked keening. And, once the deed was done and his sire had departed…of his holding it, the Syrene's freshly blackened body flaccid and desiccating in his grasp as he hugged it, begging it to come back, to not be dead. The rush of feeling with those memories was as strong as if Metaxi had just now been terminated, and Quroc cursed his kind, cursed the eidetic memory that was their characteristic. He hated feeling.

Burning with the unaccustomed yet too familiar ache, Quroc turned away to stare blindly across the banks of now charged cylinders, their pastel-colored catalyst maintaining nonexistent occupants. His Metaxi. It was the one act for which he'd never been, never be, able to forgive his father—the killing of Metaxi.

Anger again overcoming him in his pain, Quroc hissed and slammed a fisted hand into the vitriform of Metaxi's cylinder, the sound reverberating through the chamber. He had despised them all since then—all Syrene. He despised their treacherous, insidious way of getting to him, of gaining access to his most private thoughts and feelings—their empathy while they remained entire; their lifelessness, their insensitivity once stripped devoid. Yes, he hated all of them.

And therein lay his problem. He couldn't afford to hate them anymore. He couldn't afford Metaxi's haunting any longer. And there was absolutely no way that medically his eidetic memory could be canceled or removed, not even pieces of it—not without destroying everything that made him Q, everything that made him Verdajan and Xentauri on the inside. He'd be just a body, then, with some jelly for a brain—unacceptable. Death was better. Healing was preferred. He had a stake in life—a good stake.

Quroc had trained, then tested for and gained the rank and office of megan primus kathon, the top command rank below a regulus in Fleet. As that, he was qualified for shipmaster and even navarchon, master of fleet, should some regulus break Service Protocol and name him to that capacity. And that meant he would have to work with the Syrene—work closely with them— something he'd been spared as mach-lead. But he *couldn't* work with them. Not after Metaxi. Not like this. And the experts said he had to face it, resolve it, or his career was ended.

It was Metaxi...it was his father who had caused his problem—Quroc blamed them both. But it was he who suffered the consequences of it. He was the one whose career was jeopardized. It was his team members' lives that it threatened. And he was the one who had to face it, purge it. Or leave Fleet. The medicals said so.

Quroc struck another blow, harder this time—hard enough to make the hollow tube-like bones within his hand spring.

A squeal.

Anger immediately checked, Quroc's ears pricked stiffly, rotating toward the direction of the sound. Fear froze him—just for an instant. The sound was so much like Metaxi's had been when it had been just minor that, for a millitat, terror, mixed with hope, rose inside him.

Rational thought prevailed at once, though, and, chagrined, Quroc chuckled at himself. A battle commander scared by the squeak of a grograt. And, at that thought, Quroc's mind blinked.

A grograt? In here? In a chamber sealed for seven ita?

His limp fur came alive, all of it standing on end at once. Then, intelligence and innate curiosity overcame natural timidity. Grograts could hibernate for a hyper-extended period. It was possible, though in what condition the creature would be....

Quroc struck the vitriform another blow, and, again, a faint scream answered. But the sound wasn't that of grograt. It was Syrene. Of that Quroc was almost positive.

His mind balked. That was impossible. All the cylinders had been deactivated. The sound, though, that was real enough. And it had come from near the farther wall where the service tables stood.

With a specific twitch of ear, Quroc again engaged his sensor implants—all of them—scanning for any telltale biofields, that of something living or Syrene, glad that he'd spent the extra credits to purchase the most advanced implants, the most sensitive and far-ranged. But, implants or no, no fields showed. He hit the vitriform another blow.

There. The sound was there, again—fainter, this time—and, for the briefest moment, a feeble flash of fields registered—Syrene fields. Quroc felt his blood quicken—excitement…and a new fear.

Slipping between the series, he reached the offending cylinder.

o   o   o

19

IT WAS WEAK—DEBILITATED—its counter-frequency silvery-bronze sheathing showing the thin transparency of energy depletion that preceded termination by deprivation. The cylinder's indicators showed bright lucid—critical.

Shaking, Quroc's pads raced across the encasement's controls, pushing the catalyst's feed ratio up to supercharge until the unit's safety governors checked further rise of catalyst at seventy. More would be critical, he knew, watching the minor feed greedily on the energy, but, still, Quroc had to fight an overwhelming urge to override the governor. Seventy was so low a rate, and the minor was beyond weak—so weak, in fact, that Quroc wondered if he shouldn't just terminate it to end its misery.

Taking a closer look, he decided not to—not quite yet. He would give it time since it didn't seem in any pain. He could always end it quickly should it start to show distress.

Quroc watched for signs of suffering, marveling all the while at the minor's ability to survive. It was so small. It had suffered such distress. Yet, it was still viable.

Already encased within the mold meant to shape it to the Orcon physiology that was traditional for Syrene—obovate head, arm- and leg-like limbs, long neck supporting the huge pseudo-cranial sphere—it was too young, too small, for that—too small to already have been forced to the conforming that the miniature shackling and training lattice surrounding it demanded that it take. It should still be amorphous in shape, its only feature that of a single unlidded orbital. Instead, it was already shaping to a perfect version of a conformed significant with its two lidded eye-like orbs the most conspicuously prominent features of its tiny face below the cranial dome. This minor was perfect, except for one small blemish, one small glint of sparkling golden glimmer that winked from within its plasma near what was now its shoulder internode. Just one small, strange flaw in a nearly perfect bio-.

The governor released its check, startling Quroc. Anxious, he watched the feed increase in increments to full.

He wasn't sure how long he stood there watching it, but, not until the indicators turned from lucid to yellow and then, finally, to the naug that signified fragile stability, did Quroc become conscious of himself, again, and of the fact that he was stiff from standing over the cylinder for so long.

Questions rose—questions for which there were no answers. How long had the minor been here? How had it been forgotten, its maintenance disengaged? And what was it doing here, anyway? His father had no need for Syrene, now. All Quiloc's work was accomplished from this residence, except for those rare instances when Consul ships would come to whisk him off to some formal function at Ita. Everything else was done by trans-interspacial comlink—holomorphic semblancing—just as good, almost, as being there in body. Quiloc had no need for a Syrene to take him through the Interspaces that separated universes from one another. Quiloc especially had no need or use for an untrained minor.

Untrained—that thought struck Quroc. All the trainers had been long since dismissed from his father's employ. Quroc had checked that fact upon arrival, hoping that Metaxi's trainer was still about. No trainers—not even old Mardoc, his father's senior trainer—had graced the household roster, though. Further, there had been no inventory of Syrene.

An image from the Fleet dispatch he had received via ship-com just decitar before making planetfall niggled at him. It couldn't possibly be, but, suspicious anyway, Quroc cautiously opened the cylinder's seal—the vitriform shielding lifting back to let him penetrate the inner containment field that surrounded the still dormant, feeding minor. The catalyst tingled oddly as he penetrated. His fur electrified, small sparks of static bleeding off to swirl around until they hit the containment field and dissipated by merging with it.

Quroc knew he should be wearing gloves with one so young, not chancing the tearing of its fragile plasma sheathing with his touch. Withdrawing his hands, he felt beneath the unit and found a pair of the pliant coverings still stored in there usual place. Slipping them on, he reached.

At his touch, the minor's orbs opened, spooking Quroc. He was surprised. One just off critical didn't usually rouse. He crooned to it to calm it, and it blinked. "So you have function, little one," he kerred, warbling his words to temper his voice's somewhat graveled character.

The minor flinched, then relaxed when Quroc just kept stroking it. "Can I see?" he asked.

It blinked again, inclining its head slightly to the side, obvious curiosity and question mirrored in its orbs. The tiniest of tactiles, the minor's plasma forced to stream by the conforming lattice that encased it, rose like fine threads from just below the terminal internode of its left upper limb's completion where the shackle encircled it.

Quroc let it explore. When it seemed satisfied, he touched the detention field off and released the bind against its shackles that kept it pinned. Then, he lifted the minor to turn it over.

The minor squealed, then writhed, its body strobing in a terror that was obvious. Its shocks were mild, but Quroc laid the minor back inside the cylinder all the same, unwilling to stress it further. He'd seen all he needed, and what he'd seen revolted him. "Sss," he hissed gently as it continued to struggle. "You'll deplete your energy, again."

The glimmer at the minor's shoulder flared brightly for the briefest moment, then faded. The minor stilled, its orbs concentrated in their focus on Quroc. At once, a fleeting sense of displacement and detachment overcame Quroc, bewildering him until he realized that the minor had probed him—probably for intent—if he was accurately remembering the mental taste.

The feeling was gone as suddenly as it had come, but a slow growl rose in Quroc's throat. Unnerved, he quickly closed the cylinder and sealed it, not bothering to engage the detention field.

Collapsing against the cylinder behind him, Quroc closed his eyes, fighting the fear and panic that threatened to overwhelm him. Weak though it was, the minor was powerful—more powerful than was natural. Like Raganth had been. Like Metaxi. And the dispatch had said that the minor stolen from the Ita Academy was of rare and unusual type, a charan color.

This one was that minor. Of that, Quroc was sure. It was the charan color. It was of Raganth and Metaxi's unorthodox subtype. And it was here. In his sire's residence. In what was supposed to be Quroc's residence some turn.

Long breaths later and finally calm again, Quroc looked back to the cylinder and checked the life supports, then stripped off the gloves. There had to be a reason for the minor's presence—something to do with Quiloc's position as High Consul. Maybe, having been recovered, it was stowed here until it could be returned to Ita. Maybe its life support had been turned off accidentally by household help unused to the fact of Syrene on-premises. Quroc sought any reasonable rationale for the circumstances, circumstances that otherwise could mean disaster to the Q Dynasty. And he knew there was none.

Quiloc would have immediately sent some dispatch off about recovering it, had its presence been legitimate. The Academy's hunt was full on and operational, though. Quroc had heard the status coming in, and that was decitar ago, so no dispatch had been sent. And none would.

He would have to find his sire, though. He would have to know.

Intent on thoughts, and, more, intent on questions that he feared the answers for, Quroc failed to pay attention to his sensors. Hurriedly, he stuffed the gloves beneath the unit, then turned…to find his husky, black-furred sire watching him.

o   o   o

20

QUILOC'S EYES WERE HARD AND GLISTENING. So were his fields.

Quroc's lank fur rose. Just as suddenly, it fell, flattening itself against his skin to expose every gaunt angle of him.

Feeling very much the naked youngling, Quroc shrank away inside himself even as he damned his father's power to intimidate him. Then, he doubly damned himself for succumbing.

Forcing himself to a composure he didn't feel, Quroc bowed. "Father," he said stiffly.

A feeler adorned eye ridge twitched on Quiloc's face, this as the brow arched just a fraction. It was a moment before the black-furred patriarch nodded acknowledgment to Quroc's formal greeting, but, once he did, he shifted completely from frigidity to welcoming father—too welcoming. "Quroc," he said. "It's good to see you. My congratulations on your successful testing and promotion."

Relaxing against one of the cylinders, his thick pelt shimmering in the low light of the chamber as his heavy muscling rippled it, Quiloc tipped an ear toward Quroc. "Megan Primus, now, isn't it?"

Chafing still, Quroc inclined his head.

"You're young to hold the highest archon position in Fleet. "Has anyone offered you a command, yet?"

The biofields surrounding Quiloc showed a tenseness, a guardedness, that belied the amiable tone of voice, the interested pleasantness of face below the eyes, the calm lay of fur, and Quroc realized that his sire was as uneasy in the confrontation as he was. That knowledge comforted Quroc somehow—the mighty Quiloc unsettled by his lowly bastard son. But, then, no wonder, considering the presence of the minor. Quroc straightened his narrow frame and stood to his full height that was just slightly taller than his father's. "No," he said. "I haven't been offered a command. Not yet."

Quiloc nodded knowingly, then said, "Shattam is thinking of trying you. At least, so I've heard. He's losing one of his top archon."

Flex threatened Quroc. He controlled it. But he didn't want his sire using influence to get him posted. He said so—quietly, firmly.

His father shrugged, then stood free from the cylinder he had been lounging against to glance around the chamber. "I thought I'd find you in the holding," Quiloc said, his ears flicking in distaste. "You always liked it here when you were a youngling, though I never knew why." Bringing his focus back to Quroc, Quiloc smiled, his voice softening, though his eyes still glittered, their pupil slits narrowed. "I'm sorry I missed your homecoming. I was otherwise preoccupied."

By his sire's antics, Quroc had to assume the worst, and that rankled him. "Drop pretense, Father," he snarled. "You know that I know." Quroc indicated the encased minor. "This is the minor stolen from Ita, isn't it? And it's not here for any legitimate reason."

Quiloc dropped his eyes—his head, as well. Not in shame, though.

Stalling, Quroc knew. Looking for some neutral answer. Quroc didn't want that answer, that manipulation of truth. "Who stole it, Father?" he asked flatly. "A political friend? Maybe their relative stole it? And maybe you thought you could somehow use Q Dynasty's influence to smooth things over for them? We'll take the firestorm?!"

"No," Quiloc said quietly, though his ears flattened in warning.

Disbelieving, Quroc shook his head, a cold rebuttal ripe. But, seeing Quiloc's mien, he hesitated, then quelled it. His sire's fields read true. His father wasn't bending truth.

...But the brand. Quiloc must have been party to it. Quroc said as much, but his father denied that.

"It's the 'Q' brand on it. Newly laid," Quroc spat. "Right below what's left of the Academy I.D. And you and I are the only ones authorized to use that brand."

The yellow eyes wavered—confirmation to Quroc's mind. There was collusion here. He knew his father, though. One thing his sire was not was dishonorable. But if honor and loyalty conflicted, Quroc wasn't sure how Quiloc would handle it. "What happened? Who laid the brand? Did someone else do this? Are they trying to frame us?"

Quiloc was stubbornly silent. His fields read darkly.

Hissing, Quroc turned away. Something was dangerously wrong. He felt it. He knew it. He knew something else, as well. It was Quiloc who had decided to let the minor terminate—terminate by itself. By atrophy. No record, then. Just a disintegration into nothingness that would never show on the outdated cylinder's operations register. "I know what you did, Father," Quroc said quietly, his own hurt, shame, and disbelief all merging into a confused incredulity. "Why?" he asked, running his hands over the minor's cylinder protectively.

Still, Quiloc gave no answer.

"Is this the way of the Q dynasty, now?" Quroc asked sadly. "Is this how you taught me to be?" And visions of Metaxi rose once more inside him.

Metaxi had been one thing, though. This was a newly formed minor—innocent, even incapable, of wrongdoing. And it was someone else's property. "Why?!" Quroc demanded, his eyes angry, but begging. "WHY?!"

A hand, its clasp strong on his shoulder, gripped Quroc, pulling him around to face. "To protect your brother," Quiloc snarled. "He stole it. He branded it. He brought it as a gift for me." Quiloc's eyes locked onto Quroc's. "Your brother Riloc stole it from the Ben-Drom."

Riloc! Angered, Quroc jerked free from his father's grip. "My half-brother, you mean. Remember? One of your true sons. Not your bastard get like me and Surac."

Quiloc slapped him—hard—though the claws were well retracted. It was a stinging blow Quiloc delivered to Quroc's face, and it made him reel. Hard hands then gripped both Quroc's shoulders, shaking him, demanding his attention. "Look to me," Quiloc snarled.

Silently, defiantly, his own ice-blue eyes stony, Quroc obeyed his father, just as he always had and knew he always would. But his lip curled in contempt.

Quiloc's yellow eyes were harsh. To Quroc's chagrin, though, something else lurked in them and in his father's biofields as well—something that Quroc couldn't read.

"So, all these turns…." his father said. And, drawing a deep breath, Quiloc looked away, though he never released his grip. Then, he sighed. "Listen to me," Quiloc said after a time. "Listen to me," he repeated, looking back and shaking Quroc, again. "You and Surac are my firstborn. Of a love-bond—a true love-bond. I cherish both of you."

Quroc hissed, then spat.

Hissing his own warning, Quiloc's grip of Quroc hardened, pinching nerve-points until Quroc, quivering now, stilled. "You have never, either you or Surac, been treated as less-than," Quiloc said. "…But neither will I treat my other children less-than for your sakes. Just as I have protected you when there was need, so do I protect your brother."

Quroc felt the old nervous tick in his cheek begin to twitch as surrender fought resolve. Resolve won. "And rouse opinion against this family," Quroc snarled, his words a whip. "I'm the one who'll suffer. I'm the one with a career in Fleet and the one you named to follow you as leader of this family. That's not just your brand that Riloc laid. It's my brand, too!"

"No one needs to suffer. Not if no one finds out," Quiloc said, his sight steady on Quroc's. Then Quiloc let him go.

Quroc did nothing as his father's hand reached to code out the unit, but thoughts, visions—visions of Metaxi writhing as his father punished him by terminating the Syrene in front of him, visions of Raganth's dying.... Blending with those came visions of this small minor's inquisitive orbs, its mutilated sheathing, plasma scars just forming, fragile in their coagulation, its terror—this filled Quroc's mind, flooding him with pain, then rage, as he watched his father's hand cancel the unit's power.

A keening started somewhere between Quroc's mind and the darkening cylinder. Tiny glowing tactiles appeared on the clear vitriform, pressing, exploring, struggling for a way out—the minor's.

Something ruptured inside Quroc then, and, never meaning to, he lashed out, his claws vicious in their tearing as he seized his father's arm in a twisting jerk that popped joints and shattered the bones of it with ugly, dull snaps.

Quiloc screamed, falling heavily. Quroc watched as if within some hideous dream—watched his father writhe, the jagged edges of broken bones and pale pink Verdajan blood that was so unlike his own, stark against the shiny black fur, the bones grinding as they rubbed against each other and the stone floor. And, even as he watched, Quroc hit the cylinder's emergency release, bursting the shielding open to grab the minor.

The minor squealed at his rough handling, adding its cries to his father's. Quroc muffled it, pressing its pliant body against his. Then, remote to himself, detached from feeling, he struck his sire a head blow that abruptly stopped Quiloc's pain and screams with unconsciousness.

A shrill tocsin was sounding somewhere, and, cursing, Quroc realized that his father wore a security alarm. There was banging against the chamber's access, now, and a rough, heavy, alien voice bellowed out—the Hellenite, Harg, head of the household guard and Quiloc's personal bodyguard.

The banging stopped, but now there were other sounds, other voices, then a strident buzzing of system overload. They were trying to force the access.

Bewildered and in turmoil, Quroc bent to his father's side, shock at what he'd done penetrating finally. It confused him. Quiloc's open, unseeing eyes...the minor squirming in the crush of Quroc's arm—all of it seemed some dream. Shaking himself to reality, to rationality,

Quroc checked his father's breathing. A rush of pent breath escaped him. He hadn't hurt his sire too badly—nothing that wouldn't heal.

Sharp pings gave warning of the access's impending breach. The minor squirmed more violently, then stilled as if dead. Quroc looked down at it. Dead or not, he wasn't leaving it. Dead or not, he had to get it out of here. Nothing but would stop the consequences, now.

With a last stroke to his father's fur, Quroc rose and bolted for the passage that led to the maze of training cubicles just beyond the holding, then through to gain the disused trainers' quarters. He made for the outer emergency access that led to the death catacombs.

Quroc found the access easily enough, but when he tried his code on it, keying it in with remembered surety, it didn't budge. Nor would it open to Mardoc's old code.

The household guard wasn't far behind now. Bellowed oaths echoed through the ancient stone of the underground complex. Quroc's hand shook as he tried any random series. Nothing. The access wouldn't give.

Pursuers were closing, pounding down passageways they were unfamiliar with in a wild search for him. Quroc had itat, maybe. Shaking, he pried the access mechanism open, his claws shearing with the effort. Its guts exposed, he tried to override the lock, bridging contact points with his digital pads, his flesh and the white fur around it stinking as it burned. Static fire erupted, and the minor, so unnaturally still until then, squealed as the arcing energy touched it. It was still alive.

The minor strobed—violently—the force of it slamming Quroc back against the hallway's opposite wall. But the minor's charge had been enough to overload something. The access opened suddenly with a bang, then, just as suddenly, started to fold shut, again.

Quroc bolted for it, scrambling…but he wasn't fast enough. The access closed—on him—pinning his legs.

He fell forward, the minor still wrapped safely in his arms. The edges of the access's contracting metal leaves cut into his legs, threatening to sever them, the pain excruciating. Quroc cried out.

Someone yelled. Something hard and cold…a metallic clang…the guards had jammed something between the closing door leaves, but the access, though impeded, kept closing.

Then, the pressure on Quroc's legs eased as old and barely functioning species specific sensor safeties finally engaged. The door leaves drew back some, just enough to give Quroc space to wriggle through. But, now, something hot and clammy—two, then three of them—wrapped lengths of themselves around Quroc's legs.

Quroc shuddered. Harg had hold of him, was trying to pull him back, the Hellenite's tentacle's constricting grip a vicious thing. But the access wouldn't give more, even when it became clear that someone was mechanically trying to pry it open, their mutterings and grumblings giving evidence to their failure.

Barked orders, and weaponsfire began to chatter against the door leaves, sprays of radiants leaking through like cold, wet light as an attempt was made to weaken them. Harg's tentacles renewed their grip.

Another appendage—a different one that seemed more sequacious than the others—now squeezed its hot, slimy mass up between Quroc's legs until it was on his side of the access. It probed, seeking solid purchase, but could find none. Giving that up, it slid around Quroc's abdomen, its facile length questing, touching as if tasting, the slime that coated it smearing Quroc's back and sides…his belly. It stopped when it reached the minor carried under Quroc's right arm.

So that was the plan. Quroc dropped the minor, pushing it away from him. His arms free from having to protect the tiny being, he began to abuse the sneaking limb when it tried to grab at the small Syrene. The limb withdrew a little, plumping itself up under his attack, its soft, mushiness surprisingly resistant to any penetration by Quroc's claws.

Abandoning his attack, Quroc fought to pull his legs free from their entrapment by Harg's tentacles using leverage and every bit of strength that he could summon. Responding, the slimy limb wrapped itself around his upper body.

Until now, Quroc had resisted the panic rising in him, but, when the limb slithered up to grasp his neck, its brackish smelling slimecoat actually brushing his face, that panic overtook him. He struck out, biting down into the snaky thing until his teeth met one another. And he hung on, despite the villainous taste of slurry that began to spew from the appendage in its wounding.

The limb started writhing. Grimly, Quroc hung on, even when the limb's whipping movement threatened to snap his neck. And he clawed his way forward, his digit-tips finding any fissure in the rough rock floor to gain a purchase.

Slowly, millimetron by millimetron, Quroc felt his legs begin to pull free, the tentacles wrapped around them stretching to maintain and even tighten their hold as they were dragged with them through the aperture.

Suddenly he was free. Quroc's legs cleared the access which now snapped shut, its old sensors, antiquated as they were, holding true to their archaic program to close on anything not Xentauri. A terrible shriek rang out from the sequacious mass Quroc still held clamped within his teeth as it jerked in spasm and released a thick, stinking syrupy sludge.

Retching, Quroc spat, flinging the heavy member from him, then reached down to peel the other, still wrapped but severed, tentacles from about his legs to let them drop, shuddering and quivering to the ground.

Sprawled and gasping, Quroc eyed the access. How long would it hold under the bombardment, he wondered? His hand reached automatically for his weapons harness and the ship codifier that should have been there. But they weren't, and he realized that he didn't have them—not the harness with its store of weapons and survival gear, not the codifier, not his uniform. Quroc's sight reached upward to the stone ceiling. Those were somewhere far above.

The minor stood watching him, its photoluminescence providing the only light, faint as it was, to the tunnel he lay in. Quroc groaned. Feeling in the form of pain was now beginning to return to his numb legs. He gritted, then ground his teeth against it, and reached to rub more feeling back into them, the pain of his action so excruciating that he had to stop himself from crying out.

He had to get up. He had to move. They would be coming for him and the Syrene, moving to cover any access port to the tunnel and the catacombs. Time was critical if he was to escape before they sealed every path to freedom.

The light around Quroc began to dim, and he looked up to see the minor wandering away, its faint luminescence fading as it moved farther and farther up the tunnel's slope, leaving only heavy darkness in its wake.

Swearing, Quroc tried to rise to follow it, but his legs buckled. "Syrene, come here," he hissed. But, after what seemed a small forever, Quroc realized that it was gone and would not come back.

The sounds of weaponsfire on the other side of the jammed access stopped. Then, a pulsing sound so deep that it made Quroc's teeth vibrate began within the very rock that surrounded the access port. The rock actually began to glow, throbbing and bulging outward at each pulse.

A slow fear permeated Quroc as he recognized the booming sound. His father's outer fortifications were substantial, but nothing, nothing, not even the thick, resilient betrad of the reinforced stone's composition could withstand an assault of Ghison fire.

Again, Quroc tried to rise, only to fall, once more. Then, he crawled, blindly and by feel, the booming throb of the bombardment to the wall behind him a grim warning of its impending breach.

o   o   o

21

SURAC WOKE FROM A VIVID NIGHTMARE at the urgent pricks of her son's claw tips. "What is it, Quiroc?" she whispered, shaking off the dream.

"I think its Grandbrother," the youngster said. "I think he's in trouble."

Confused, Surac asked, "Grandbrother?" Quiroc had never called any of his half-uncles by that title.

"Quroc?" he suggested, his blue eyes blinking in a timidity very unlike his normal nature.

Surac shook her head. "Quroc," she said, her soft voice dubious. "How would you know him? Even if he were here. You've never even met him."

"He looks just like you...like me," Quiroc said, insisting. "...And he's in trouble. I *saw*."

Suroc frowned, dipping her refined head close to sniff her son, his distress strong, but his knowing sure. Still, distrusting native ways in the face of common sense, she asked, "You're very sure?" She knew her son. He was a prankster, and very good at it.

Quiroc nodded, his eye-skin crinkling in worry, his ears and kit whiskers quivering.

Her nightmare made sense to her now—the twin connection. Quroc had been fleeing something terrible, and she had lived it with him, though not, perhaps, accurate to his reality. In her nightmare, she had been wrapped by something trying to squeeze the very life, even the very breath, from her. Cloying, sticky, awful—

Quiroc was becoming more agitated. He pulled at her, begging. "Mamman, he needs help. I don't know what to do," Quiroc cried in whisper. "Please, Mamman. I've sabotaged the security. I've closed all the accesses so Grandsire's soldiers can't get out, but now they make the rock bend."

The rock bend. That vision brought fear. And, now, Surac understood the faint rumbling vibration she felt. She placed a well-appointed hand to the wall beside her. Yes, it penetrated to the very foundations of her ancestral home. The Ghison.

Surac's anger rose. They dared destroy the sanctuary. And where was Quiloc? He would never allow this.

Sprung to standing, Surac said, "Show me," to her young genius son.

Quiroc led Surac to a room immediately adjacent to her quarters. It was supposed to be his sleeping room. Instead, it was more a workroom than anything else. Leading her to one of his mainframe computers, he sat into the terminal, and, assured that she looked on, he coded it on.

Digits dancing across the com's lightboard, Quiroc switched on a tiny robo-monitor that sat inert atop the console. It came to life, whirling upward at his touch to the lightboard. It hovered there until Quiroc cued it again, then fled the room so swiftly that, to Surac's sight, it was only a clear blur. Likewise, the screen in front of Quiroc was a whirling blur of color as Robber, as Quiroc had named his hand-built toy, flew through passageways at near kinetically-impossible speeds. Moments later, the screen cleared suddenly, giving Surac a sense of vertigo. What that screen showed, though, enraged her—a horde of house guards cowering within portable shielding as other guards aimed small hand-held Ghison generators at the Syrene Holding's outer emergency escape access. They were firing on the very founding walls of Surac's ancient home. Worse, they were firing against stone that protected the ancient warren, centuries old, of the first Q Dynasty matriarch. "Can Robber get to the other side?" Surac asked.

Quiroc's digits flew across the lightboard, and, again, a whirl of color crossed the monitor, making Surac's sight swim. Then, the viewer went dark. Surac grabbed onto Quiroc's chair for support as she lost all sense of direction. Again, Quiroc changed something, and faint images of pattern emerged on the viewer. The patterns froze suddenly, and, at the edge of them, something moved. It was a something that crawled on all fours. Surac gasped, instantly recognizing the form of her twin brother—his faintly iridescent fur.

"Why?" she said, speaking her thoughts aloud. "Why is the house guard after him? Why is he running?" It made no sense to her. Quroc was named heir-apparent—house liaison with "the Outside"—after Quiloc.

"Something about a Syrene minor. Something about something Riloc did," Quiroc said. "Riloc stole something. Grandsire did something, and Grandbrother attacked Grandsire because of it."

Surac's ears flattened. Disturbed that her son had witnessed a fight between the two house patriarchs, she pulled Quiroc's chin around to catch his sight. "You saw this?" she asked.

His eyes big, Quiroc nodded, and Surac realized that he knew the traditional implications of what he'd seen. What he didn't know was that, when it came to fights between Quiloc and Quroc, tradition did not apply. The two had always been at odds, mostly because they were so much alike…because they cared so much what each thought about the other.

"I'm scared, Mamman," Quiroc said.

"Currur," she said, agreeing. "We'll talk about it later. It will be all right."

Looking back to the screen, Surac watched her twin's crawling form, then shook her head in disgust as she wondered how she could help him. "He has to have come in on a ship," she said. "Probably his own. Where would he have parked it, Quiroc? He would be heading there."

Quiroc went back to the lightboard. "It's in the ancillary hanger," he said, turning on the house surveillance for a moment. "It's beautiful," he whispered, then flicked the house surveillance off, again. "Can we help him, Mamman?"

"I think so," Surac answered, though she was doubtful. "Maybe," she said, again. "It will be tricky, though. And I'll need your help."

For the first time, the worried look on her kit's face ebbed a little. Tentatively, he smiled, a touch of his normal rakishness returning. "I think Grandbrother needs these to get into his ship," Quiroc said, and, to Surac's amazement, pulled what she recognized as a codifier and a weapons harness from a compartment of his computer station. "And maybe this, too," Quiroc added, his eyes twinkling as he unwadded a shimmering skinsuit. "Maybe to protect him when he's flying out in space?"

Surac shook her head, displeasure and happiness mixing oddly within her. "Quiroc, you're going to have to learn to leave another's property alone."

"Yes, Mamman."

o   o   o

22

QUROC HAD CRAWLED ONLY HALFWAY through the main passage of the rising tunnel when the heavy, dull throb of the Ghison fire's bombardment stopped. That meant one thing to Quroc—his pursuers had broken through and would, once more, be closing on his position from behind. Now, it wouldn't be just trying to evade guards who were hunting inward for him from other access points into the catacombs and tunnel, it would be a matter of escaping pursuit from behind, as well—pursuit that was much closer.

Again, Quroc tried his legs, but, as before, they failed, buckling under him, his head and one shoulder smashing hard against the tunnel's rock wall as he fell. Knowing that he could never elude capture this way...that the reason for his actions—the minor—was probably already a moot one, Quroc just closed his eyes and lay where he'd fallen, face down in the musty-tasting grit of the tunnel floor. He lay there, waiting for his father's guards, the futility of crawling farther, the utter doom he felt, overwhelming him.

How long he lay there awaiting capture, he didn't know. It seemed an empty eon as measured by the ragged breaths of cold, stale air he dragged into his pre-lungs, each draught of it an eternity all its own, each one loud and hollow-sounding in the darkness. And, in those empty eons, Quroc's mind imagined ghosts—not

Metaxi's—but the ghosts of his ancestors whose grizzled, mummified remains lay within the catacombs all around and beneath him in the maze of death vaults that was this place. Those ghosts seemed almost tangible to Quroc as his scanner implants picked up vestiges of residual energy from unknown source. That brought him back to rational. The residuals weren't vestiges at all, he realized. The sensor images were real. Every follicle of Quroc's now dust-coated, filthy fur rose as his imaginings became credible.

Terror drove him, his legs tingling with its effect as he rose to try to break and run. But the fields were all around him, gold and penetrating. They seemed to smother him, to swallow him. There was no way away from them. Quroc tried to flee, but, his true sight useless in the steeped blackness of the place and his sensors overwhelmed, he only crashed against the rock surfaces that were the tunnel walls.

Suddenly, the penetration cleared as if it hadn't been. His scanners cleared. Better still, his mind cleared, and he realized that there *were* fields—Syrene fields—above and to the left. The minor, self-illumined by its own charan fields as well as by an odd golden halo, was scrambling up one of the long, narrow ducts that fed air in from the surface.

Renewed hope filled Quroc—the minor, safe and within sight—and the duct offered practical means of escape. Then, Quroc gulped, a new horror filling him. The minor was more than two-thirds of the way up the narrow duct. If it reached the top without live Xentauri escort, it would be terminated as it violated the species specific security net that surrounded every duct and access of the place.

"Syrene. Stop," he hissed, hoping no one was near enough to hear him. But the minor only paused long enough to look down at him before continuing its upward scramble.

Cursing, Quroc braced himself and tried to stand again, and, this time, his legs, tingling painfully and quivering, did hold. Pulling himself up into the duct, he had a moment's panic as the shaft seemed to squeeze shut about him, suffocating him. Fleet training rescued him, calmed him, and, feeling for purchase with his feet, Quroc began to climb the duct, an ascent that had once been a source of pure adventure for him when he was small, but now was only terrifying.

Finding old niches he had chiseled out as a kit— barely toeholds for him, now—Quroc worked his way up toward the minor, his climbing slow, so slow, dead web-hangers and nameless other things dislodging to fall into his upturned face. Dust burned his eyes. Forced to, Quroc closed them and depended on images projected into his brain from his implants to guide him.

One full eternity later, but only a third of the way up, Quroc heard the quick, quiet padding of a solitary set of footsteps in the passage beneath him. He stilled, not even daring to breathe, dread of certain discovery filling him. His pursuer would be sure to have, at least, a scanner, if not a tracer. But, moments later, to Quroc's surprise, the footsteps faded.

Resuming his ascent, Quroc neared where the minor clung, stopped for some unfathomed reason Quroc could only bless, its golden halo vanished. Quroc braced himself against the duct's dry, dusty walls, opened his eyes, then reached to grab it.

It moved. He missed.

It started climbing up again, its movements swift and sure. "Stop," he hissed out the command.

It looked down at him, its orbs seeming like voids within its glowing body, the glimmer at its shoulder gleaming like a golden star. Quroc felt the minor's probe, its reach with its mind to touch his. He shook as that probe penetrated, and he had to clamp his teeth down on his tongue until he tasted blood to stop himself from screaming.

He felt the minor in his mind, querying. A shiver coursed down Quroc's neck, his body threatening flex. He hated them that touch—this one's so much like Metaxi's had been. "Stop," he gasped. He was slipping, losing consciousness. The long fall back down the air duct loomed.

Threads, cloying threads, engulfed his face, probing at his sealed eyelids. Insistently.

Quroc ground his teeth deeper through his tongue, his pale blue blood welling up to fill his mouth. He swallowed it, the metallic taste of his own flux bringing him a rush that steadied him.

The threads retreated.

Forcing himself to look, Quroc found the minor's orbs staring into him. He felt it asking. "Unsafe for you. Stay attached to me…below my head," he croaked, hoping that someway, even though untrained, it would understand. He couldn't telepath ideas to it—something it would immediately comprehend. Not now. He couldn't even think how, right now.

Golden sparks flashed, the minor's orbitals alive with them, the glittering gilt flaw at its shoulder internode flaring out to beyond brilliant, as well. Then, the minor dropped, its slight, almost massless body floating gently downward past Quroc's face.

Quroc felt the minor's tactiles grasp his chest fur, pulling it as the tiny Syrene laced them into it, seeking purchase. More footsteps…and Quroc recognized his father's voice ordering the searchers. Quroc heard the household guard maligning him as they searched the maze of side passages. He was sure of capture, now. They would be using "sniffers" as well as scanners and DNA tracers. Unconsciously, he began to quiver.

There was a yell. A scuffling. Running footsteps. Unmistakably, unaccountably, the voices faded.

It was a very perplexed and relieved Quroc who waited until the sounds below him were just far off echoes. Then he quickly clambered the rest of the way up the shaft. He didn't have much time.

Quroc popped his head out of the duct and into the open air of the estate's paved side courtyard that doubled as a landing platform. It was dark, now. By the lay of the stars overhead, it was early nightfall—local wake-time. Quroc glanced fearfully about, fully expecting the security tocsins to sound. When, after a few moments, no alarms wailed, Quroc became even more nervous. Something wasn't right.

He looked around, seeking some cover in the open courtyard. But none offered except the hanger where his ship lay. That hanger had its access open when it should have been closed, its upper launch bay lifted to the stars. Something definitely was not right.

The minor whimpered. Quroc shushed it.

There was nowhere else to go, except back down the shaft. That Quroc wouldn't do.

Fighting the knowledge that he was heading straight into a trap, Quroc heaved himself out of the relative safety of the duct, pressing the minor to his body to make certain its shackles were grounded to him as, together, they passed through the security net. Then, he sprinted toward the hanger, his mind a blank in the fear of anticipated capture.

He made it. Disbelief flooded him as no one challenged when he sprinted for the open hanger. No assault of stunners.... It was uncanny. His father's security was much better than that. And the thought crossed Quroc's mind that his father was playing him. It was the only answer.

Feeling the fool on some macabre holomorphic training stage, Quroc dropped and rolled, keeping the minor close and protected in the curve of his curled body as he dove for cover behind a land skimmer parked just inside the gaping hanger door. Then, he waited.

But, again, no challenge, no stun-fire.

Stealthily, Quroc eased toward his waiting ship, scanning for biofields…expecting.

No fields showed. No sentry system engaged to assault him.

Cautiously, Quroc poked his head up. "This is ridiculous," he grumbled. And, getting up, he boldly walked, calm and resolute, toward where his ship lay. And he kept expecting, kept waiting for, his father and a guffawing house guard to step out from some hiding place and capture him.

Reaching the side of his warbird, Quroc waited. But, still, no one came forward to end the charade.

He glanced toward the security monitors, walked over to one and touched it. It was dead. More charade? Or was someone helping him?

He looked back to his warbird, then just stood there dumbly, trying to figure out a way to get inside the Veerwing Quadstar Harrier without a codifier.

The minor—. Glancing down to the Syrene still curled against his chest, the protective crook of his long arm cradling it there, Quroc contemplated it. It seemed quite strong despite what it had been through. Maybe he could convince it to strobe again and short this lock, as well. It was worth a try, though Quroc doubted much success on the warship's much more intricate technology.

Clambering up the Harrier's side, he reached the portal…only to have it open just as he reached toward the locking mechanism. A hand grabbed at him. He smashed down on it instinctively, jerking back to crush himself against the Quadstar's fuselage to avoid the weapons discharge he was sure would follow.

"ROWL!"

Quroc frowned, recognizing the scream. That was Surac's voicing. He was certain. "Surac?" he hailed, still cautious.

No answer—just an ominous silence.

Scared, frustrated, and getting mad, Quroc set his teeth, hissing quietly. This was impossible. Surac would never betray him, would never aid his sire against him. They had been through too much together. …Unless Quiloc was using Surac's son as leverage. Surac would betray him for Quiroc. And she—her DNA so identical to his own that the computer might disregard the minute differences—was the only one who could possibly hazard accessing the ship with the codifier, though it would still be a chancy thing.

"Surac!" he hailed again, worried now more about his twin being assaulted by the ship's cabin security weapons than about being captured.

But, still, there was no answer.

Terrified for Surac, now, Quroc eased toward the open port. What if the ship's scanners, having sensed him and gotten a measure of the few differences between them, the most obvious being their respective sexes, had already fired on her?

Quroc peeked around the edge of the portal. His twin was there, curled into a small ball of still and silent blue and white striped fur. "Surac!" he yelped, launching himself through the portal, uncaring whether it was a trap or not. Surac was hurt.

Leaping to reach the com, Quroc slammed his palm down on its security override, then turned to see to Surac. He pivoted just in time to see the port sealing shut, its lock clicking into place, and Surac springing to her feet, a snarling menace. "You *bastard!*" his sister snarled. She was rubbing her arm.

Her good arm snaked out, claws bared, and Quroc barely twisted away in time to protect the minor who still clung to him. Surac's claws caught him across the shoulder, blooding him once just lightly, then withdrew.

Warily, Quroc turned back. He fully expected to see a stunner in his sister's hand. "Surac?"

She held nothing, no weapon against him. She only glared. "You bastard," she repeated. "Here," she hissed, shoving toward him the weapons harness, the codifier, and uniform and boots he'd left in his room.

Quroc stared down at them, unthinking, and, in his mind's sight, saw the hanger's dead security monitor. He looked to her, then, his blue eyes misting. And, not for the first time, Quroc blessed the fact the had a twin—a smart, loyal twin. "How did you know I was in trouble?"

"Quiroc. He figured it out. He saw you fighting with Quiloc, then woke me. Then Harg was brought up minus half his software."

Harg. Quroc flinched just thinking about it. But Quiroc…"Quiroc doesn't even know me. He's never met me," Quroc said.

Surac laughed somewhat bitterly, yet there was relief there. "Well, considering," she said, bending an arm to lay it next to his so that the length of their stripes matched, each bend, irregularity and swirl a mirror image to each other, "it wouldn't be too hard to figure out."

Quroc tipped an ear, then indicated the ship com. "You took a chance," he said. "The com could have decided not to make exception for your sex."

"Quiroc said it wouldn't as long as I used this along with your codifier," she said, holding out a small, obviously homemade device. "And I believe my son," she added haughtily. "But you certainly took long enough in getting here. …The ship's prepped and ready. Fully charged."

Quroc took the small device from Surac's hand and turned it over and over, a soft hissing whistle pushing through his teeth. "Did Quiroc make this?" he asked.

"He did. He makes a lot of things like that. He's the one that subverted the house security system." Surac stopped as Quroc raised astonished eyes. She laughed. "He's just like you, Quroc. Temperamentally, I mean. He's a lot smarter than you were, though. Or me."

"This is genius," Quroc said, handing the device back to her.

"He's that, too. And it worries me. But enough of that. Get yourself gone while you still can…before the guard figures out they're chasing Quiroc, not you."

That jolted Quroc. "They're after Quiroc?!" Then, in his mind came the re-echoed sound memory—the set of solitary padfalls in the tunnel. They made sense, now. "But the tracers!" he said. And Quroc began to try to pry the minor from its wrap around him, intending what he didn't know yet, but something, some way…. He had to help the youngster.

Surac put out a restraining hand. "It's okay. Even if they catch him, they won't hurt him," she said. "But they probably won't catch him," she added, and she extended her leg to expose the inner surface of her thigh.

A patch of fur was missing—quite a large patch. "He's got a bit of help to confuse the tracers and such they're using. The guard should be lost in the catacombs for at least a small moon's turn or so."

Quroc stopped, then grinned and shook his head, loving her. "Surac…. Thanks."

She kerred faintly and ducked her head, then pushed her way passed him to the portal. "You won't be able to come back, you know," she warned. "Not for awhile, anyway."

Quroc nodded, then reached to grab her, the minor squealing as he crushed her against him. "I love you."

"I know," she muttered, squirming a little. She kissed him with her tongue, then, just lightly on the nose as sisters were prone to, then firmly pushed him away. "Now get out of here before it's all in vain," she scolded. "And when you get the chance, transcom me all the why's of this little situation."

"I will. When it's all over," he promised, coding open the sealed port.

She was gone, then, slipping down the side of the ship and out the hanger's access. Quroc watched her go, then sealed the port, strange sorrow filling him. Surac was right. He couldn't come back. Probably not ever. His father would disown him. He'd probably be lucky to keep his career in Fleet when his father had finished with him. But the Dynasty was safe. And so was the Syrene, he thought grimly.

Quroc glanced down at the minor. So much like Metaxi…. No. He wouldn't change things. He didn't need another one to haunt him. He didn't need another Syrene to ride his memories. How to get it back to its rightful owner, though—the Ben-Drom, his father had said—without implicating himself or the Dynasty.

Both his ears flattened. He couldn't see a way, not with the brand seared into it.

The ship's com blinked on, its defenses automatically coming alive to target whatever the nonstop seek/find sensors identified as threat potential. Quroc checked the monitors to find a strange Xentauri and a Vischurian Silver slipping toward the household. Their fields read as thieves only, nothing more harmful, nothing deadly. Quroc let them be. They would only prove more diversion, and that could be a good thing…for him, for Surac and for her son Quiroc.

Quroc slipped into his place at the harrier's con, the minor climbing off of him as if it understood the need. Switching the ship's controls from automatic to manual, Quroc canceled the targeted weaponry that was honed on the two intruders, then fired the atmospheric thrusters and outed with a practiced, easy grace.

As the ship cleared the hanger's launch bay, Quroc got one final look at his ancestral home, its sprawling angles and curves. The two upturned faces of the thieves showed surprise. They pointed at him. Actually, Quroc realized, they pointed at the minor who clung to the viewscreen, watching everything. And Quroc's sorrow at another spurious leave-taking from his father welled up inside him, bringing an uncomfortable tingle to his eyes, and to his chest and throat until he felt as if he'd drown in the sensation.

Rotating the harrier, Quroc angled it toward space just as his father and the guard emerged from underground. Pausing it a moment, he tipped a wing, acknowledging, then punched it, his destination decided in that instant.

○   ○   ○

23

THEY HAD MISSED IT. Matac swore. They had all missed. First Modoc and Che'eert had let Riloc and the minor slip past them, and, now, the Cadre mach had missed Quroc. "Incompetent fools," Matac hissed. She was angry.

Leaning back into the snuggle that was the only item of comfort beyond the necessary in her techtronic-laden apartment, Matac ran through the entire situation again, looking for some escape from the inevitable, some contingency or countermeasure she had overlooked. Finding none, her ears sagged. She was defeated. The operation was a wash.

Matac didn't like to lose. Matac liked to win, and, best, she liked to win alone. She had told no one about her operation—not Pryr, not Belamy—no one. That was her way. Once she had an assignment, how she carried it out was no one's business. The less minds that knew, the better. That assured a tighter, cleaner operation, with less chance for failure from security breaches, intentional or otherwise.

But this operation had gone wrong, and it was her fault. Matac rarely ever depended on others to do her work, but, this time, she'd had no choice—not without breaching the Academy herself, something Belamy as Fleet Director had strictly and vehemently ordered Special Operations not to do. So she had used Riloc. And Modoc. And Che'eert. And, then, the Cadre mach. And, true to Hadron's Law, the quarry was lost—too many operatives.

So, the operation was blown, and, now, she had to stop Quroc from taking the damned minor to the authorities—authorities who would destroy the minor to glean its memories, which would lead them straight to Riloc, which, in turn, would lead straight back to Matac…which, once those same authorities finished their interrogation of her, would blow the whole Cadre organization wide open—something that could *not* happen.

"Miserable, bungling idiots," Matac growled, and swore, again. Modoc's miss she could understand, but it was inconceivable to her that an entire network of Cadre machon, their sole and very specialized mission being to intercept and seize or destroy, could miss so plain a target as Quroc's fighter.

Without a Syrene significant with him, Quroc couldn't cross the interspace, and that meant that he'd had to use one of the few ring bridges that physically spanned the Betweens from universe to universe—specifically the ones whose frequencies were designed to bridge from Universe Xi to Universe Itae. How hard could it be to intercept a target that had only several options instead of an infinity of them?

Still, though they stalked and chased his wake, the mach had missed, and, even now, Quroc was out there somewhere in Universe Itae's intergalactic expanses, heading straight for Ita Centralis and the very authorities

Matac feared. "Canis!" Matac snarled again, frustration bringing her to flex. "So *what* if Quroc's running the Edge?! Run it, too. He's not *that* good." And, though she knew she wouldn't, Matac wanted very much to punish the Cadre mach for their fear, legitimate as it was. Who would have ever thought the conservative Quroc to run the dangerous Edge. Who would have thought him to escape his father's house with the minor? Matac flipped through the file on her computer screen. It was against his every profile.

Matac shook her head, fighting back her body's urge to spit and flex and strike. Forcibly, she calmed herself, resigned to present circumstances. There was nothing for it. The minor would have to be destroyed, Quroc with it. The slaughter of the innocents—it was one of the unavoidables in war.

She was ready for what she had to do. Matac was always ready. A touch of her pads across the comboard brought up the necessary images. She sampled all of them, constructing image- and sound-bits into exactly what she needed to accomplish the final operations task.

It took only moments to do, and, like all her technical work, it was perfect. No one—especially not the Grundian, Frigog—would suspect.

Matac rose and brushed her fur to lay, then took her place within the holomorphic stage, a portacom patched to main in hand. She would have to do this live, on-stage. Nothing less would do when it came to Frigog.

Matac touched on-link. Instantly, her call went through, Base Commander Frigog's visage appearing in holo- immediately in front of Matac, the Grundian's garishly veined features of pulsing green vascular networks laid on raw and sticky-looking blue skin repulsive to every one of Matac's natural instincts. "Mega-Commander Frigog," Matac said.

"Regulus Poteck, sir," the Grundian replied, her vocalization a muffled ratcheting as it reverberated through the membrane that coated the top of her superior cavity.

Upon Matac's indication of impending orders, the Grundian did the expected. She involuted, exposing her coby-sense, comparable to an audio-visual recording device, only, in this case, completely biological. Matac was glad to see that. That coby function would accomplish two things. First, the minor would be taken out. Second, the Regulus Poteck, a degenerate rank-abusive, would soon no longer hold his post in Fleet. That coby would ensure as much, and Frigog, a good commander who had been passed over for promotion many a time, finally might advance. Matac practically purred, the computer translating the action into a match for Poteck's characteristic sanguinity. And then she— Matac-as-Poteck—gave the order, her only sorrow being that Quroc would go down, as well. He had been a good, if regulation-bound, commander. It really was too bad. The slaughter of the innocents..

o   o   o

24

IT WAS A TROUBLED MEGA-COMMANDER FRIGOG who contemplated the orders given her by the Regulus Poteck. She knew Poteck. She knew how debased and self-serving Poteck was. "Intercept and destroy," Poteck had ordered, and a regulus order, regardless, was law—to be followed by Fleet no matter how it may violate Omniversal law.

Repeatedly, Frigog replayed her coby of Poteck's orders. Repeatedly, she failed to find a chink, some loop-hole, to use to legitimately amend those orders. There just wasn't any.

Dumping her coby imprint into one datachip, then into two more just for safety's sake, Frigog sent a concentrated pulse from her brain to another set of waiting chips, imprinting them with her own orders. Then, she paged her second-in-command. "Where is Metan Rajan?" she asked when he appeared.

"Gone to pick up Kahn," the second replied once his phasing-through solidified. "They're both due to come on-duty, and Kahn should have been back by now. 'Jan thought it best that he go after him. Kahn's in rut."

"Mmm," Frigog hummed, cringing inside herself. Rutting Droms were *most* notorious. "Well, set these orders to Rajan's ship com," Frigog said, handing over one of her own cobied datachips. "Make sure he understands that his fliers, including Kahn, follow these, my orders, exactly. I repeat, exactly."

The second looked to her a moment. He looked long and hard, then said, "Exactly, Megan Frigog." And Frigog knew that he knew that there was trouble coming.

Frigog watched her second dissolve to exit. She was glad to have Rajan. Rajan as lead, Kahn his second, was exactly what she needed. Trouble-makers though they were, their talent and their targeting was absolute. And Rajan could hold the inept elements of the wing in check. Rajan, she knew, would make sure her orders were executed correctly.

o   o   o

25

"Hssc, Kahn. Must go," Rajan whispered to the Altan Drom who was his wing and comrade. "Come."

Kahn rolled over, trying to ignore the saurischian's insistent hiss. His blood-high long since spent, Kahn's usually tightly cord-strung body was flaccid with fatigue. The she had been demanding, and, now, Kahn only wanted sleep. Rajan should know that. They had been friends too long not to know each other's kind-needs. And, right this itat, Kahn's need was sleep.

Rajan did know that, but Rajan also knew that night was near, and night would bring the Low Drom klah to wakefulness and movement. So, if they didn't out from the household soon, they would be caught, and caught meant they would be dead meat hanging from some Low Drom's talons. Low Droms were very possessive of, even obsessive about, their she-s…not that *that* fact had ever stopped Kahn when he found a willing she he wanted.

Kahn had snuggled further in beside the she with a growled demand for Rajan to "let-alone and go away." To that, the soft, pliant green skin of Rajan's broad, flat snout wrinkled up in amused disgust. His long, tapered tail twitched. "Hssc, Kahn. Must go now! Klah wake," Rajan insisted. And he snaked that heavy, prehensile stretch of ridged, serrated tail along Kahn's side to find one of the few soft, vulnerable places of Kahn's body—places where the plating that underlay the hide met at juncture.

"HrrAIGHT!"   Kahn jerked upright, talons clearing sheaths as he struck out.

But Kahn found no mark.   Judiciously, Rajan had moved.

"YOU STUNG ME!" Kahn bellowed.

"Hsssss, Kahn," Rajan warned with a nervous glance toward the inner access. "Quiet. You rouse klah guards." And, carefully, Rajan listened for any telltale sound of movement from beyond. Luckily, the walls were thick. Luckily, the security system had been subverted.

Now, Rajan's sight caught on the Low Drom she. She lay quiet and unmoving, not having roused or even twitched to Kahn's yell. That worried Rajan. And he didn't like the look of the she. Her biofield flux was very low to his naturally spectral-sensitive sight. "She h'okay, Kahn?" Rajan asked, his long lips crinkling in an anxious fluttering wave that ran up and down his snout.

"Hmmrr. Why shouldn't she be fine?" Kahn grumbled absently as he groped about for his castoff eye-shields.

"You venom poison maybe?" Rajan asked, as, cautiously, he reached to check the she's vitals with one bare-boned hand, the raw, puce colored nerve-net that covered it supersensitive.

The Low Drom she's feel was clammy, but there was strong lifesign to her, Rajan found. What was normal for her kind, though, the saurischian didn't know. What he did know was that the unnatural act of Andromedan's performing heterosexual mating, whether Low or Altan, was rough in the mildest sense. Sometimes it was even deadly.

"CHO'TAN, DON'T TOUCH HER!" Kahn bellowed, striking Rajan's hand away. "SHE'S FINE. JUST SLEEPING."

This time Rajan hadn't been quick enough. "Sssss. You quiet, Kahn!" he said through clenched teeth as he tried to shake the sting of Kahn's slap out of his hand's nerve-net that was now livid and visibly throbbing.

"Hmgrr," Kahn grumbled, still trying to find his shields.

Spying the mislaid eye-shields, Rajan picked them up and held them out.

Irritably, Kahn snatched them away and slipped them on, sealing them to his face with an easy movement that belied the fact of their intricate fit beneath his heavy browplate. As those shields slipped in place, a flash of static energy set off by contact melded them to Kahn's face, their scanners immediately engaged. And the read those scanners gave, showed Kahn that his saurischian friend was truly worried. "The she's just fine, 'Jan. Just sleeping," Kahn said, then scowled. "Like I was, you sorry j'hurad. And outworlders aren't supposed to touch she-s. You know that!"

"This be normal?" Rajan asked with a dubious glance toward the yet unmoving she. Her stillness really bothered him.

"For Low kind," Kahn rumbled, locking his weapons belt around his flanks. "Come on," he urged. "Let's get out of here. Why'd you let me sleep so long?!"

Rajan tipped an eyeridge toward the Dromedan, but held his silence. He was well used to Kahn and the sublimations his ego demanded.

"Where'd you leave our transportation?" Kahn demanded as they fled the emergency safety access to gain the alley, Kahn moving as if he was drugged—sluggish.

Rajan cast his head directionally. "Ship be—"

Weapons, two of them, pressed against Rajan's flesh, silencing him immediately. Strangely, he'd had no forewarning, which was unusual for him. With a glance, Rajan saw two more weapons pressed against Kahn's hulking form.

"On your bellies, both of you," a gruff voice said.

Both Rajan and Kahn ignored the command.

A glimpse backward showed Rajan a host of Low Andromedan he-s—at least eight of them—their weapons drawn and leveled, the energy from the body shielding glowing in the deepening darkness.

"You're under klah arrest for trespass, slimies," the nearest Drom said.

"We were guests," Kahn said, turning round to face the speaker. "Ask the she," he said, inclining his head toward the now sealed access.

Rajan groaned. Doing it was one thing; admitting it, another.

"Both of you?" one captor sneered.

"No. Just me," Kahn said easily. "The j'hurad, here," he said, indicating Rajan, "just came to get me. We've got duty."

Laughter, harsh and caustic, greeted that remark. "No more, you don't," said another voice—a deeper, harsher voice—its owner boldly stepping toward them, though no haze of body shield surrounded him. The obvious leader by the way the other Low Droms rendered passage to him, this Drom reeked of the bitterness that Rajan recognized as burrite, an addictive that gave its user a twisted form of ecstasy at any stimulus, including pain. This one was dangerous.

"The klah-lead will have your blood," the stinking, drug-saturated Drom sneered. "That she's his property. You're both dead." The leader turned toward Rajan. "Your fluids should be especially pleasurable to let."

Malicious laughter again spread through the group, and Rajan's hide gave an involuntary ripple. Low Droms, unlike their Altan cousins—Kahn's kind—were notorious. Slighter, weaker, and, in most cases, except, perhaps, for Kahn, shorter than their larger relatives, Low Droms made up for their deficiencies by sheer treachery. Honor and fair play were not Low Andromedan traits like they were the Altans. Nor was following the law. And, in truth, neither Kahn nor Rajan had broken any laws. The she had let them in. Voluntarily. It had been she who had subverted the special house security. That evidence alone would clear them at a hearing…should they make it that far. By the look of circumstances, though, they weren't going to get that chance. A look toward Kahn's fields showed Rajan that Kahn, too, realized their dire predicament. Rajan let another ripple shimmy down his hide, this one, a signal.

Kahn struck, his talons ripping at the leader's face to lay the flesh of head open from auricle to jaw seat as his spiked heel kicked back to connect with one of his guards, the kick's force shoving that Drom into his startled partner. Both guards went down as Kahn found a third and fourth.

Rajan had rolled as Kahn struck. Engaging body armor with veteran ease before his guards had time to fire, he drew his own disruptor as they finally reacted. Their weapons-fire stopped immediately, though, as they danced wildly to avoid their own fire that had been deflected back on them by Rajan's armor. Then, warily, they began to back away. To assault now was futile, they knew, their stun weapons useless against Rajan's heavy machon body armor, their shielding no match against the force of his disruptor. They retreated, and Rajan, his ruby-colored eyes glowing with battle-fever, spun to help Kahn…and froze.

The leader, his lower jaw severed and dangling in a tattered mass of flesh and spurting bronze flux, just knelt there watching Rajan, his talons poised over Kahn's still body.

Rajan watched those talons as they hovered, their threat to pierce between the plating just above center belly where Kahn's heart complex pulsed. The talons lowered infinitesimally, one millimetron, then another, the Low Drom eyeing Rajan, his rabid eyes daring.

Chancing one long look to appraise Kahn's condition, Rajan saw that both the heavy front and side flexor cords had been severed on Kahn's massive legs, the cords' membrane coatings torn and pulled away from Kahn's hide. All of it lay in a shimmering iridescent mass on the dark ground. And, like the legs, Kahn's arm cordage was equally devastated. Kahn was down, and, though awake, thoroughly immobilized.

The talons kept descending, the Low Drom leader's yellow eyes squinting at Rajan as they watched him through broken shards of remnant eyeshields Kahn had shattered. The Drom jerked his head at Rajan's disruptor, the movement bringing the dangling jaw to swing wildly, scattering more flux.

Comprehending, Rajan acted as if to comply. But he didn't trust the Drom.

The talons plunged.

Reflexes faster than the Drom's, Rajan fired, blowing the Drom's descending mitt away at wrist-like juncture, then re-angled his weapon toward the beast's mid torso where the plates split in front to make him vulnerable. When the Low Drom didn't down, Rajan doubled, then trebled his disruptor's power, raising it to sure-kill disintegration level. He held it there, the weapon beginning to glow with overload.

The beast took it, defying him, defying the disruptor, when it shouldn't have been able to. The Drom rose and lumbered toward him, seemingly unaffected, though the disruptor burst hide, then shattered plating, severing molecule from molecule as it ate its way through the beast until the Drom's body became an eviscerating mass.

Rajan stood his ground…kept the disruptor trained on the Drom, despite the weapon's hot sear to his hand, despite the fact that the Drom, huge and menacing, was almost on him.

Finally, the beast staggered. Fell. But, still, it crawled, its other arm grasping at him, the three main dactyls of that remaining mitt clawing at Rajan until it connected with his armor's sear. Only then did the body still.

Rajan stopped firing and stepped back, gingerly twitching his foot clear of the now relaxing mitt. Then he saw why the Low Drom's body had been able to maintain mobile integrity under the disruptor's fire. The Drom was mostly techtronics, held together by retainer fields— probably a long time victim of Cheran's disease.

Rajan shuddered. Cheran's victims—the living dead. Someday that would be his fate, just as it was all career mach, if he didn't make sure he took fatal fire, instead. And, seeing the Drom, he would make sure.

The silence around Rajan had grown eerie. All his aesthetic instincts began screaming inside him, warning him of an impending something. Death? he wondered. It had that feel.

Slowly, Rajan looked around, his eyes still glowing. He scanned, expecting, and he was unafraid. His soul was clean. He could die.

The remaining Dromedan guards were there, but they just stood by staring at him, the smell of their fear strong and acrid. There was nothing else. His disruptor still glowing hotly, Rajan silently tipped his snout toward the wary guards.

As one, they cast head.

He tipped, again, and they took it as leave, slipping slowly, one by one back down the alley to disappear around its farther curve, that backward retreat as much done to show him respect as victor as it was done in fear. They took their injured cohorts with them, but they left the dead leader's body where it lay.

Rajan eased as the last of them vanished, his bright eyes dulling to half-glow, then turned to Kahn. Stepping cautiously around the dead Drom, leery of residual movement, Rajan holstered his disruptor, then squatted next to Kahn.

The Low Drom's severed mitt lay strangely upon Kahn's chest. Rajan ignored it for the moment.

Kahn's fields were faint to Rajan's spectral sight. He reached to touch a pulse place in the skull furrow. There was viable life there—just.

Rajan checked the place where the Low-bred's taloned mitt had fallen, and the remaining glow in his eyes went dead. Be it because he hadn't been fast enough in his fire or because of some ill-destined fluke of the mitt's fall, the talons of the severed mitt had somehow perforated between the plates of Kahn's chest, anyway. There were, at least, one, maybe two, deep punctures. Rajan detected an unnaturally erratic rhythm to Kahn's heart-pulse sequence—a fifteen count instead of the normal twenty-two.

Reaching to touch Kahn's lower torso, then, again, the head furrow, Rajan checked them against one another. While there was just sufficient pulse above, there was almost none below where most of Kahn's vital organs lay. Kahn needed help—fast.

Careful not to disturb the impaled talons, Rajan pulled a medic-aid kit from his weapons harness, selected a specific canister and released its contents on and around the severed mitt, the plastoid instantly adhering to and immobilizing everything it touched. Then, with the Low Drom's mitt cemented in place, Rajan began to render aid, pressing down upon the split in armor plating that underlay Kahn's husk-like hide. Rajan pressed just so to force the body's flux through and out the inferior chambers of his friend's heart-complex and into the lower body.

Rajan didn't dare move Kahn to his ship, and he couldn't call the thing to him. The alley was too narrow.

Yet, he had to get Kahn out of there and to a medic station. Now.

Pausing his compressions, Rajan pulled a portacom from his harness and touched a sequence into it. Moments after, he put the device away…and hoped help would come in time—Cadre help

o   o   o

26

THE SHELTERED ALLEY WHERE KAHN'S BODY LAY was deep in the heart of one of the Low Drom territories of Galaxy Ita Centralis' Andromedan sector, on the artificial planetform called Regar. Its territory split between the Altan and the Low, Regar was a patchwork of hostility, the Low-breds being severely antagonistic toward the Altans, their ancient ancestors. Regar practically bristled with animosity, and the civilian police who were stationed there to maintain some semblance of order were tough and not known for following the code of Omniversal law. They couldn't—they would have been dead. Therefore, any situation they encountered, they approached with deadly force.

Rajan knew that. He also knew that the civilian police were especially prejudiced against fleets and would not hesitate to take advantage of his and Kahn's vulnerability. The Cadre knew that, too, but, despite the danger, Cadre members were sworn to help each other, and they took those pledges seriously. So, when Rajan's coded call for aid came in, Cadre liege scrambled, and among those answering the call was a mean-looking Draconian named Gor.

Between assignments, on temporary leave from Fleet, Gor was hanging out around the Cadre's Ita-based ready-room as was his want during idle times...when he wasn't whoring or so drugged he couldn't function. Gor was there when Rajan's coded call for help came in.

Veteran tough, Gor had been trained in Special Operations as an infiltrator before an incident had taken half his face. Now, carrying too much synthform and biotronics not to be detected and immediately identified, he had been retrained and promoted to a mega-commander in the tachon—the tactical service specialty.

But Gor didn't consider his new ranking a promotion. To him, regular service, except for the machon and mechon specialties, was for cowards who preferred to fight behind the shielding of a translight or from within the heavy armoring of a battle cruiser. Gor preferred to take his enemies face on. That he was permitted this irked him. So, when the Cadre formed, Gor had jumped to join it, happy with the chance to work the underground, again.

Gor was good. It was he who reached Rajan and Kahn about the same time that the civilian police were starting their penetration of Rajan and Kahn's position. And Gor, not knowing that it wasn't the police who were the threat, downed the lot, all four—swiftly, silently, and thoroughly—before Rajan could stop him.

"Trouble, now," Rajan hissed as the rest of the Cadre team joined him and Gor beside the comatose Kahn.

"Not if we make it look like the Low Drom did it," Gor said. And the others agreed with him.

"No good come," Rajan repeated, then tried to tell why.

But Gor cut off Rajan's explanation with a silencing hiss, telling him, "You just mind Kahn and let us to our business, Mach." And when Rajan began to object again, two of the Cadre team leveled stunners on him.

They—Gor and his team—destroyed evidence and manipulated other evidence. Then, they were gone. All but Gor. They transported Kahn's body out with them before Rajan got another chance to tell them about the eight Low Drom guards who could witness contrary to their evidence manipulation, guards who could testify that the dead Drom hadn't downed-out the civi-police. He couldn't have because that Cheran-devastated creature had been killed by a Ghirran saurischian and his short Altan Dromese partner long before any police ever arrived. That left Rajan as culprit since medical evidence would show that Kahn also had obviously been down.

"Come on," Gor said, forcing Rajan out of the alley to his ship.

Reaching the corsair under Gor's insistent escort, Rajan was shoved into it with an urgency. "Get gone and out of here," Gor snapped. "We'll cover you from civi-monitor and police patrols until you're clear to base. Kahn should already be on-station by now. In the Med." And with that, Gor stepped back, then melted himself away in a haze of transfer.

Obediently, a stunned Rajan fired his corsair, turning its antique nose to his home base. But he knew he was in trouble, and, this time, he was afraid. Nobody got away with assaulting civi-police—not anyone—and he was the one sure to be charged with it once the incident began to be investigated and the Low Drom guards talked. Rajan and Kahn were unique—easy to identify, easy to find. The authorities would come straight for them. And, when they did, it would be all over for Rajan.

RAJAN MADE IT BACK TO POST without incident or challenge. He checked on Kahn down in Medical, then retreated to the sanctuary of the base's lounge, feeling sick and dead inside. The Draco Gor was Cadre, and what he'd done, he'd done from a sense of loyalty and duty to the Cadre's own. It was understandable, as well, considering that civilian police of Regar—civilian police anywhere—held bias against Fleets and would take any opportunity to brutalize and even kill them. But that didn't alter circumstances. Rajan was going to lose his freedom. It would be he who was blamed for taking down the four civilian officers…unless the eight Low Drom household guards who had witnessed the original fight were killed.

Long tail twitching in agitation, Rajan curled a lip. There was no way he was having that on his soul. That much he knew. But, equally, he understood that he couldn't turn himself in. Authorities would want truth. They would demand truth—getting it out of him one way of another. And they had ways. But Rajan couldn't let them have that truth. The Cadre would be discovered, and that would breach his pledge to it.

The Cadre being a secret organization, Rajan was pledged to hold that secret, just as he was pledged to its ideals. More, he couldn't break the tacit covenant that bound all Cadre members. He was soul-sworn not to. Breach that by exposing Gor, and he was just as dead as if he'd broken the Machon Code. More than dead, if there was such a thing. And Rajan believed there was.

Rajan saw no way out. He could look to no one—not to the authorities, not to his Fleet superiors—not when it involved the Cadre. The only thing he could do now was to let the Cadre find him sanctuary far from the reach of Omniversal authorities. Ultimately, that would mean an end to him, though, for the Cadre's answer to a plight such as Rajan's was to give him a totally new identity. The Cadre would give him a new name and history, after altering his physique, then turn him loose to be a Runner, forever fleeing possible discovery. Or, if he agreed, they would offer him the ultimate protection, changing his DNA and his brain patterns—his memories, too—so that scanners...nothing could identify him as who he was...who he had been. He wouldn't even know himself when they had finished—a necessary thing in a realm where technology's pervasiveness was complete.

A shudder ran Rajan's full length. He'd seen that done. There was nothing left of the individual that had been. And all of it—any way they did it—meant an end to his career—an end to friendships and to familial ties;

an end to purpose and fulfillment…an end to flying. To Rajan, it meant an end to living, being, and that he couldn't face. He'd rather really die.

"Yo, 'Jan."

Rajan recoiled, barely stopping himself from striking out.

Moliére LeSerge, affectionately named "Jaeger" by Kahn for his tracking talents at tachon, stood looking down at him, his eyes showing the typically Tellurian pinch of hurt to Rajan's reaction to him.

"Hsc!" Rajan hissed. "You not sneak, Jaeg-. Not nice!"

"I didn't, you green, sly, long-snout. I hailed you when first I came in. You just didn't hear me."

The tall, black-skinned Tellurian stepped down into Rajan's cubicle and nervously ran a pink palmed hand through his coarse, white, kinky hair. He was waiting.

When Rajan finally tipped his head in consent, Jaeger slid into the cubicle to sit across from him. "You okay?" Jaeger asked, worry crowding the skin around his dark-on-white eyes. "Heard about Kahn," he said softly.

"'Jan h-okay," Rajan said lightly.

"Cut the cover, Rajan," Jaeger snapped. "We all know better. Kahn's your wing and glove, and he's hurt bad. We all understand."

Rajan curled a lip, then gave it up. Jaeger was friend, and, though the Tellurian didn't ken Ghirran custom of never speaking of another's pain or worry, Rajan knew he meant well. "Be fine once Kahn back fly," Rajan said. Then, leveling a ruby eye toward the talkative creature, Rajan warned, "No want talk."

Jaeger nodded, then punched up a drink for himself on the table synthesizer.

Rajan watched the amber colored fluid foam inside its vitriform shell as the synthesizer formed it. It was a mild intoxicant, specific to Tellurians. They called it ale, and Rajan wrinkled his small, delicate nostrils in distaste at its pungent stench.

"You want something?" Jaeger asked. "I'm buying."

"Hnc, no. Just come to duty soon," Rajan replied.

Rolling eyes until only white showed, Jaeger laughed. "What's it matter if you have a drink?" he scoffed. "How often do any of us get action on this post? Especially machon."

Rajan dipped his head. It was true. This post was where fleets were sent who were either so incompetent that no one wanted them or who didn't play the game right—those considered liabilities to status quo control because they wouldn't conform to Dictate and Protocol's demands. Rajan, Kahn, and Jaeger numbered among the latter. Each of them was there, quietly reassigned and neatly stowed so they couldn't influence other fleets, isolated on a nowhere post that was more formality than functional, a relic of a time when Ita's defense depended on its spaceports and the machon stationed there.

"How many times does Ita Central, much less Ivalan, get attacked?" Jaeger asked, then laughed into his drink as he swallowed some.

"Hnc, Jaeg-," Rajan said, snapping his long tail. "You no tell 'Jan. No get good fly, yet, since been here," he said, showing teeth in moment's fury.

"Well you might just get a good fly, now, Machon."

Both Rajan and Jaeger flinched. It was the base's second-in-command who, no warning given, had just phased in beside them. "Commander Frigog wants to see you, Metan Rajan," he said. "Immediately." His tone was grim.

"Odds it's nothing," whispered Jaeger, despite the presence of the subcommander.

And, normally, Rajan would have agreed, except for the Second's biofields, those, and the sign the second gave him—mach-sign for intercept/destroy

o   o   o

27

CATCHING A RIDE ON A TRANS-UNIVERSAL freighter had saved Quroc from having to chance a stop at a Fleet outstation to get a shift Syrene. His ship nestled safely inside one of the freighter's voluminous holds, Quroc had made the trip through Universe Xi and into Universe Itae in good time. The freighter's shifting through the Betweens had been rough, as was usual for the big haulers, but the ride, expensive as it was, had meant the difference between centar and itar in getting to and, then, through, Itae. That freighter had taken Quroc all the way to Galaxy Ita, Universe Itae's largest and most central galaxy, and, had he so wished, Quroc could have ridden it right into Galaxy Ita Centralis. Quroc's instincts had told him not to ride the freighter in, though, so he had begged off at an Inner-Perimeter stop.

Free of the freighter, with his ship recharged thanks to the hauler's friendly captain, Quroc had finally placed his careful call. On a special frequency, scrambled sub-link, Quroc had spoken to his commander-in-chief, the Fleet Director Leon Belamy, spilling his story and begging Belamy's help. At first, politically-minded Belamy had been visibly shocked and silent, but, just as Quroc had guessed, he was more than willing to help. "You were right to call me," Belamy had said. "This would destroy your father. ...And, of course, we'll make sure this doesn't touch you, either." And, when Quroc had asked about penetrating Ita's Perimeter Nets, Belamy had assured him that he had nothing to worry about. "Civilian Defense Net doesn't even know about the minor. Fleet wanted to keep it completely in-house. As for Fleet, I'll take care of it. Fly straight in." It had been a smiling and much relieved Quroc who'd flown fast and hard, just breaking Edge, to Ita Centralis. Quroc chose to ride the chancy Edge for a second time in the trip because the moment his contact with Belamy had been severed, a ghostly fighter squadron had appeared—a fighter squadron very similar to one that had chased him from the Xentauri system outbound until he'd had to push his ship dangerously close to shift speed to escape them.

Just like the last time, Quroc made good his escape from the mystery fighters, losing them in the swirl of arcing, warping space that was the Edge. Now, safe and whole, with help from Belamy a guarantee, Quroc was approaching Galaxy Ita Centralis, a small, artificially constructed intra-galaxy that resided at the core of Galaxy Ita. Where once, long ago, a black hole had existed, but had subsequently swallowed itself after eating all of Galaxy Ita's core, Omniversal engineers had constructed a small and, as yet, incomplete artificial inner galaxy to serve as neutral location for the Omniversal government. Ita Centralis as it was called, contained, at present, nineteen completed systems, with others— multitudes of others—still under construction. One of those finished systems—Ivalan—was the designated High Fleet Headquarters, and, in Ivalan, lay the planetform, Iban, where both Fleet Academy's Main

Syrene Holding Complex and FleetCom with Belamy were located. Both were Quroc's destinations.

Coming into Galaxy Ita Centralis, Quroc angled his ship between two Sentinels, cutting close, the prick of their scanners tangible as they checked his body, brain, and biofields for identity. Redundant, repeatedly redundant, the Sentinels were the bulwark of Ita Centralis' Civilian Defense Network's, or CivNet, security perimeter. If the Sentinels didn't like you, they neutralized you by generating both a stasis field that knocked you out, and an interference wave that knocked your ship dead as they tractored you to temporary holding until Security got there…unless they really didn't like you. But, then, you never knew it if that happened, having been already vaporized to had-been.

Quroc didn't like the Sentinels, but neither did he fear them. They were necessary in a time when the Omniverse was still suffering aftershocks from the last civil war. They would be necessary for a long, long time, if not forever, and they served their purpose effectively, efficiently, and without bias. It didn't matter who or what you were, which was about the only circumstance within the Omniverse where that was completely true.

Quroc glanced toward the Syrene minor which had finally fallen into what Quroc could only compare to a sleep state in living beings. It had played most of the trip, toying with the ship controls, exploring lockers, even handling weapons that it came upon within those lockers, though Quroc had put a stop to that immediately. Quroc was worried about the little thing. If it had seemed recovered earlier, it was exhausted, now. Curled up beside him, its small body folding oddly within the confines of the conforming lattice that surrounded it, the minor was noticeably paler and weaker, the gleaming gilt flaw that seemed embedded at its shoulder internode brilliant in comparison. The minor needed to get to a charge berth soon. Luckily, Belamy had offered to have one ready.

Once through the Sentinels, Quroc received automatic clearance from a CivNet controller for the High Fleet system of Ivalan, and, point-zero-five decitar later, he was successfully passed the High Fleet Cyber-Sentries, weaving his way through the docking networks that surrounded the Ivalan system beyond the outer boundary of its photo-transmission web.

The High Fleet Cyber-Sentries, or DeathNet as fleets called them, had been the first real tricky part if his call to Belamy had been intercepted. Safely through that, now came the second chancy part—getting passed Fleet Perimeter Security. If Belamy was being straight with him, Quroc would be given cursory authorization. If Belamy wasn't, Quroc was prepared to take evasive action.

Quroc placed the call through to Port Control, requesting clearance through the Perimeter Net for a planet-side landing at Iban, one of the six gigantic, artificially topoformed planets that comprised the Ivalan system.

"Destination, Sir?" an obviously bored Fleet controller asked.

"Admin' Landing-port Sida," Quroc replied, naming the port nearest Belamy's office at FleetCom.

"Cleared for Perimeter penetration, Sir," the controller said, just as Quroc cleared the docks, the planets and the photo-transmission web that encircled the Ivalan system known as The Ring coming into plain view.

Quroc always enjoyed this part of the fall to Ivalan: The Ring, a ribbon of blinding glare on the far side of the system; the planets with their perfect hexagonal tectonic plates of varied topography; and, closest, the lacy silhouette of the backside of The Ring, each lumen strand of it shielded to spaceside. Slipping his warbird over that back-shielded web of light strands and into the clear space between it and the planetforms, Quroc remained ever vigilant, at-ready to evade and escape. This was the Gap, the last defense zone before planetfall and one of the most heavily scanned.

Although he was suppose to, Quroc didn't drop his shields for scan by Fleet Security, depending on Protocol's privilege for the first time in his career. Though strictly against regulation, Quroc supposedly didn't have to drop his shields, a perk that went along with his new rank and grade as one of the top archon in Fleet...as a member of the prestigious High Command. Tight, now, for there was little chance of escape here, Quroc waited for challenge.

No challenge came, though, and, soon, Quroc relaxed, again. He even reached to stroke the dormant minor.

o   o   o

28

Leon Belamy stood staring out at the view afforded him by his open atmosphere office high atop the gargantuan FleetCom edifice. That view of Iban's suspended ribbons of cityscape was magnificent. It was usually inspiring to him. Not so this itar. Belamy didn't even really see it. He was deep in thought.

A shimmer...trails of color: the scheduled fly-by of machon warbirds caught Belamy's attention. He watched as the high-tech quads spun their silent, twisting flight down through the atmosphere, then leveled out as they tore through Iban's artificial troposphere at what was called sub-wave velocity, their passage only detectable because of their relatively slow speed and the fact that they used colored vapor.

The machon patrol was strictly a ceremonial show now that Iban was defended by three stages of out-perimeter security nets, and, beyond that, by Ivalan's Sentinels, all of it redundant to Ita Centralis' own heavy security precautions, but the warbirds were still a beautiful if somewhat menacing sight—deadly Harriers notorious for their pin-point strikes, their arsenals capable of annihilating an entire planet in itat, a city in a thousandth of that time.

Belamy watched those machon and thought of Quroc. He would be flying a ship very much like them. In fact, at first glance, Belamy had thought that the movement in the sky was Quroc. But it was too early, yet, and Quroc certainly wouldn't be using colored vapor.

Returning to his desk-console, Belamy again sank deep into thought. Quroc's sublink had surprised him. Quroc's story had not. That surprise had come earlier with the panicked call from a very frazzled-looking High Consul Quiloc, his arm slung and obviously in need of medical attention. Worried about the consequences to his eldest son and prime heir, Quiloc had related the whole story to Belamy, and Belamy had promised to try to help. But the situation, starting from Riloc's theft of the Ben-Drom's minor, did not make sense. For one, Belamy knew Quiloc's youngest son. Riloc just wasn't smart enough or skilled enough to break into the Fleet Academy Syrene Holding, not by himself, so someone had to have helped him—someone skilled. And that brought up the second question: Why specifically had someone helped Riloc steal the Ben-Drom's minor just now, right in the midst of the Cadre operation? Immediately, Belamy had smelled a covert operation, however well-intentioned, gone awry, and he was betting it was Cadre, but, so far, he had been unable to find the catalyst.

Belamy touched a personal paging code into his console. It was a Cadre summoning code, and it was directed to the Special Operations agent, Matac. If anyone could get to the bottom of this, she could, and Belamy wanted some very clear answers. Then he paged his secretary. "Kiel," Belamy said. "Can you get me a line to the Ben-Drom?...Quickly and on scrambled private link."

"That might take some time, Director," Kiel said, his distaste at the mention of the Altan clear. "You know he is absolutely impossible to reach, even for a Fleet priority.

"Well, do your best."

"As you wish, sir. Anything else?"

"No. That'll do."

"Then you might want to take a look at your screens," Kiel said. "Something exciting seems to be happening in the Gap."

Startled, Belamy turned to the bank of mostly ignored monitors that lined the side of one curve of office wall. There he saw it, bristling machon fighters closing on a target that Belamy, quickly punching up the magnification, was sure by the insignia was Quroc's ship.

"Kiel, get me the machon base commander. *NOW!*" he barked.

○   ○   ○

29

NOT UNTIL THE WARBIRDS, weapons on full, began to close on him did Quroc think about the possibility of danger from the outstation machon. By then, it was too late, though. By then, the mach were spinning around him, their weaving flightpaths cutting into his as they drove at him like angry viperwasps.

Quroc evaded, his ship's movements violent enough to tumble the unrestrained, sleeping minor from its place by his side. The tiny Syrene, its orbs wide with fear, clambered back to him, grasping at him.

A ship-to-ship broke through. "This be Metan Tertius Rajan ab Ghirran, wing-lead. You charged be infiltrator. By order, the Megan Tertius Frigog, you land Core Ivalan," a lisping voice demanded in broken Omniversal. "Not h'obey, you be has-been. Down, now." It was audio transmission only—a warning that this was to be taken seriously.

Infiltrator.... Stunned, Quroc watched the warbirds wheel around him. His first thought was that Belamy had betrayed him. But that made no sense. He'd gotten through the Sentinels, the DeathNet, and Perimeter Security. So it was another mach error. Spaceport mach were notorious for their ineptness and known for mistaking targets. Whatever the reason, it didn't matter. Quroc's course was laid. He could prove who he was, and that he did have the Fleet Director's sanction to bring the minor in, his link with Belamy on-copy, ship datacom.

Quroc touched open his comlink. "This is Megan Primus Quroc ab Verdaje, Kathon," Quroc said. "You have mis-identified, mach. I am no infiltrator."

"Possible, Megan," the Ghirran said, coming back on-line, this time on visual, as well—a long, broad, green snout; dull red eyes. "That why you still be 'live. Megan Frigog give chance you be you—this h'against orders, Regulus Fleet Command. Now, you down now, h'else we take down."

The link went dead, again, and the fighters, their arching, four-point wings refracting the harsh light from the photo-transmission web, pressed Quroc a little closer—too close for their erratic flight.

Flicking his scanners to broad receive, Quroc listened to the machon banter for clues of their intent as he held his own ship steady, his skilled hands on ship's con unconsciously reacting to every nuance of data input so to float and twist the ship safely amid the gyrating antics of his would-be attackers, attackers whose flying showed most of them to be exactly what they were: wobble-danglers. And, for a few tense moments, Quroc thought that they would *all* go down—him with the machon—not intentionally, but by the mach's sloppy handling of their ships. Some of the bobbing ships came so close to Quroc's own that, several times, Quroc caught himself unconsciously reaching for weaponry to blow them off. Finally, the warbirds settled to stable flight, the

Ghirran cursing them, ordering them to steady running...threatening to take them out himself if they didn't. And Quroc breathed a grumble in relief.

Quroc's ship riding center of the mach formation, they flew a neutral course, riding the Gap, empty space between The Ring and the six revolving planets of Ivalan. More confused than really worried now that the mach had settled, Quroc chewed on what the mach-lead had told him.

"Give chance you be you," Quroc mouthed, trying to make sense of the Ghirran's broken Omniversal. That, coupled with the "orders, Regulus Fleet Command," and the infiltrator part. If this attack was on the orders of a regulus, then Belamy couldn't help him, except by sanction of the Omniversal High Consul. Regulus had extraordinary powers.

Worried now, Quroc re-opened the link and, as calmly as he could, used the truth. "I have permission from the Fleet Director himself to land at Iban," he said. "I'll copy-to you said-same, Mach."

Again, the Ghirran. "Copy-to perhaps you fake," he said.

Quroc growled, angry, now, because he had noticed something—a very large detail that proved the mach in error. "Mach, you and yours are vector-warped," he snapped. "In case you haven't noticed, Fleet Security's not on me. If you have a target, you've got the wrong one. Suggest you have your wet-brains checked."

In answer, the mach-lead loosed a burst across Quroc's Quad. It was a well-aimed charge, the light plasma diffused enough to have already liquified before contact. It ran off-shields in blinding rivulets—harmless, purposely harmless.

Then, the Ghirran came back on-link: "If we be wet-brain, Megan, then you free once clear by FleetCom. Now you land Core Ivalan."

Surprisingly, the Ghirran's eyes still held the pall of boredom; his voice was still fact-of-matter, not angry as Quroc had expected of a cull mach to such insult. The Ghirran's flying was point-to-purpose, too—also a surprise.   Maybe that was why the Ghirran was wing-leader. At least he knew a little of how a Veerwing Quadstar Harrier was supposed to be flown.

The link had gone dead static: "End transmission. No more talk; no more time" in mach-sign. It was a language Quroc understood too well. And Quroc realized he was in trouble. The mach weren't kidding, and they weren't taking no for answer.

And they could "down" him, cull flyers or not. He'd waited too long. At this range and sluggish speed, they could and would burst his ship's shields, then atomize him with concerted fire. There would be no contest.

But Quroc couldn't land at Core Ivalan with its military as well as civilian police bases. Not with the minor with him. Politically, it would be all over for the Q Dynasty once the fact of the minor's existence in-possession was recorded by authorities. No one could protect Quroc, his father, or the Dynasty, then. And Quroc hadn't come this far just to lose.

The fighters were in closed formation about him, now, escorting, forcing, him down toward the Core—the gravitational center of the Ivalan system where the high security detention area was cloistered. Quroc let them force him, seeming to comply. That gave him time to think.

Precious moments…Core Ivalan in clear sight, now, "shadow-side" of the planets where they shaded one another from The Ring's light bulging ripely above and all around him, huge. The fighters were hazing him, their ships so close to his….

In that eternal blink of still-time that comes at-crisis, Quroc's old mach instincts fired. He knew exactly what to do. He flicked his weapons off—a sign to his captors that he did comply. Then he waited.

And when his escort seemed lulled into thinking he'd capitulated, Quroc made his break-run.

With a single lightning touch, Quroc brought his ship's weapons back on-line to deadly full. Simultaneously, he drove his ship down upon the fighter just beneath his and rolled obliquely out, spinning his Veerwing right through the midst of the startled flyers.

Running a chaotic course to avoid any strikes coming, either, from the mach or from Fleet Security, Quroc opened up a link just one more time, this time on broad-band for all to copy. He told them—told them all—that he'd land at his original destination or die, then dared the mach to try to stop him. "I'll take you out," he promised. "Live or die, I'll take you out."

And the mach believed him: They dropped back. All of them but one. One mach ship hadn't dropped back, hadn't been lulled, and it was on him, shadowing him, bating him, whirling around him. But it never fired on him. Instead, it warped the space matrix they flew with its wake until Quroc's ship shuddered with the effects of sheer. By itself, that one fighter, forced Quroc back toward The Ring and away from Ivalan and Iban. And that one flyer, Quroc realized, was no dog, but a real machon. It was the Ghirran, and he was holding to the Machon Code: weaponry only at last resort. It was only one ship, though, and Quroc figured that, of the two of them, he, a veteran combat fighter, was the better flyer. And they were very near The Ring.

o   o   o

30

Leon Belamy was frantic. While he had successfully managed to quell any movement against Quroc by Fleet Security, he seemed powerless to stop the machon, even when he placed an emergency call-stop through to Base Commander Frigog. The machon were under a mission lock-down, by order of Regulus Poteck, the Megan Frigog told him. She couldn't call-stop even had she had the power. "I'm giving you the power," Belamy snapped.

"And I am telling you, Fleet Director, that anyone, everyone, including Regulus Poteck himself, is now powerless to stop them. Their orders were sealed. Their communications are locked-down. All of this by order of Regulus Poteck, Sir. I am sorry, but there is nothing I can do."

"Copy-to those orders," Belamy said icily.

Frigog had paused at that. The order was not without precedent, but it was irregular. Belamy was only the civilian Director. He was not Regulus. Then, hesitantly, she did so. "These are the original orders I received," she said as she transmitted.

Seeing those orders, Belamy blanched. Poteck or whomever was responsible for them had been thorough. Voluntarily, Frigog then cobied-through her orders to her machon. Only those gave Belamy room to hope. For some reason—and, right now, Belamy didn't care why—the Megan Frigog had changed the original orders. She had changed them just slightly, but that seemingly insignificant change could be just enough to save the Megan Quroc.

"Who is the mach-lead, Megan," Belamy asked with bated breath, glancing back to the viewscreen that monitored the chase-down.

"The Metan Tertius Rajan ab Ghirran," Frigog replied.

"Rajan," Belamy whispered, watching both ships head back toward the blinding Ring. Belamy knew Rajan; he knew Frigog's orders. Hope lifted and sank simultaneously. Profile, skill, and judgement would seal both flyer's fates unless Belamy could somehow stop them. And he was helpless to do that.

o   o   o

31

ONLY ONCE IT WAS CLEAR that the lone warbird, dogged in its pursuit of him, had really forced Quroc to yield—only then did the other machon rejoin the chase, splitting off into two factions in anticipation of covering Quroc when he committed to cut to one side or the other of the phototransmitter.

Quroc laughed. They thought him ignorant, fool enough to fly right into the perimeter defense artillery's range field. They were the stupid ones, though—all bluff and no menace for a real combat flyer like he'd been for eight full turns and more. Only the Ghirran was a threat, but one-on-one against the Ghirran was just like a hassling run in the mach corps, and Quroc had been, was, no ordinary machon. He was Mach Elite. It would be no contest.

The Ring was close. Quroc drove for it, plunging through its strands of blinding multi-spectrum light so disorienting to most pilots. And the fighters—all except the Ghirran maverick—dropped back, again.

And, still, the Ghirran didn't fire. The Machon Code—he was holding to it.

Quroc shook his head, grinning. It would be fair, would it? "Okay," he muttered. "Now to lose you."

The Ghirran in hot pursuit, Quroc punched through the energized strands of lumen that formed the phototransmission web, then wove an erratic course through those blinding rivers of light as he targeted Iban and the FleetCom edifice there. Course laid to com, he jumped his ship to hyperspeed just long and hard enough to breach the gap between The Ring and the planet's surface, but not enough to split the matrix to plunge through Edge to the interspace Betweens that lay as deathtrap to any who dared break the cosmic laws of physics without a shift Syrene to help them.

Concussion blanket-fire—Quroc felt its impact against his heavy shielding as the cull flyers tried to knock him out by luck alone as they realized that his drop from sensor was illusion because of speed. Predictably, their fire missed him completely. They had lost. He had won. And no one, nothing, had been hurt. Quroc smiled within himself. …Except for egos.

o   o   o

32

POWERED DOWN AND USING THE RING'S voltaic output as camouflage, Rajan had watched his quarry weave flightpath through The Ring. The flyer was good, but not that good, having overlooked the fact that his choice in taking to The Ring necessitated abandoning his scanners momentarily while he completely focused on his flying. That gave Rajan the opportunity he needed to drop out to set ambush. Rajan's on-board computer logged the quarry's error.

"TARGET LOST," the com indicated as his quarry jumped to hyperspeed, and Rajan waited, his sight seeking the position on his con selected as most probable to be taken if the target-intercept was actually the real Megan Quroc as decided by the ship's analysis computer.

Rajan's orders were explicit: If target didn't hold to profile, take it out. So far, the evidence was insubstantive.

Every flyer had a flightprint—a distinctive and uniquely individual way of handling their ship, as well as characteristic tendencies in their moment-to-moment, in-crisis decision-making. At present, Rajan's com's analysis indicated that the target had exhibited some of the Megan Quroc's characteristic flightprint, but nothing absolutely conclusive—nothing that stood out and substantively marked the target as either infiltrator/imposter or the actual Megan Quroc ab

Verdaje. And Rajan needed absolute proof, as measured by his com against the Megan Quroc's old machon flight profiles.

"TARGET REACQUIRED," the com indicated, and Rajan smiled. His quarry had chosen exactly as the Megan Quroc would have. Still, however, the analysis computer was not satisfied. More proof was demanded.

Obedient to his orders, Rajan powered up and made his own jump.

o   o   o

33

QUROC DROPPED OUT OF HYPERSPEED in-atmosphere, down low on the far side of the planet, right amidst the cityscape that was Iban, Omniversal High Fleet Headquarters. He was on the inside, now, his calculations perfect, his luck holding—no disintegrating percussion telling him that he'd obliterated something, either ship or structure.

Now, Quroc concentrated on his flying, wheeling, sideslipping, skewing his scrappy Veerwing's flightpath to avoid collision with a blur of obstacles that, at speed, his sensors only identified as solid. He was base-final, now, and happy. He would make it.

A beacon loaded. Quroc swore. The pesky maverick was back—had jumped after him—the chase, the battle of skills, returned.

The flyer was harrying him, now, pushing him to stretch the limits of ship tolerance, forcing him to take chances that could kill them both, and, perhaps, a host of others, too, as the flyer repeatedly bore into him, compelling him away from any quarter that would give him freedom enough to maneuver. And, still, the Ghirran didn't fire—odd.

They were driving deeper into the complex…lower, into the congested gridwork of concourses that fed pedestrian traffic back and forth on lifts between shuttle landing platforms and various Fleet offices. The flyer wouldn't fire on him here in the deeply populated administrative quadrant of the planet, Machon Code or no, and they were way beyond that code's restrictions, now. But there were other ways, and the feisty flyer used them.

Quroc knew what the maverick was doing, but he was at a loss to stop it without killing himself and a host of others if he took the Ghirran out. And to escape now, to achieve his objective, Quroc knew he'd not only have to outsmart, out-fly, the Ghirran, he'd probably have to down him.

And it was in that moment that Quroc realized that, still, no Fleet Security defenses had engaged to stop him…that Fleet Security wasn't after him, at all and, by this time, it should have been, else he'd already be blown from atmosphere. It was only the machon who were bent on turning him from target, and images of the ghostly fighter squadron that had chased him earlier in the journey flashed in his memory-sight. Why?

Quroc looked toward the Ghirran's ship, seeing it clearly for the first time. Why?! And then he saw the ship for what it was—a customized Quad just like his, if a little newer—customized and battle-scarred. The Ghirran was not just a real mach pilot, Quroc realized. The Ghirran was Mach Elite—combat-tempered Mach Elite. Like Quroc had been. Like he still was, Quroc reminded himself with gritted teeth. He was still Mach Elite, despite his move to kathon and the rank of high commander. In that moment, Quroc knew that one of them was going to die.

The Ghirran spun his ship into Quroc's, again, and, again, Quroc managed to avoid being obliterated while making sure he didn't himself obliterate anything. FleetCom itself—an edifice that was more a monumental feature of landscape in that it covered a full sixth of the giant planetform that was Iban—was registering on Quroc's com, now, and he looked for a way—any way—to achieve objective.

Touching on a schematic of FleetCom, Quroc saw the weakness, his battle-high brain homing on it: the transport shuttle shafts, the ingress tunnels. He picked one of the larger ones. He picked a main one that his com said was engaging. And when, once again, the Ghirran spun his ship into Quroc's, just as the tunnel gate was ready to open in preparation for an approaching shuttle, Quroc star-rolled, his ship's wings like gears between the Ghirran's wings, then punched his speed, aiming for it.

So did the other flyer, matching him.

Quroc swore. He had the line. The other didn't. Quroc swore, again. In Iban's relatively heavy gravity, the Ghirran would crash if he didn't pull out. Now.

In a single millitat, that option ended. The flyer was committed, itat away from certain death. And Quroc did not give way. He held his space.

Unconsciously, Quroc prepared himself, his mind weighing, against the Machon Code, the act of doing nothing, of letting the other flyer crash.

Images: The Ghirran's ship...the tunnel...the wall—the solid, unending span of over-vertical that was the FleetCom edifice. Images: There was no time left...no time for Quroc to give quarter. In his mind, Quroc saw the crash already—the impact and the blow-out of the Ghirran's ship to a billion bits of nothingness. Waste.

o o o

34

LEON BELAMY COULDN'T QUITE BRING HIMSELF to accept what he was seeing. He had watched two ships, dwarfed by the surrounding cityscape, weave and dart between, under, and seemingly sometimes through the chaos of obstacles that was Iban's planetary megapolis. He had watched them come at-speed straight for him from around the giant planetform in millitat, the chaser driving at the chased as if to purposely force a crash that would kill thousands. Watching, Belamy had flinched until their was no reaction left in him, and, still, he'd watched, Frigog still on line, Matac there, too, having come to summons.

It had taken barely an itat for the darting ships to make the turn around the planet. From the time he'd seen them in the Gap heading toward The Ring till now, only a moment's blink in time. And now was ending: two ships driving straight for the solid wall of the biggest, most structurally solid building yet constructed in all of Ita.

Building alarms wailed.

Belamy closed his eyes. He braced himself.

o   o   o

35

THE ANALYSIS COMPUTER FINALLY CONFIRMED. In himself, Rajan always had been sure, but knowledge based upon aesthetic senses did not hold with FleetCom and especially not with a regulus. So Rajan had needed to gather the empirical proof. And now he had it. The computer finally agreed with him that the target he was playing was indeed the Megan Quroc and not some replicated, infiltrator be-alike. Rajan could let his quarry live, and he was happy.

Transmitting his computer's decision to the main computer banks at FleetCom took just a touch of one of Rajan's ungues. In a micromillitat, transmission was complete. The Megan Quroc was finally, ultimately, safe from Fleet Security annihilation. But the single millitat that had passed in the proving and transmission of that proof was the critical last one Rajan had to roll away from certain death. Now, the wall of FleetCom itself loomed and so did the tunnel—still closed, but due, in exactly six millitat, to spread.

Rajan idled, time and motion slowed as it always was when he was fighter-high at-critical. He wondered if he'd live or die. He didn't care. But, then, he did. If he lived, he lived his troubles. If he died, he'd die the way he'd always wanted to—in combat flight—and all his troubles would be dissolved in a soul-freeing instant's flash of material disintegration. Life or death was under the Megan

Quroc's claws, and that was only fair since the Xentauri's life had for so long hung in the balance of his ungues. Rajan flicked his weapons off. And, on a whim, his shields, too.

Alert, but relaxed, his prescient senses neutralized by balanced probabilities, Rajan waited for the Xentauri's verdict, his brain and hands at-ready.

o   o   o

36

QUROC SWORE. AND THEN HE MOVED, damning himself for his heavy conscience. Realtime now, the Ghirran's destruction imminent…and ethical according to the Code.

Cursing the Machon Code as he did it, Quroc shifted his ship just enough to fit them both through the tunnel. He was taking the chance of killing himself doing it, but Quroc would not purposely let a fellow machon die, even if that dying didn't break the fighters' maxim. And, as he did it, Quroc hoped against odds that the Ghirran was skilled enough, quick enough, to pull it out. If he wasn't? Well, Quroc's conscience would be clean. He'd given out the chance, slim chance that it was.

There was a momentary image, frozen in time, of the uniformed bodies of ceremonial guards stationed just outside the opening tunnel's maw hitting deck, then, he was in…*they* were in, the tunnel barely big enough to take them both.

The Ghirran *had* been quick enough. And, grimly, Quroc hung his digits on the con, using both his own skill and the ship's computer to fly him. Two ships side by side in a tunnel barely big enough for them was enough to make a rock sweat.

Anticipating the touch that was almost sure to come with both ships' wings intermeshed in the tight quarters,

Quroc braced for shock, hoping he could compensate just enough, not too much, for any jolt of touching when it happened.

But no shock came. And Quroc and his adversarial wing careened through the tunnel at breakaway speed.

Not one shock of inadvertent wing-touch came…even when Quroc braked to subwave speed. And they hurtled through the multi-kilometron-long tunnel locked together, matching speed for speed, their ships in a forced formation so close that any mistake would send them both to their deaths in a grisly wreck that would grind them both to powder, despite shields or armor, despite retention field or stasis.

Com indicators showed that Building Security had now reacted to unauthorized presence. The tunnel's inner fortifications were engaging. Shockwaves of concussion blanket-fire began to hit in wave after wave, and Quroc knew it could only be moments before the Ghison began…as soon as all the barriers were closed to protect those upon the inside from the Ghison's devastating effects. And a barrier maybe one full itat in front of them at their present speed was closing, its interlocking shutters snapping shut. The com showed nine millitat only in which to safely stop before the Ghison would engage.

Quroc signed, both audibly and on visual, then hit the foils, braking. The Ghirran matched his act, each ship mirroring the other's deceleration perfectly—not a wobble. Quroc checked his com readout. Yes, they would make it. They would stop in time. And already Building Security computers had reacted to their "surrender." They were standing down the Ghison.

The tunnel walls began to take on characteristic as his ship slowed, and, grimly, Quroc smiled. He was on the inside, just where he needed to be. Having breached FleetCom was sure to land him in in-house detention, and that, with his rank, would ensure him his audience with Belamy. There would be safety for the Q Dynasty and the minor. Belamy would fix things. Belamy had the power to do that…now that Quroc was where he had to be so Belamy could…now that Quroc was on the inside, having taken a Veerwing Quadstar Harrier where one had never ever been or been meant to go—up the very throat of Fleet itself.

Quroc looked to the ship right next to him: two— he'd taken two Quads in. It had to be a first of some kind—that, in an Omniverse where firsts of any ilk were likely "nots". And Quroc chuckled, his grin turning real…though how this first would look upon his file wouldn't be exactly good for his career in Kath.

BOTH SHIPS CAME TO ALL-STOP, Quroc's and the Ghirran's, just this side the now-closed gate. They came at-rest, hovering next to one another. And Quroc was glad the Ghirran had lived. Life—all life—was precious.

Quroc looked down and stroked the terrified minor whose tactiles, threaded through the fabric of his skinsuit now, were clutching at him. Even that which was not alive, just vivified, was precious.

After a long moment, Quroc's com indicated a ship-to-ship transmission. He touched it open.

Glowing ruby eyes…. The Ghirran grinned at him, the mouth just open enough to expose the rows of gleaming ivory teeth within. "Megan Primus Quroc ab Verdaje, Kathon," the Ghirran hissed, acknowledging him. Then, the flyer saluted him, one Mach Elite acknowledging another. And there was laughter there. More, there was respect mirrored in the Ghirran's glowing eyes. And joy—real joy. But there was also a strange sadness.

Quroc saluted back, matching grin for grin just as Fleet's M.P.'s and some reporters from the NewsNet joined them.

A huge shadow rose up in the Harrier's viewscreen, and Quroc's smile froze as he gulped. It was the Regulus Primus Omega Ben-Drom who stood looking in a him. It was the beast himself, big and tall enough to stand beside a hovering Quadstar Harrier and still seem as if he looked down in.

"Sir," Quroc whispered of old habit, even though the Drom couldn't possibly hear him through the shields and hull. And, unconsciously, Quroc reached to shield the minor from its monstrous master.

o   o   o

37

"WHAT IS THE DAMAGE TO IT?" the Ben-Drom asked, retreating to place distance between himself and what did disturb him—the minor's circumstances. The Ben-Drom was angry. What he saw sickened him. Such mutilation of a Syrene, especially a minor, was beyond his acceptance.

Though, upon recovery of it, the small Syrene had, to all outward appearances and despite its obvious mutilation, seemed happy enough, even healthy, it soon became plainly evident that it was not—that its seeming stability was but the result of the presence of the Sier within it. The moment that the golden gleam that was the Sier began to extract itself from the minor's body, the minor had started to thrash and keen, using its own scant energy to try to stop the Sier's disengagement. To the Ben-Drom's learnéd sight, the minor's potential potency had become immediately manifest as being another Syrene identical to, or even more powerful than, Raganth. Even though so small and weak, the minor effectively shattered the Sier's integrity as that energy sentient had attempted vacancy. From a consolidated point of light rising clear of the minor's photoplasm, the Sier had been stretched into a strand-like extrusion as the minor tried to pull it back. That extrusion had turned instantly to snapping webs of exotic lightning that danced about the room's heavily catalyzer-saturated atmosphere once the Sier did finally come free.

At the moment of the Sier's final separation, the minor had stilled, seeming to become almost comatose. Ka had infused it with a compatible energy, and that had stabilized it physically, but, still, the lights and liveliness that had been so distinct in the small thing itat earlier were gone.

Watching, the Ben-Drom knew what damage had been done to it was more than physical. It had affected the minor's still fledgling psyche. The Ben-Drom knew that, not from the minor's response, but from Ka's.

It was obvious to the Ben-Drom that Ka was deeply troubled. The Ceoheician's wide-set headcrests were fully reared, arching so stiffly from brow to the vee-ed rooting place at the bottom of his strong neck that the sheeting hair that covered those sweptback, horn-like processes pulled away in leaves to bristle. And, beyond that martial posture which was only a more pronounced version of Ka's normal bearing when in risky environs, there was something else: Ka had shown absolutely no reaction to the minor's condition—not on Iban, not when regaining the privacy of the Ben-Drom's residence on Regar, and not to the violence of the Sier removing itself from the Syrene. While, publicly, a complete lack of emotion was normal for magus-warriors, and especially for Ka, such complete dispassion was *not* normal once Ka was alone with the Ben-Drom. Except when conditions were at-critical. It was from Ka's complete and utter inuredness that the Ben-Drom knew the minor to be badly harmed.

"What is the damage, Ka?" the Ben-Drom asked again as he watched Ka's delicate, if calloused, hands at their work. Skilled and dexterous, those hands were presently attempting to free the shackling from the minor's body.

To the second asking of the question, Ka raised his sight, his face a mask, his dark eyes hooded in their stare. His hands paused, but he said nothing.

"Is it that grave?" the Ben-Drom queried.

Ka gave but the most imperceptible acknowledgment, then returned his attention to the small Syrene.

The Ben-Drom re-approached the cushioned workplace where the minor lay to stare down at the pale, plasmic mass quivering under Ka's ministrations. Then the Ben-Drom touched the magus-warrior's arm, the course, black material of the Ceoheician's robes stinging even to the Ben-Drom's tough-hided dactyls. "Ka?"

The magus stilled completely at the rare touch. Then he turned his head aside, away from the Ben-Drom's searching sight.

"Ka?"

A breath. Then, turning toward: "The minor has known such pain and terror," Ka said quietly, "that I fear it may never be reconciled."

Ka's voice was hard. His verdict puzzled the Ben-Drom. The Altan dipped his head in another, this time silent, query, but the magus did not respond.

"Reconciled?" the Ben-Drom asked, pressing for explanation.

"To us. To everything we are, we think, we do. To shackling, to the idea of obedience, to—" And, here, the magus just stopped.

The Ben-Drom's gall rose. So did his voice. "TO THE SHACKLES?! WHAT WORRY THAT?! WILL IT SURVIVE?" he demanded.

Deliberately, Ka pivoted to face, his normally quiet eyes hard and glittering dangerously. "Lord," he said, his voice a hush, "it can survive, but, unless I can heal its confusion, its anguish, it will never serve unless stripped devoid."

"*Serve!*" The Ben-Drom spit out the Dromese word that Ka had used. What angered the Ben-Drom most, though, he did not dare address. Should he, he would address it with a strike, not words, for stripping was, to him, the greatest scandal. "After such harm as has come to it, I would not expect for it to serve!" the Ben-Drom growled, grinding the words out. "Can it be set free?!"

"No, Lord."

Surprised, then irritated by the Ceoheician's uncompromising decisiveness, the Ben-Drom started to berate the Blackblood, then forestalled. Instead, he demanded reason. "Why?" he asked.

Again, Ka stilled his work, pointedly turning his sight to the Ben-Drom's. "Because its experiences confound it," he said in answer. "It cannot comprehend the rationale of why it did receive such hurt as it has suffered. It cannot understand us."

Ka dropped his gaze, and, touching the shackle that bound the minor's neck, demonstrated its extreme response, the tiny Syrene flinching with a squeal. "It would, in essence…." Ka turned to face, again. "It will, in essence," he corrected, "enter madness, can I not offer it respite."

"Explain to it, then," the Ben-Drom rumbled.

"It cannot understand. It is too immature to understand us our ways."

"It is intelligent."

"Yes, Lord," Ka said, his hands and sight again returning to their work upon the shackle. "It is that and much beyond. That is the difficulty. It has no frame of reference." This last was said with the flatness and quietness used only by Ka when he was overwhelmed.

Gently, firmly, the Ben-Drom reached to stay Ka's hands. "What can be done, then?" he asked, his husky voice a hush. Ka's headcrests sank, the heavy cartilage that formed them flattening as the blood beneath receded. And Ka let his fields disclose for the first time. "I know not, Lord," he said.

And the Ben-Drom saw within Ka's fields what he had guessed: the magus-warrior's deep distress.

The Ben-Drom looked away, disturbed. As a Syrene handler and trainer, Ka was the best the Ben-Drom knew, and he knew many. If Ka did not know, there would be none that could.

The Ben-Drom's sight caught upon the ethereal form of the Sier hovering just beyond, the gilded blush of its energy bright against the steeped darkness of the Syrene laboratory. The Sier was calm, now, as it had not been when first it had divested itself of the minor. If the minor were in such dire straits, surely, the Ben-Drom reasoned, the Sier would not so be. "The Sier seems not concerned," the Ben-Drom observed.

"The Sier is not Syrene," Ka said. "Nor does it comprehend beyond the moment. Scarring, be it physical or quintessential, it does not ken. It sees no significance of past upon any present or future, should it even admit existence of all such things."

Irked by Ka's indictment of one of his most precious assets, the Ben-Drom's temper reared, again. "It knew enough to stay with the minor until it was returned!"

"And caused what anguish to you, Lord?" Ka replied caustically, green fire blazing suddenly in his so dark eyes. It was a precipitous vehemence so contrasting Ka's previous dispassion that it jolted the Ben-Drom. The Altan stepped back as if pushed.

"The Sier cares not—" Ka stopped, then sighted the Sier and shook his head. "Nay," he said, amending himself, "it comprehends not how its own actions can hurt others, for it perceives not hurtfulness in its any movement. It can only recognize that another is expressing displeasure, and it reacts to that only as it sees fit. There is no conscience there," Ka said. "Your prize is ruthless, yet does not even know that it is thus."

"It stayed with the minor!" the Ben-Drom repeated emphatically, having collected himself from his shock to Ka's fervency.

"Its choice was arbitrary," Ka replied. "Why did it not stop the minor's theft? It could have. More, it could have led us to it, saving both the minor its torture and you your desperate anxiety and sickness."

"I AM NOT SICKENED, KA."

To that bellowed declaration, the Blackblood Ceoheician just bowed, then began, once more to fit a keying shaklan into the binding mechanisms of the fettering that encompassed the minor's neck-like lumenals, shackles that compressed them. Ka was trying to release the manacles the minor wore without the shackle's unique and individual key—a difficult thing, at best, on a significant's larger shackles, and, here, on miniature varieties, almost impossible.

The Ben-Drom watched awhile, helping as he could until the stiffness between he and the Ceoheician eased. "I will not argue with you, Ka," the Ben-Drom said a long while later, once they had finally succeeded in releasing the lumenal manacle. The Ben-Drom did not like to fight with the being who was his only friend. Indeed, even though they often disagreed, the Ben-Drom valued Ka's opinions. It had taken long turns for Ka to begin to speak truly with him.

Speaking beyond the absolutely necessary and, particularly, speaking a judgment, was against all Ka's magus ways, and the Ben-Drom knew that the devotion the Ceoheician bestowed upon him was the highest for Ka to break that long ingrained convention. The Ben-Drom knew himself honored that Ka had chosen to join him, much less befriend him, then, break ethos for him. And, while the Ben-Drom felt that he deserved-not that honor, he was glad for it. Without it, he would have been truly alone in the cosmos.

"What of the minor, Ka?" the Ben-Drom asked a long while later, once all the shackles had been removed.

"I know not," Ka said, repeating his earlier sentiment.

The Ben-Drom reached a digit out toward the tiny Syrene, the thick, dark member with its rugged hide a strong contrast to the tiny being's pale fragility. "Is there nothing?" the Ben-Drom whispered. "What of Sitad?" he asked. "Can Sitad not help this one some way?"

At that, Sitad, who had been silent and withdrawn, turned its orbitals to the Ben-Drom and said, "I have communicated to it, Ben-Drom, but it does not find within me what it seeks."

"And what is that?" Ka asked, his interest peaked, his attention riveted now on the tall significant.

Sitad turned its focus toward the Ceoheician. "Experiential empathy?" it said, its look to Ka something the Ben-Drom could only name as penetrating. There was a message there, he knew, but he could not read it.

It was obvious that Ka understood Sitad's meaning well, however. A shiver crawled across the Ben-Drom's skull hide, for he saw the Ceoheician's fields seem to fracture into shards for just millitat before returning to their ever-neutral. "Ka?" the Ben-Drom queried, at once leery.

The Blackblood dropped his head and shook it, then reached to stroke the minor, that touch seeming to soothe it. "There is interfuse," he whispered, and his sight sought Sitad's, once more. But the Syrene significant just dropped the lid-like sheathing down to cover its orbitals and turned away.

Looking to both, it was the Ben-Drom's turn to still. The room echoed with an almost palpable thickening that frightened him. What Ka suggested was bonding, mind with mind, feeling with feeling, memory with memory, that Blackblood Ceoheicians shared only within kind, and, then, only with their most trusted—usually only with their mate and their master teacher. Even the Ben-Drom, who was Ka's closest comrade ever, did not share that intimacy. "I cannot sanction such," the Ben-Drom said.

"You cannot sanction," Ka acknowledged with a searing hiss, his gaunt face so drawn, now, that his alternately flat and pointed teeth showed momentarily. "It is mine, only, to decide. Leave me."

The imperative—so rare in Ka. The Ben-Drom backed away, then left the chamber to stalk the dark, cavernous hallways of his large residence. He was worried—worried for Ka, now. "Damn the minor," he swore, his words a whisper to himself. "Damn Ka's Destinies."

         o   o   o

38

ALONE WITH THE MINOR, except for the Sier and Sitad's reserved and silent presence, Ka contemplated the small Syrene. It was so fragile, and the Ben-Drom cared so much.

It troubled Ka that the Ben-Drom cared so much for this Syrene—for all Syrene—their plight the Altan's passion, their autonomy his goal. It was that caring that disturbed Ka most. He was unsure that he could save this tiny one, yet the Ben-Drom trusted him to do so. Ka would not, could not, fail that trust. But to interfuse—a thing forbidden except within gens, with master, or with mate—and to do it with a creature so very alien to himself—a creature that, though considered non-sentient by most, Ka knew to be so highly evolved that thought was no longer a process in it, but a state of being *of* it.

And what kind of thought?

Ka had heard stories. He knew the warning: Those who knew the mind of a Syrene knew madness. Ka knew the truth of that ancient admonition. He himself had fought, did even now fight, the madness provoked by such a touch that had for so long threatened to destroy the Ben-Drom—the long ago touch of a Syrene elder's mind that even yet brought his lord to the very brink of rabidness at each unusual stress, at each thing the Ben-Drom found to be irrational or a mindless cruelty.

Ka knew as truth what Sitad had spoken as the minor's need. Moreover, he knew that the Syrene significant would not suggest a thing that would threaten him. Syrene would never intentionally endanger. Syrene would never give harm.

Again, Ka stroked the minor, his touch soft upon its fragile sheathing, though his hands were hard and calloused from his turns of weapons training. This was a minor, yet virgin-minded—undeveloped. Perhaps with one so new, a merging would be safe. Is that what Sitad recognized? Could he safely mesh with it? Could he meld, sharing his mind, his very being, with it, without losing himself to it completely?

Would he survive? Would it? Or would one, the other, or both cease to be?

Ka looked to Sitad, but the significant still remained aloof.

And Ka knew his true fear. It was not death, not madness, that he feared. It was the memories of his own youth that terrified him—those that Sitad had hinted of when it had spoken of experiential empathy. It was the remembering—remembering the darkness, the hatred and the mutilation of him by his father, that Ka feared. To feel, again, the fires of the Ramath De, to know the wandering; to see his mother's death at his father's hand because he was spawned a Blackblood of the throwback genes of both of them—they both blooded white, but carrying the seeds of a much more ancient race—these memories Ka did never touch. Not ever. They were the only thing he feared. But these would be the memories kindled were he to complete interfuse with the Syrene minor, for it was them that likened to the minor's cruel ordeal. It would be those the minor would feed upon, grasping at Ka's learnéd, forced acceptance of them and the reasons for their happening. That feeding would shake his understanding from him. This he knew. The minor's touch would finally shatter every resignation that he held within him of those incidents. It would finally be as his teaching master, Bota Ghiza, had foretold so long ago as necessary: He would face his anger and confusion at his father…at all his Whiteblood heritage. He would live the experiences—all of them—again, and truly come to peace within himself about them…or die the mind's death, trying.

Ka shuddered, both his inner nictitating membranes and his outer eyelids closing. What would be the use? What could the minor or his lord gain should he fail?

Nothing.

No. He could not do it.

Ka turned away—from the idea and from the minor whose questing orbs watched him almost as if asking…as if it understood. He turned away, and started to address himself to readying a charging berth for the needy small one.

At once, the Sier who had been quiet, began to radiate, sending curtaining waves of auric brilliance about the chamber. Ka's mind, his sight, was captivated and drawn away from the bitterness and terror that still held him—pulled into the Sier's mesmerizing, anti-rhythmic pulses.

Ka became immersed within that strobing. He listened to the silent waves—a random chaos of contra-positive light-sound that was the Sier's true communication.

Nothing translated. No impressions, no assurances—nothing—etched themselves upon Ka's consciousness. There was just the light-sound. He became submerged within it until nothing—nothing—Was. Except *it*.

A touch brought him release from the Sier's reverie. It was the minor. It had risen, floating upward to bring itself level with his face, the murky depths of its orbitals watching him. Now, its tactiles stretched to begin sifting among the many folds of his raiment until they threaded through and touched his skin. It wanted life. And sanity. It knew somehow. He felt that.

Drawing a harsh breath, Ka retreated to the inner silence of his training, thinking nothing, knowing nothing, not even self...aware of nothing. And, there, immersed within his own self's deepened stillness, he decided and began to prepare himself to try.

o   o   o

39

IT WAS A SCREAM THAT RENT THE BEN-DROM to his very core. He ran, loping through the passages until, once more, he faced the access behind which he had so many long and troubled moments before left Ka. Now, the scream had died, and, in the emptiness, there was only death-like silence, utter and complete.

The Ben-Drom stopped, frozen by his fear for Ka. At once, cursing and angry at himself for hesitation, he slammed the access mechanism.

Inside, only the glow of Sitad and the Sier broke the darkness of chamber interior. There was sign of neither Ka, nor the minor.

Stepping through, the Ben-Drom queried of Sitad. Bowing, that Syrene turned and led the Ben-Drom through and upward to where Ka's private sanctuary—his shoto—lay hidden.

Never before had the Ben-Drom entered Ka's inner sanctum. It was a forbidden thing in magus ways. Now, stepping to its open access, the Ben-Drom paused. To violate Ka's place was to violate his friend. "Ka?"

There was no answer. There were no fields evident to the Ben-Drom's scanners. And the Ben-Drom, who was never one to hesitate, hesitated yet again, then tentatively stepped into his friend's inner realm.

It was a strange place, the shoto. In the diffused lighting, the Ben-Drom recognized the glyphs and symbols that he had once blindly read by touch alone in the mysterious cave where Ka's teaching master, Bota Ghiza, had kept the Ben-Drom imprisoned after his madness struck as a result of an encounter with Syrene elders. That had been on the planet Jenai in what was now known as the Rin System, and the Ben-Drom not only had been mad, but had been devoid of every one of his senses except touch and voice. Yet, he recognized the emblems immediately, though he had not known them since and had never seen them.

The Ben-Drom stepped further into the nearly empty chamber, crossing the polished stone floor, his tread loud and echoing though his feet were bare. Still, there was no sign of Ka.

Only his eyeshield's proximity sensors warned the Ben-Drom of a wall. Neither his sight, nor his nearing and farthing senses, perceptives he depended on that were unique to Altans and hyper-sensitive, warned him of it, and he reached a mitt out to isolate the position of its all but invisible surfaces.

The wall was thin, free-standing, and almost impervious to any variety of detection, save that of tactile contact. Behind the wall lay an alcove, its only feature a bare dais and a single hovering pillar of dark light. Upon that dais lay Ka's antique, ceremonial light jian—both of them—along with something Ka called a tanto—a short, knife-like weapon that was a remnant artifact from Ceoheician kind's early pre-history. It was here the Ben-Drom found the minor hovering, it's glow gone faint.

It was here he found his friend, the magus fallen in an untidy heap of layered robes, no movement discernible to his body—not of breath, not of heartbeat. Neither were biofields apparent, excepting those that showed gross life. "Ka?"

No response.

Easing himself down beside the collapsed body, the Ben-Drom knelt and touched the magus. Sparks flew from his dactyls to the body, Ka's body at negative charge. At those sparks, Ka's eyelids opened to expose the tightly sealed nictitating membranes just beneath. Then, those translucently opalescent membranes slid away, as well, to expose the naked surfaces of the eyes. Those eyes were vacant. The eyelids' response had been involuntary.

The Ben-Drom turned the magus' limp body over. He had seen this catatonic state in Ka's kind before. He'd seen the ministrations that the Blackblood Ceoheician bota—the wise ones—used to bring them out of it. And the Ben-Drom, memory exactingly intact as only an Altan's could be, reached with surety to press the nerve-points he'd seen pressed as he began to utter the alien sounds of a prehistoric Ceoheician language that he did not understand.

And as his dactyl tips found the places necessary on Ka's body, that intimacy also a violation of everything Ka was, another part of the Ben-Drom's extensive scope of duplexed brain began to plan. He was truly angered, now. It was that dangerously quiet anger of his Altan kind. It was the anger of resolve—that which catalyzed certain action. The Academy, the Megan Quroc, the Xentauri house of Q—he would take them down. All of them.

A hand reached up—Ka's. That hand shook. It was deathly cold. "No," Ka whispered, the sound a croaking hiss. "You…do not…understand."

o   o   o

40

ON-SCENE, LIVE IMAGES OF QUROC snarling and trying to shield the minor from media reporters as he emerged from his Quadstar Harrier, as well as a clear image of the Ben-Drom accepting his stolen property from the Xenti—it was the most excitement Ita had seen in ita...since the "mysterious" destruction of the Hoy and Nettite civilizations. The holomorphic replays of the event were all over the NewsNet.

Those images did nothing to help Belamy's dark mood. Neither did the panicked call from High Consul Quiloc. The sometimes difficult Xentauri was angry—very angry—about his son's arrest.

"You can stand down to your regular activities, Matac," Belamy said to the Xenti queen who stood by. She had told him all, the entire secret operation. "We'll handle it from here."

"Yes, Sir," Matac replied softly, and, when next Belamy noticed, the Special Operations agent was gone, having slipped out so quietly that not even the security system had noted the change. Only the room's monitors showed the difference—occupied, then empty space.

Switching off the NewsNet, Belamy turned his hearing to listen as Lurad continued to attempt to calm Quiloc, that Xenti raging and snarling as his holo- semblance stalked up and down the office. The speech was native Verdajen Xentauri—all grumblings and growlings.

Unfamiliar with the language, Belamy could only guess what was being said, and, though curious, he stopped himself from touching on his translator.

Abruptly, Quiloc's form blinked out and Lurad shifted orientation to face. "Matac should not have ordered the Megan Quroc destroyed," it said. "That small indiscretion could have cost us the operation. It could have cost us the High Consul Quiloc's devotion to cause had it been discovered. It potentially still may. Is Matac very sure that her orders to Frigog cannot be traced?"

Unconsciously, Belamy nodded in his kind-way, then, remembering himself, said, "Yes," to the waiting Lurad. "Frigog cobied, it seems, but what she cobied will lead to blank space—Metan Matac's ever clean work."

The Yulandan was quiet for awhile, its fluid-filled, sack-like body clear-colored and unmoving except for the interplay of minute life-process bubbles that misted out from its interior. Thankful after so much chaos for the quiet, Belamy just let his eyes stare at those bubbles, his mind in neutral.

"You are distressed," the Yulandan observed.

Belamy snorted. "Matac ordered the death of an innocent. Yes, I'm upset! This isn't what the Cadre's about. We're about stopping things like this from happening."

"Matac understands her error," the Yulandan replied.

"That's nice to know."

"The operation is not forfeit," Lurad said. "It goes forward, Matac's efforts to secure the Ben-Drom's minor to us adding benefit. The virus should, by this time, be undetectable, even by the most skilled means."

Belamy could only stare. Lurad was so coldly dismissive of everything past, so analytically oriented, that it disturbed Belamy's sense of decency. "And what about the Megan Quroc's situation?! For God's sake, Lurad, he's up for court martial."

"It is none of our concern," Lurad said, calm as ever to Belamy's upset. "He chose his course upon Xentauri and knew the chance he took."

"I promised to help."

"That was also an unfortunate error, but I will help you complete such pledge to the precise extent necessary. Once fulfilled, all requirement of conscience on your part will be satisfied."

Dropping head to hand, his retainer buzzing its usual objection, tiredly Leon asked, "What does that mean?"

"Your actual question being, 'What destiny awaits the Megan Quroc,'" Lurad observed, then paused until, finally, Belamy looked up. "All—the Megan Quroc, the Megan Frigog, and the Metan Rajan—will most probably suffer dishonorable discharge."

Belamy began to erupt, but Lurad boomed out, "There is no help for it," drowning all objection. "However," the once more staid Lurad continued, "it has been arranged that the Megan Quroc will be offered posting as a top commander in the private Xentauri fleet. The High Consul Quiloc has already begun proceedings for such arrangement's accomplishment. The Megan Frigog, likewise, will be offered posting in a prestigious private fleet, one that will offer higher ranking than she could ever enjoy in Fleet service and at a substantial increase in service credit."

Shocked at the manipulation of lives, Belamy could only listen, his senses reeling.

"Rajan," Lurad continued, "is Cadre. And he is first and foremost a pilot. This is his love. This is his reason for entering Omniversal High Fleet service. This is his very reason for wishing to exist as a life-participant beyond his species' domain—very unlike a Ghirran. If our operation is successful—and it will be—Rajan will be flying full capacity for Cadre cause, supported and sustained by Altan credits."

Belamy sank down into his chair. Lurad had it all worked out. Of course. And that was the Yulandan's way. But Belamy couldn't stop the growing feeling that the Cadre itself was turning rotten and corrupt.

"We understand your sense of violation," Lurad said as if it had heard Belamy's unspoken thought. "But please remember that your Tellurian kind do tend to worry for the individual more than for the organism. Your kind are also prone to unwarranted extremes of guilt and conscience, and unwarranted lack thereof, depending upon rather arbitrary determinations of worth and loyalty. Reference your glee at entrapping K'har by utilizing the Bjen Dvorkahn as contrasted to your despair at the fate of Quroc. As Cadre leader, you must work around your flaws. Now, however, it is time to address fulfillment of your pledge to Megan Quroc."

o   o   o

41

QUROC LOOKED DOWN AT THE INHIBITORS encircling his arms and legs—so much like Syrene shackling in every way, except that they only knocked your nervous system out temporarily instead of killing you. That, and they didn't adhere, either. Quroc shuddered as, again, visions of his Metaxi's dying rose to haunt him. Their crimes so similar, his and his Metaxi's—both guilty of following their instincts; both condemned for it. Well, he was no Syrene, entire or devoid. He had rights. His only hope, though, was that Belamy would find a way to clear him.

Quroc had made it to in-house detention. Fleet Security had thrown him in the brig there, instead of shipping him to Core Ivalan—a matter of his rank. That was after the long interrogation session. That was after they hadn't gotten him to talk.

He'd held his silence like he'd been taught to do at 'Cad when in enemy capture. Of course, the Academy hadn't meant for that discipline to be used by its own against its own. His interrogators had pointed that out. "We aren't the enemy," they had screamed to his continued silence.

Their frustration had been a source of strength for Quroc. If they screamed, if they threatened, it was a good indicator that he was winning. His only answers had been the required ones, plus his demand to speak with

Belamy in private. They had denied him that, but he knew his rights, and, finally, Belamy had come.

Belamy and he had talked, and Quroc had told Belamy everything he safely could. The Fleet Director had seemed, not dubious, as Quroc had expected, but irritated. Belamy had seemed distant, even cold. Both reactions Quroc couldn't understand.

Shaking his bald face, Belamy went away, then. His fields, on leaving, betrayed him, strangely, as sorrowful. "I think, Megan Quroc," Belamy said just before the detention portal sealed, "that your career in Fleet is over." It was the darkest itar for Quroc.

But Fleet Director Leon Belamy had come back, now. And what he'd brought with him—a Legal, and a message from Quroc's sire—showed Quroc that Belamy did believe him about the minor, that Belamy did care. But there was a difficulty, Belamy told him. That was all the Tellurian said before withdrawing to leave Quroc alone with the best legal counsel Quroc's sire could secure.

The Legal, a brindled Xentauri she, introduced herself as Celac, then promptly proceeded to tell Quroc that there was enough evidence, one way and another, to convict him of the actual theft of the minor. That, along with a lesser charge of trafficking stolen property could put him in a penal core forever. "Luckily, your Fleet Director has convinced Fleet not to turn you over to civilian authorities for criminal prosecution, but—" Here, Celac spread her elegant hands. "As you know, theft of a

Syrene carries with it a life-term punishment, so this is the very good news. Now for the bad."

With barely a pause, Celac consulted her portacom, then plunged on: "Technically, the case is one of liability. Actually, however, it's all political. As you've probably seen on the NewsNets, one Regulus Primus Omega Ben-Drom, owner of the stolen Syrene, has filed charges, not against you, but against Fleet Academy. He has publicly embarrassed them. As a result, it's the Academy that's coming after you." Celac's brow feelers arched. "The Academy doesn't like its image sullied," she said dryly. "And the notoriety this case is getting is doing just that, so you're the designated votive offering."

It came down to charges of Disgrace. The fact that Quroc was logged as present at the Academy Syrene Holding at the time of the minor's theft, the fact of Quroc's family brand upon the minor, and the fact that Quroc had been in possession of the minor and had tried to evade capture were all embarrassments to Fleet and to the Academy. Quroc would be tried for violating Fleet Conduct Ethics, and, if enough evidence was brought to substantiate the charges in the judgement of a Peer Review Board—and there was plenty enough of that— then Quroc's career in Fleet was ended. "Instead of a criminal charge, it is a complaint against you, your character, and this is a very hazy area of law. I'll do my best, but, considering how much worse it could be, I suggest you not fight the charges of Disgrace and subsequent discharge from Fleet. Should you, then, with the evidence against you, the Academy and Fleet could very well change their minds and turn you over to the civilian authorities for criminal prosecution."

A knot had tightened in Quroc's gut. "But it's all not true," he whispered when finally Celac had quieted long enough for him to say something.

At that, Celac's ears had folded precisely and neatly back. "Czzt, Quroc! Let's be reasonable, shall we? You were present at the Academy Syrene Holding at the exact time of the minor's theft. The minor has your brand on it, its legal Academy one cut out by your very own Xilarn blade. Then you were caught trying to escape Ivalan with it. Add to that the charges that could be brought against you for endangering so many lives in that *stupid* skirmish flight around Iban, and, in the civilian quarter, you'd be prosecuted to the fullest extent the law would allow." Celac showed teeth to him, her anger and disgust at him very pointed. "You are very lucky to be who you are—the son of a powerful High Consular and a member of one of the most prestigious Xentauri dynasties. If you weren't, I'm sure that you would soon be enjoying a lifetime of banishment to a penal core inside the most miserable planet that could be found in the Omniverse." Celac's ears came back up, and she now smiled sweetly. "Let's accept the happy tidings of the minor discomfort of a Disgrace and Dishonorable Discharge from Fleet and get on with our pampered, spoiled life, shall we?"

Quroc had risen during this last, his body flexing in anger. "I'm not guilty," he said stiffly. "I don't like your attitude, and I don't know where you've gotten your information. But it's all wrong, and there's proof of that! So, unless you're willing to represent me to that effect, you are dismissed."

That had still-stopped the snippy queen. There was a moment of stare down between them, but it was Celac who finally relented with a skeptical and clipped, "All right. Tell me your version."

Quroc took a deep breath. He had to be careful. He could safely only reveal so much without jeopardizing his family, so he decided to circumvent anything that touched that end of it. "First," he began, "I don't know anything about my being at the Academy Syrene Hold at the time of the minor's theft. As to a Xilarn blade, I no longer own one and haven't since my youth. And, I wasn't escaping Ivalan. I was in-flying Iban when the machon challenged my permission to land at FleetCom— permission I received from Fleet Director Tellurian Leon Belamy."

To this last, Celac gave a vigorous shake of head, and Quroc snapped: "Check the flight recorders of my ship. Check those of the Ghirran mach who chased me in. Check with Fleet Security, the machon station itself, Fleet's DeathNet, the CivNet, even the Sentinel cybersentries that ring Ita Centralis." Quroc was snarling at Celac by this time. "Then there's the freighter I took from Xi U through to Itae U, then on into main Galaxy Ita. All of that substantiates it." Tense and quivering, now, Quroc forcibly stopped his flexing and drew a large, shaky breath. "And that alone should shed enough doubt to clear me."

Celac still looked incredulous, but she kept her silence. What she did do was to touch her portacom and, once satisfied with whatever lay upon its face, she handed it to him.

Seeing it, Quroc collapsed to his cell's bunk, his mind reeling with what was disclosed there. "It's all a lie," he whispered to himself. Then, to Celac: "It's all a lie."

Again, the queen's brow feelers arched. "Oh? You're telling me that the entire Omniversal High Fleet has a conspiracy against you?"

"What I'm telling you is truth," Quroc said. He said it, but, inside himself, he knew already he was defeated. Silent for a long while, Quroc just stared at the evidence on the portacom. And, though he didn't like her, he was glad the Legal stayed with him. She was Xentauri kind and Dynasty, and, as kind, she didn't offer any word of comfort; she didn't feed him words of false hope or encouragement. She just settled her short, lean frame against a wall.

Finally, Quroc roused himself to hand back the portacom. "Thank you," he said. "I guess I'll settle for it your way—the Disgrace and Discharge. It's better than the penal core."

Celac nodded to him, paused, then nodded, again. "That's the smart way," she said. "...But it's not the way we're going to do it."

Quroc's teeth clicked together in his astonishment. "What do you mean?"

"I mean," Celac said, "I believe you. I don't suppose you'd be willing to undergo a BT scan?"

Quroc looked around the cell. There were bound to be monitors listening to the conversation, even though there weren't supposed to be. "No," he said, unable to tell her why. Then, "There's Xentauri reason."

Celac immediately indicated understanding that Quroc knew that which would break the Xentauri ethics code of speaking out against kind. A BT scan being open for public scrutiny was, therefore, an impossible thing for Quroc in his present circumstances.

"I understand," said Celac. "But it's all right for you to speak to me. I *am* Q Dynasty by blood and birthright, just like you, so you can tell me anything. And I have already assured we are not monitored," she added.

"Prove both?" he requested.

Celac brought out a prohibitively expensive sensor that did prove them unmonitored. Then she held out her hand, palm pad down, and he saw it faintly there—the pinprick tattooed needle marks, seemingly just skin mottling, that identified her as the Q. He touched them, and the microscopic implant just beneath the scars erupted, emitting a small beep within his inner ear. If Q Dynasty touched Q Dynasty, the distinguishing gene-code matching, that sound erupted in both their inner hearing. Quroc nodded, satisfied. If she wasn't Q, he couldn't prove it.

Celac settled down into a waiting pose and turned on her portacom, again. "Now, slowly, completely, and from the beginning, I want to know everything that got you involved with the Andromedan's Syrene," she said. "That means every detail of every move you made, as well as every move you know of that was made against or for you by anyone. Anything I can use to corroborate your story. Remember. Every detail. I have a feeling that the details are the only things that are going to give us a fighting chance."

Real hope came to Quroc. Not because of Celac's words, but by her fields. She really did believe him. She was interested in a way that was more than cursory. She was on-scent and hunting as only Verdajen queens, the warriors of his kind, could. And Quroc began to speak.

o   o   o

42

AT FIRST, CELAC HAD VIEWED QUROC as just another of High Consul Quiloc's spoiled and wayward children, products of a permissive queen-mother so typical to Verdajen dynasts. Quiloc was always employing her to get them out of scrapes, and, to Celac, Quroc's case was no different.

Seeing the eldest son, though, listening to him, Celac had realized that Quroc was different. Somehow, he'd managed to become responsible—probably the result of Quiloc's training rather than his queen's, for, if Celac's memory of that branch of the Q Dynastic history served her accurately, Quroc and his twin had been born of a love liaison between Quiloc and some Nadejan Xentauri warrior queen some turns before Quiloc had officially taken mate.

Having met Quroc, Celac felt for the blue and white striped Xenti whose azul-blue, very Nadejan eyes were so, so serious. He was such a relief from Quiloc's other, 'legitimate' children. Quroc was definitely worth fighting for, and, maybe, just maybe, if she could get some breaks, she could help him.

Criminal defense law was Celac's specialty, and she was good at it, even if she did wind up using it mostly to kit-save Q Dynasty delinquents. Well, here it seemed was a real case, and Celac salivated just thinking about it.

But the odds against winning the case were overwhelming. The laid Q brand and the Xilarn blade evidence was damning, none of it helped by the fact that Quroc admitted that he had indeed been inside the Academy Syrene Holding at the exact time the Syrene minor's tracking brand had disappeared from premises. The evidence was solid against him, unless Celac exposed the real truth—that Riloc had stolen it, and that Quiloc had attempted to destroy it.

Much of what had actually happened could be proven: Quroc's finding the Syrene in the House holding in termination status, Quroc's breaking of Quiloc's arm, and the amputation of pieces of Quiloc's body guard. Unfortunately, most of what was provable would break Xentauri covenant and jeopardize the family, so, even if she'd wanted to and Quroc would allow it, Celac couldn't use it. That left finding the "ghost squadron" that Quroc claimed had chased him outward from Xentauri—'silent runners,' he had called them, "coming out of nowhere." It left the freighter. And it left the in-run—officially an out-run according to Fleet. And that discrepancy—a falsification of record, she hoped—would be where Celac would start.

Why Fleet would falsify a record that was so easy to verify, Celac couldn't understand…until she tried to uncover that falsification. Deep within FleetCom's archival pits, Celac discovered something that every common fleet knew: Fleet was tight. When it wanted to suppress something, it did so effectively, efficiently, and thoroughly. Every record convincingly showed the same thing: Quroc was out-running when he'd been captured. There was even visual evidence to prove that. Those visuals were so convincing that Celac caught herself doubting Quroc's claim that he'd been flying in.

Celac left FleetCom angry with herself and in awe of a giant bureaucracy that could move so quickly to cover itself. It had taken skill to create all those various visuals, and Fleet had done it in an impossibly short time. ...Unless Quroc actually was lying to her.

Back in her office, Celac put through several high security calls to the Civilian Defense Net, requesting every record they had of traffic, both ship and communication links, from their controller stations and cybersentries. Thanks to her reputation, she didn't have to get an order. The records were opened to her office immediately, and Celac at once set two full teams of investigators on those entries. She was very thankful that Fleet and the CivNet were at odds with one another and uncooperative.

Celac also ordered a full copy of records from the Xentauri System's private military defense complex for the time surrounding Quroc's supposed fly-through. She even bothered with the Fleet outstations there, though she already knew that she wouldn't find anything to help her.

By the end of the itar, Celac had evidence contrary to Fleet's, all of it gleaned from CivNet, that Quroc had indeed been traveling into Ita. The records from the cybersentries even showed the minor in transit with him—a good thing that would belay any claim by Fleet that Quroc had been running empty at that time, actually in-transit to collect the minor.

And there was more: Though Fleet records from their outstations at Xentauri failed to show any pass-through by Quroc's ship, either in or out of Verdaje, Xentauri records did. As an added bonus, those same Xentauri records showed that, while Quroc had indeed had the minor in his possession outbound from Xentauri, he hadn't had it with him when, earlier, he'd come in.

That evidence didn't particularly clear Quroc of Disgrace charges, but it did establish Fleet's falsification of record. That alone could get Fleet to drop its charges with the right maneuvering by Celac. Protecting Quroc from retaliation by Fleet was Celac's primary concern, however. Even were she to get formal charges dropped, Quroc would still be vulnerable to repercussions from Fleet hierarchs. She needed something, some lever, by which to force them to leave him alone. She needed something to stay Fleet Academy which was using Quroc as a foil against the Omega Bjen Dvorkahn's suit against them. The Academy needed to prove Quroc guilty to release itself from culpability. If it succeeded, the Ben-Drom's suit failed. If it didn't, the Academy would not only lose face, it would be paying a heavy penalty of credits to the Ben-Drom, and it didn't want to do that.

If Celac could convince the Ben-Drom to drop his suit, however....

Celac shook her head. It was impossible. The Ben-Drom was famous for his mercenary sagaciousness. To even hint something like that to him would only spur him on.

Equally, it would be impossible to prove that Riloc had actually stolen the minor since neither Quroc nor Quiloc would cooperate with that tack. Xentauri loyalty, especially in-family, was absolute, even when the actions of one jeopardized another. It was one of the reasons why Quroc had taken the minor away with him in the first place.

Ears wilting, Celac sighed. "Why didn't you just let Quiloc terminate the damned minor," Celac growled. "It would have saved all this." And, suddenly, Celac's ears pricked. The minor! Its memories. They would substantiate Quroc's stories...if she could subpoena them, then use Quiloc's position and privilege as High Consul to cleanse them of anything incriminating to the Q Dynasty.

CELAC PLACED THE NECESSARY CALLS to Civilian Judiciary. She would force the Bjen Dvorkahn to release the minor to them, then demand the minor's memories drained. Quroc wouldn't like it—the destruction of the tiny thing—but Quroc was more important than any biodroid, regardless of its rarity. A living sentient took precedent over a plasmic programmable in any circumstance.

"Celac."

Celac looked up to see her head investigator standing in the access. "Yes, Virnoc," she said, motioning him in.

He declined, leaning in the doorway, instead. "Nothing we've found overwhelmingly verifies that Fleet altered their records. And we can't find the freighter Quroc claims to have crossed with into Itae. It will be a stand-off. Fleet could claim that we had the civilian records altered in our favor, especially since our client *is* the first son of an Omniversal High Consular who is also the influential head of the Verdajen Q Dynasty. There's precedent for that happening over and over again, and all Fleet as to do is get one CivNet head to admit the possibility. And the Fleet Director himself is tight with the top CivNet administrator."

Celac knew that, but she had also hoped that, between the Xentauri records and the CivNet records, there would be that one item of overwhelming evidence to prove her argument beyond doubt. Obviously, there wasn't, so, now, it would come down to a matter of judgement on the part of the Fleet Peer Review Board who would hear the case. It would be they who would decide who they thought was lying, and Celac knew better than to delude herself into thinking that her claims had a chance there. She had to have solid proof.

"Czzt!" Celac spat, then swivelled her chair to view the notes she'd made of her interview with Quroc. "I need some evidence that Fleet has tampered with the records, Virnoc," she said, and he agreed.

"I'll keep working on it, Celac," he said, excusing himself.

Celac touched open her office intercom. "Gre'Or," she queried.

A sniffing sound, then, "Yes, my lovely Celac," whuffled back to her.

"Sorry to bother you, but who would be most easily bribed or bluffed in Fleet."

"For what?" the disembodied voice responded.

Celac told him.

A pause, then, "Who do you have?"

Celac ran through the list.

Her law partner's response was immediate. "The Ghirran mach," he said. "Not the easiest to intimidate or bribe, but easiest to get to. There are very few Ghirran saurischian's in Fleet," Gre'Or said. "And fewer still flying machon. Fleet cannot hide a Ghirran well. Try it."

"Him," Celac corrected as the intercom canceled. "Him," she said, sinking into thought. She sat up and touched her maincom. "One Metan Tertius Rajan Tag Ajin ab Ghirran, Machon," she said, reading off the Fleet records she had copied. At least Fleet hadn't changed that, though they easily could have. Their mistake.

Celac smiled and tapped another touch-point on her com. This call she placed to an old friend of hers—the local captain of the civilian police force here on Eaena. He owed her, and he would be glad to repay a part of his debt by rounding up the machon.

∘   ∘   ∘

43

HEAVING A SMALL SIGH, Rajan made his way out of Medical, this visit with Kahn no more encouraging than the last. Kahn was Not. There was no consciousness, no cognizance, within Kahn's body. Only the body's own vital fields, transparent and fluctuating, showed themselves to Rajan's spectral sight. Kahn was still comatose, though the meds assured Rajan that this was normal for Altan Droms who had suffered heart complex injury. "That's how they heal so rapidly," the medicus in charge of Kahn's recovery informed him. "He'll be as good as new once he wakes up. And that will be soon. You'll see. Then, it will just be a matter of restretching his leg stringing. He'll need you for that."

The medicus was trying to reassure, but that didn't alleviate Rajan's gloom. Rajan needed Kahn awake. They had always shared their troubles—all of them—and, now, Kahn wasn't there to share.

Rajan needed Kahn's sneaky-mindedness to get him out of peril. If anyone could figure a way out of Rajan's dangerous predicament, Kahn could—especially when it came to a matter of problems with authorities. Kahn, or, rather, Kahn's associations, could easily get the entire matter of the Regar assault on the civi-police dropped completely, and that, Rajan figured, was his only hope.

Rajan hated being reduced to graft, bribery, and tail-stroking, but that was the only recourse left to him.

Fate had decided he was to live, and, so, he had to face the reality that living brought him—a reality where trouble was not only tracking him, but was very close to closing claws about him. That he knew. He felt it in the hollows of his bones. And Kahn had the contacts to save him.

Another small sigh broke from the saurischian's lips. He not only needed Kahn, he missed him. Kahn was his comrade, both at-arms and off-duty. They played together, ate together, bunked in the same cabin, and they always flew together—had since their first assignment together after the Academy. They were a fixed team—inseparable—having assured that by registering themselves an element—a legally unbreakable team of flyers who had to be assigned that way to whatever wing they were attached. The only thing Rajan and Kahn didn't share was she-s, Kahn's mating appetite for females—any who were compatible, and even some who weren't—insatiable, while Rajan's was non-existent.

Despite his worry, Rajan chortled, minute saliva-coated bubbles of the helium gas by-product of his respirations escaping from between his lips. That was the one good thing about Kahn being fighter-down—he couldn't taunt Rajan about his celibacy.

"What's the chuckle, 'Jan?"

It was Jaeger. Rajan groaned inside himself. "No much," he answered. "Just thoughting."

Typical to his kind, the black skinned, white-haired youth bobbed his head, then asked, "How's Kahn?"

Rajan tipped snout. "Same," he said.

"Oh. Too bad. You think he'll be up when time comes to space-out?"

Frowning, Rajan looked askance. "What mean?"

Jaeger waived a small, flat, black square of transcommunication matrix at him and grinned. "The Ben-Drom's summons, that's what I mean, you ugly long-snout. Haven't you checked your T-Mail lately?"

"Hsc," Rajan affirmed. "Kahn's, too. No get summons from Ben-Drom."

Sobering immediately, Jaeger dropped eyes and started shuffling his soft-slippered feet. "Oh," he muttered, his fields showing him embarrassed and uncomfortable like he'd just as soon wing-over and fall-off as be there now.

"You get summons?" Rajan asked, pushing for information before the Tellurian could follow through desire.

Jaeger shrugged, the embarrassment evident in his fields worsening.

Rajan let him off. "Good news, Jaeger. Not feel bad. You get gone this place," he said, forcing through a grin. "When space?"

"A little less that three dectar," Jaeger mumbled. Then, the Tellurian's good character rose. He straightened and brought his eyes to level. "I'm sorry, 'Jan," he said, meaning it. "I just thought, for sure, that the Beast would have you and Kahn back. Everybody thought that. After Donjon and all." Again, embarrassment flooded Jaeger. "Well, I gotta go. Got duty," he said, even though 'Jan knew he didn't.

"Hnc," Rajan responded, tilting an eyeridge toward the Tellurian's fast retreating back.

Jaeger's mention of the famous battle of Donjon only made the scald of being passed over by the Ben-Drom more potent. Donjon had been Kahn and Rajan's first real firefight. It had been a battle-first for Jaeger, too. It was where the Tellurian had earned his name, Kahn hanging the moniker on him in a drunken ceremony celebrating their victory. That battle had also been where Rajan and Kahn's friendship had been sealed—they who had for so long been antagonists at the 'Cad, and, then, reluctant members of the same element of a wing, assigned that way by the Ben-Drom himself because of their enmity toward one another.

That was two ita previous. To Rajan it seemed much longer than just two ita, though. It seemed forever since the Ben-Drom had dismissed his crews with a promise to recall anyone who wanted to fly with him and his again once his new fleet was built. Rajan and Kahn had been biding their time till that happened, taking shabby assignment after shabby assignment without complaint. Now it seemed the Ben-Drom's fleet was built, but they wouldn't be a part of it. Obviously, the Ben-Drom's promise had not been meant for everyone. At least, it hadn't been meant for Kahn and Rajan, since it couldn't be an oversight. Not now it couldn't be an oversight—not after having just seen and been seen by the Altan on Iban after the intercept of the Megan Quroc.

That Kahn and he had been excluded explained to Rajan why the Ben-Drom had seemed so frigid and aloof to him at Iban, though. It all fell into place, now.

Bitter and depressed, Rajan made his way back to quarters. That those quarters were cold and dark suited him. He didn't bother to bring them up to comfort. He didn't bother with his weapons harness, either. Uncomfortable as it was picking-up against his scales, he left it crossed about him and just curled into his hole-like lair of a bunk, his hearing shut even to the singing gems he'd brought with him from his home-world that were, usually anyway, such therapy for him.

Rajan tried to sleep, but couldn't. His mind wouldn't stop its fretting. He couldn't escape his misery. After a small while, Rajan gave it up. He would escape. He just needed help. And the saurischian started to dig into one corner of his self-made lair, his long, wicked claws picking away at a careful riddle of stones he'd ceremoniously fitted there.

The conundrum came apart with its usual difficulty, the time passing in the ticks of Rajan's claws as they lifted each puzzle-stone out in order. Finally, the deed was done, and, with carefully whispered words, Rajan lifted both the gem-studded, fringe-wrapped, brown bone pipe and its scaled bag of herb from the hollow he'd so carefully designed for them.

He handled both with a reverence, for they were sacred to him—the pipe made of a bone gifted to him of his nurturer, the bag cut by him from his own skin.

Gently, he loaded the pipe with contents from the bag, then brought the long stem's mouthpiece to his teeth, clenching it between their jaggedness before closing his lips about. Drawing, he lit it and sucked long pulls of the heady, blissful herb. He loved the Hevra. It was his one illicit pleasure. And, letting go, Rajan allowed himself to sink into its rapture, his sight watching the heavy curls of blue-green smoke caper and swirl about him.

The Hevra—it stopped time; it stopped the humdrum hurry that was life; it stopped the pain, and put wonder, even ardor, in its place. Just for a time. Just for a little while. And, for a little while, Rajan could lose his worry for his troubles and his misery at the plunge his career was taking…his regret.

And, in a breath, he was flying, once again—not routine circuitous patrols in mundane space around Ivalan, but really flying, breaking Edge, his ship, a strange ship—only three wings instead of the four of his Quadstar Harrier—a shimmering, void-black, tri-winged fighter that barely warped the matrix.

At once, Kahn was there, toying with him—flying a ship just like it—three wings. Kahn was begging for a hassle—insisting on one—contesting Rajan's superiority.

Taking challenge, Rajan tumbled his ship through and down, spinning round Kahn's ship, his wingtips meshing with those of Kahn's like gears as he rolled his tri-wing over and around the other in one of the most dangerous maneuvers ever.

But Kahn rolled out before the game was played, and, with a snarl, Kahn snapped, "Fighters high at alpha-twelve-dash-three. Six of them."

And they met them three for one, straight on, their weapons-fire bursting, silent screaming, on their enemies, the squall of an alarm that warned, "IMPENDING RIVE," urgent in Rajan's auricles as he pushed the Outer Edge, the plunge into the never-ending chasm of Betweens threatening.

The attacking fighters veered off—dropped out-space—and Rajan eased off. But the alarms still wailed.

Screaming, screaming, never-ending screaming. Rajan checked his readouts, searching wildly for the riving Edge of which the alarms warned, but nothing showed. Anywhere.

Kahn was bellowing…cursing…ordering him to— Come to attention?!

The bubble broke, the dream's reality shattering in a million shards of star-strewn space and fighters' wake.

"METAN TERTIUS RAJAN AB GHIRRAN. I REPEAT: COME TO FULL ATTENTION. AT ONCE!"

It was Commander Frigog's voicing. Wildly, Rajan looked around to see, with sweet relief, that, at sometime during Hevra's plunge, he'd already safely stowed his pipe and bag. Hevra safe, Rajan shot, belly slithering, out of lair to jerk himself upright in obedience. "Sir…Madam…Yes, Sir," he said, his lisp vanished in the moment.

It was the comlink. The Grundian's visage was brilliant there in her urgency, her green veins bulging out with pulsing fluids as her membrane hummed with tension. Frigog was practically sizzling. "Get your stagnant, rotting hide down here, hyperspeed, Machon," she snapped.

"Sss'rr," he acknowledged, his lisp back.

"On the Quad," she added quietly, visage blinking dead.

Alone, again, Rajan heaved shaky breath. His legs wanted desperately to buckle. He resisted. Well, at least, Frigog wasn't really angry. Just playing-look that way. That Rajan knew. Her speech had told him something: that he didn't have to hurry all that much. Frigog's use of loose-speak instead of formal jargon meant as much—a code within the mach that others didn't ken. He had to get there, but he did have time to get himself in order.

Gathering his scattered wits, he fumbled with the riddle-stones, then, aware that time was slipping, just jumbled them in place. They would seal themselves about the pipe and bag. He'd just have Tangler's Testing when next undoing them. And, as he quickly put his lair in order, dissipating smoke and other traces, he wondered what would make the usually quiet Frigog act so tight. It wasn't like her, and she was the only good thing in this place.

Rajan's mind was clear, now, of the Hevra's influence and euphoria. Gone with it, too, was the feeling of well-being that usually stayed with him long after. In its place, foreboding once more crept its icy claws into his spine.

Sticking his badge to shoulder, Rajan checked it, then stepped to the old transfer pad embedded in the deck floor by the cabin's access and engaged.

The coordinating transfer com materialized him on the Quad decks just outside Frigog's office, and, as his brain came functional, he knew what had caused Frigog's sizzle. His latest nightmare stood there manifest. They had come for him. They'd caught him.

"Your escort," Commander Frigog said as she indicated the six staid-faced civi-police beside her. "You will accompany them. My orders."

o   o   o

AEROS

44

"ENTER, PLEASE." IT WAS A THROATY, well-modulated voice that emanated from a speaker in the outer access of an obviously expensive suite of offices. Skin furrows wrinkled forward in vee's atop Rajan's flat, grooved skull, the finely laid, tiny scales there shimmering in the evening light.

Rajan was flummoxed. The civi-police had taken him, not to Core Ivalan or some other penal holding as expected, but into the Aesthenian System itself with its five hugely magnificent garden planets that were the very heart of Omniversal government. Set down on Eaena, the fourth planet, high up on a landing ledge of a building that was more a gigantic piece of sparkling artwork than it was practical workspace, Rajan stood looking around at a view of a multi-kilometron park, a few scant, equally artistic buildings the only occasional break in nature-scape. And Rajan wondered why he had been brought here.

The access slid open, and the six officers who had escorted him—really only *had* escorted him, not roughed him up or killed him as he'd expected—politely gestured for him to enter. Suspicious, Rajan twisted head and tipped a wary eye, scanning the interior.

"Come in, please. *Do* come in."

It was the same voice. Tentatively, Rajan did as bid.

A brindled Xentauri she, her fur curling in interesting swirls all over her body, stepped forward. She greeted Rajan with the Omniversal gesture of welcome. Rajan returned the greeting, but guardedly.

The Xentauri female nodded as if satisfied after looking Rajan up and down. Then, she motioned the six escorts toward a small sitting area. They began to argue quietly with her, indicating Rajan, then his weapons belt, but, obviously, their arguments failed. The Xentauri excused them to the waiting area again, and Rajan took note. The Xentauri obviously had clout.

She turned to him and formally introduced herself. "I am the Xentauri Legal, Celac Q ab Dijevan ab Verdaje," she said. Then, "Won't you please be seated?" And she indicated a remoldable suitably pre-shaped to fit Rajan's species-type situated just in front of a large, polished desk mounted with an inset comscreen and stage that masked its data from observer's sight.

The preformed remoldable was a rare politeness, and this point was also not wasted on Rajan. He began to relax, but not much.

The she's voice, her demeanor, was too pleasant to Rajan's thinking. Neither matched the hardness of her fields. Rajan smelled an attempt to trap. He also felt completely powerless to avoid that trap. He was guilty— guilty, at least, of allowing the Draco Gor's machinations of the evidence—and, though he couldn't speak, he also couldn't lie just to defend himself. It was against his soul-way.

Having taken her place behind her desk, the Xentauri was now watching him closely, her brown eyes steady on him.   Rajan bowed stiffly in strictest Ghirran kindway. "Xentauri Celac," he said politely.

She smiled, inclining her head. "Please do sit," she said, again indicating the seat he was to take.

Again, Rajan ignored the politely phrased demand, instead letting his senses scan the room's interior and its furnishings.

The place eked of high prosperity, yet it was a working office. This Legal, Rajan realized, was one of the more successful ones. Not by graft, though. This one was no sluggard. Everything about her and her surroundings reinforced Rajan's impression that she was dangerous to him. His schooled sight easily picked out all the special places that were vaults, as well as where the sensors lay hidden for the remote monitors he felt recording him. The large room was loaded with them, though, by design, they would have been invisible to most.

Noticing that the she-creature's eyes still watched him, following his gaze as he assayed her territory, Rajan ignored another motion from her that he seat himself. She rose, then, and rounded the desk to approach.

Rajan stiffened. The officers over in the waiting area grew still, and one of them began to rise from where he sat.

There came a scent of fear and nervousness from that quarter, and Rajan began to realize that they were afraid of him. The machon reputation.... That fact registered in his mind. It would make them extra cautious, extra kill-happy.

The Xentauri again motioned the police officers off. "It's Metan Tertius Rajan Tag Ajin ab Ghirran, Machon, to be more accurate, isn't it," she said, her eyes steady on him, her face—her body—close. The six escorts anxious, their breathing caught and held, the room grew heavy with tension.

The she was inviting Rajan to sit again—inviting him with a graceful movement of her hand.

Rajan watched that hand, its four fingers and two offset thumbs darker when compared with the rest of her body, excepting her pricked ears which were equally as dark as the hand's digits. And, as always when he encountered a Xentauri, Rajan found himself intrigued by the set of double thumbs that graced each hand, his own hands nerves twitching in wonder at what it would be like to be thus structured.

"Metan Rajan?" the Xentauri Celac queried. And she touched him.

Her touch—it broke the trance-like, slow-motion spell that had come over Rajan. And he knew he'd fallen into battle-ready without even knowing it.

Purposely, Rajan forced himself to relax. He did it with a gentle breath, audibly expressing it to ease the tense civilian officers. Then, he shuddered skin, that act loosening the hard muscles just beneath. And, to the

Legal's once more repeated indication of a seat, Rajan inclined his head and sat.

"Please be comfortable," she said.

In control of his anxiety, now, Rajan watched the Xentauri again take her own seat behind the desk. She smiled at him, yet again. "You didn't indicate if I have gotten your true naming right, Metan Rajan," she said. "Have I?"

Rajan inclined his head—an acknowledgment, but just.

"You seem very nervous. Is it that I'm Xentauri?"

The civilian police were still on guard, their tenseness stinking.

"Not," Rajan said softly.

The Xentauri smiled too sweetly. "Because I'm a civi-, then, as you Fleets like to call us."

"Not."

A frown crossed the Xentauri's face, wrinkling fur at brow. "Because I'm a Legal," she said flatly, her voice hardening to an edge that clipped her words off.

Rajan raised snout a little at her tone. "Hsc, yes," he replied.

The she's lips set, tightening around her soft, furred mouth until the tips of her longest canines showed. "Would you like your own Legal before we begin?" she asked coldly.

"Need I?" Rajan asked just a coldly. "What this be concerning, She?"

The Xentauri's brow arched at the "she," her fields flaring out to Rajan's sight. "A certain incident with a client of mine," she answered.

Involuntarily, Rajan jerked, the visage of the dead Low Drom and the four police troopers downed in Regar's dark alleyway coming vivid to his mind. "What client?" Rajan asked quietly.

"The one you are credited with apprehending, Metan," the Xentauri answered.

Rajan blew breath in his relief, unintentionally filling the office with teeming numbers of tiny helium bubbles. So this wasn't about the Regar problem. Rajan relaxed immediately and completely. So did the police escort. They turned their backs with only a few after-glances and began to entertain themselves again.

"Everything of in-run in log, Counselor," Rajan said, then added, "Find them FleetCom, Iban."

The Xentauri leaned forward, her face taking on a conspiratorial appearance. "So there was an in-run," she said.

Rajan tipped snout, confused by both her manner and her words. It was as if she pounced, yet he had given her no reason to. "Hsc, there was," he said, maintaining calm.

"And it was not an out-run? It didn't start as an out-run from somewhere in System Ivalan or elsewhere within Centralis?"

The she's fields had fired like a mach's would when closing on the kill. Rajan tipped snout again in silent asking. Her reaction baffled him. And, when she didn't offer explanation, then his own snout dropped, and he matched her menace with his own. He would not be prey. "I say in-run, She. Log show in-run, She. What you want?"

At once, the Xentauri sat back as if satisfied, but her finely manicured claws extruded to tap the obdurite surface of her desk. "What I want, Metan Rajan, is truth. You keep referring to the log. Suppose you tell me which log."

Getting irritated with her antagonism, Rajan snapped his tail in warning.

Behind him, the police, all six as one, jerked, then rose, tense, again.

"Ship log," Rajan answered. "Mine," he said. He leaned forward. "You not stupid, She. H'I not stupid."

Rajan stood. "Not play game, this, with you, Xentauri Legal!" And he moved to leave.

All six civilian law officers stepped toward him, threatening. Rajan bared teeth, then turned a scalding look to the she. "H'I not free to go, if want?" he asked severely.

"Sit down, Metan," the Xentauri Celac told him, her voice hard.

Rajan weighed his options. Then, he moved—one smooth, quick movement forward, one hand brushing body-armor active.

Rajan slammed his long, white, skeletal hands down on the Xentauri's desk, all thirteen bony dactyls on each spread wide, their claw-like ungues arching evilly as he began to dance them on the desktop surface in clear and obvious warning, the delicate-looking nerve-net that covered those hands turning from puce to surprising livid. "You, civi- she, want talk Rajan, you courteous be! Ask, no tell."

Directing one eye toward the police who now, belatedly, had their weapons drawn, Rajan kept the other eye focused on the Xenti Legal. That eye warned.

Rajan used bluff, playing on their fear of machon. "You be dead, She," he said to the Xentauri, "before they kill H'I. You tell stand-down," he hissed malevolently, tossing his head toward the six frozen troopers. And he popped a hand against the desktop to emphasize himself, his other hand all the while maintaining the sinister distraction maneuver. "NOW!" he snapped.

Though she hadn't moved, the Xentauri's ears flicked back and forth in nervousness as she tried to watch Rajan's face as well as both his capering hands. Then, with a sideways glance toward the still frozen troopers, the Xenti Legal carefully sat back.

Her fields held fear, but her eyes were warrior hard. "If they do, Metan Rajan, will you talk, then?" she asked softly, her voice cold. "Talk honestly?"

Rajan studied her, his hands shifting now to move in a mildly ominous stroking movement. Though frightened, the she had courage.

He chuckled, then, and tipping an eyeridge toward her, nodded. "They think 'Jan hurt. H'l no hurt, but no be hurted. They stand-down. Close access. You seemly be. If this, then maybe," Rajan said.

The Xenti stared at him, one brow twitching. Her eyes measured him. Then, relaxing, she flicked an ear toward the officers. They vehemently indicated negative. She flicked the ear, again.

"Door open, at least enough that we can tell if you two are brutalizing one another," one of the troopers said. "We don't want anybody hurt. And you two aren't exactly on your best behavior."

The Xenti growled. Rajan cast an eye, then gave assent, and the troopers settled back, one of them partially closing the door between the office and the waiting room, but not before giving Rajan warning stares.

Xentauri Celac nodded to Rajan, then. Rajan sat back down, and the legal took a deep, deep breath. "Now, Metan Rajan, Machon," she said. "Does the stipulation requiring good manners work both ways?"

Her eyes challenged him, and Rajan grinned. She was courageous. She was feisty, too. He leaned back, relaxing into casualness. "Speak, Xentauri," he said amicably. "Rajan listen. Answer what can," he said. Then, with a leer, he added, "If answer not make 'Jan look bad."

The Xentauri shifted in her seat, her eyes dropping momentarily. When she looked up again, she tipped one ear, then began to question Rajan anew, this time genially.

o o o

45

"THEN YOU'LL TESTIFY?" CELAC ASKED a decitar later, her brain whirling from the description Rajan had given of his flight against Quroc. Her notes were full of details from Rajan that couldn't possibly be faked. More, they matched those in Quroc's deposition exactly. The Fleet's Legals would have a difficult time discrediting them.

What Rajan had shared, he had volunteered—things that Celac would have never guessed to ask, things that would be invaluable to Quroc's defense…if Rajan would testify. But, to that question, the saurischian was mute. He just watched her.

"What?" Celac asked, a little unnerved by his continued silence.

The Ghirran drew a deep, quiet breath. "From what you ask," he said, "Fleet not be pleased to lose case. H'l be not liked if help H'l you."

Despite her best effort not to, Celac dropped her eyes. The mach was canny, not just a rowdy gadget-master like she'd been told most were, their quick reflexes their only functional capacity. Nothing Celac had said had actually suggested that Rajan's testifying could bring him disapproval and possible recrimination from the organization he served. Celac had been very careful of that. She was too good a Legal not to be. That he'd caught on from the gist of her line of questioning didn't please her.

The mach had been honest with her, though—candid, in fact. Furthermore, Celac liked him, despite their bad beginnings, bad beginnings that were partly her fault. She had treated him as a hostile witness, with justification, of course, especially considering her other dealings with Fleet and its Ita Academy in this litigation…especially considering Rajan's own evasive behavior at the onset of their meeting. And, then, of *course*, because he was one of the notorious machon. "That's true," Celac answered finally. "Fleet will not be particularly pleased with you were you to help clear Quroc."

"Would not flight log be enough?" Rajan asked.

"If there was one," Celac said, "it would help. But there isn't. All record of the event, including the ships' logs of both your Quadstar and the Megan Quroc's show him making an out-run. That is why your testimony is so valuable."

"Would not flight log be enough?" Rajan repeated.

Celac canted an ear at Rajan. "What are you saying?" she asked, realizing that there was meaning behind his words.

"If H'I produce flight log? Real flight log?"

"How could you do that? It was my understanding that you mach had to turn in all your logs after each patrol."

The saurischian grinned, ivory points of innumerable sharp, hooked teeth glinting wickedly. "Keep H'l all originals," Rajan said. "Learn hard way, H'l do, this."

Celac's own smile appeared. Things were looking up. And she decided that she *definitely* liked this mach, lisp, slither, and all. "If I could get a copy of that, it could make a big difference," Celac said, then hurriedly added, "…But I'd still need you to testify. Fleet has faked their logs, and the claim could be made that these are just as faked." And, here, as hunter stalking jittery prey, Celac stilled. She could force Rajan to testify, but she didn't want to have to resort to that. Better if he remained cooperative.

The Ghirran grumbled. Then, after a moment's hesitation, he dipped his snout. "You no need H'l just testify, Celac," he said. "You need guarantee H'l tell truth. You need BT scan."

Not quite believing what she'd heard, Celac remained silent, watching, hoping that the mach would commit himself further.

Resignation dropped the Ghirran into slump, but he said nothing more.

Neither would he, Celac realized after a few moments. "Would you really be willing to submit to a BT?"

The Ghirran's snout raised to level. "Could," he answered. "Sound like Quroc not have chance without, and H'l can no let other fall by doing not. H'l be soul-sworn not to do."

Finally Celac understood what drove the Ghirran, and she nodded to him. Celac was not religious, per se, but she understood the motivations of those who were. Most of the time, religiousness—quasi-religiousness, at least—interfered with a defense, simply because the religious so identified good as residing with god and government, and, therefore, with the prosecution's side of things. Usually, Celac hated working with them. In this case, however, she was extremely grateful for Rajan's beliefs. As one of those few whose religious principles pushed them beyond normal obligation, he would even jeopardize himself to help another. He was rarity.

Touching her com board, Celac said, "I'll arrange for one."

Again, a grumble.

"What, Rajan?" Celac asked gently, thinking he was having second thoughts.

"There be way you make look like force Rajan to do this?"

So he was having second thoughts, then. But he was also offering a way to honor his offer. "Would it help?" Celac asked.

"Since Fleet against you…." Rajan said hesitantly, then stopped and dropped his head, again. "Bad could be for H'l h'if look like helping," he mumbled shyly.

He was ashamed to ask, Celac realized, and she felt for him, but Omniversal law was very clear. It would be highly irregular for her to petition for a BT scan for a case like this. Quroc's case was not one of murder. "Normally, Rajan," Celac said, "BT scans are strictly voluntary, except in the most extreme cases."

"And this not be extreme," Rajan said, drooping further.

She knew his problem. She knew it could go really bad for him if she didn't give him a way out. But to do so, she would have to resort to things that she ordinarily would not. She did know a judge or two, though.

Celac pondered a moment longer, weighing the consequences to each of them, then said, "I'll get a subpoena for the BT."

Celac watched the Ghirran brighten immediately, and she was glad. "That good, Xentauri," he said. "H'I no cannot h'obey, hnc?"

"That's true," Celac replied.

"Now, you come with H'I to post to get flight log?"

Thinking he was fooling, Celac laughed. Then she saw that he was serious. Startled, she said, "I can't. I...I hate ring gravity. It's worse than weightlessness. I get totally sick at the sight of someone moving counter to my own orientation."

To her words, the mach had started snickering. Now, he actually doubled up with mirth, laughing outright. "Not be, She," he informed her when he finally recovered himself. "Base old. No have ring-grav. Single down, only. Not different, much, from planetside, but less."

Celac, who had pinned her ears in humiliation, muttered a small growl. "Why can't you just transcom it to me?" she snapped. "Or, better yet, bring it by later?"

The Ghirran's eyes began to glow a little, and, for the first time since their earlier fracas, the fact that he was a giant reptile, a natural enemy of Celac's kind, surfaced. "Not take chance, She," he said when finally he spoke again. "Fleet know soon you, H'l, talk. They stop H'l. Maybe find Rajan log, too. Log no more, then."

The saurischian dropped his snout, angling his head around until just one eye watched her, and Celac squirmed under that strange scrutiny. "Stop that," she said.

"Then go both, now," he said. "With troopers. While CO not know you be Megan Quroc Legal. Then be h'okay."

Celac knew he was right, but, still, the thought of taking space, especially with so alien a creature, disturbed her. Ultimately, though, she did agree. She needed that log. Only that and the minor's memories that she had demanded of the Omega Ben-Drom could prove Quroc's case.

o   o   o

46

THE BEN-DROM HAD FOUGHT AND LOST. Civilian Judiciary had compelled him to honor the Legal Celac's motion demanding the minor's memories. The Ben-Drom *had*, however, successfully gotten Judiciary to agree that he could procure the memories and didn't have to turn the minor over to authorities. It had fallen to Ka to execute the ugly deed—Ka who was yet fragile from his attempted interfuse with the minor.

Miserable, the Ben-Drom focused his attention upon other problems to keep himself from dwelling on what was happening elsewhere in his residence. His crews were his main concern, and finding his fleet commander the most pressing problem. Somewhere, somehow, some one or several were harboring against him. That this was the doing of the organization of which K'har had warned, the Ben-Drom was as yet unsure. To him, it seemed to be conspiracy in Fleet. It was Fleet that was keeping his crew selections from him, and he was bound to fight them.

He'd found Jastim. By happenstance. He'd seen Rajan, the machon having run to ground the Megan Quroc carrying his stolen minor. The Ghirran had seemed friendly, though the Ben-Drom had tested that by maintaining an aloofness. The Ghirran's fields had gone confused at that detachedness, however, and that would not have been had the saurischian been served summons and subsequently ignored or denied such. The Ghirran would have known reason for disdain, then. To the Ben-Drom, that evidence was exactly what he needed to convince himself that his suspicions were not idle. Dra and Gor, Jaxim, Methol, Kahn and Os, all of them, hundreds of them, were out there somewhere, waiting for him, and if he was to hold the pledge he'd made them after the battle of Donjon—that all who wished could serve with him again when time had completed his new fleet—he would have to find them.

With a stroke of talon, the Ben-Drom set an order to his solicitors. They were to secretly send agents forth seeking all those who Fleet had claimed as no-shows or no-respondants. Especially the Orcon Dra.

Dra—that being's disappearance truly troubled the Ben-Drom, for he desperately needed his fleet megarchon. He did not want a replacement, especially one maneuvered in by Fleet…or by the designs of conspiratorial others. And the Ben-Drom did not dismiss the possibility that the conspiracy of which K'har had warned could be located within the very service to which the Ben-Drom was conscripted.

That Fleet could possibly be so infiltrated stunned and stretched credibility, though. Rebel organizers were not usually so capably consolidated in their cause, able to control a regimented hierarchy without cooperation from the regulus command, its ever watchful, if self-serving, oversight. And the regulus command was not interested in causes. It was only interested in preserving its power and, thus, the status quo. So it would take a cause that avoided the regulus command. It would take a cause that catalyzed the lower ranks to move in some heretofore unheard of coordinated complicity to successfully infiltrate and utilize the resources of Fleet bureaucracy.

The Ben-Drom scoffed. Impossible. It couldn't happen. Yet something in him at his core thrummed at possibility, far-fetched though it seemed. If it were so, then this force could be more dangerous than surmised. And, for the first time, the Ben-Drom realized that, perhaps, the K'har's warning carried merit. Here, maybe, was something that required more than ordinary inattention.

"Lord."

It was Ka, finally returned from the Syrene habitat, and the Ceoheician looked more drawn and wan that ever had the Ben-Drom seen him. "Ka?" the Ben-Drom queried, worry bringing him to rise and approach the magus. But, as the Ben-Drom neared, the magus raised his headcrests, warning him away.

The Ben-Drom halted. Never had Ka so warned him. Never had the Ceoheician been so dangerous-feeling to the Ben-Drom's nearing senses. The Ben-Drom struggled to quell an involuntary rise of venom. Succeeding, finally, the Ben-Drom tried for openness. "Is the minor terminated, then?" he asked.

Ka's eyes shut momentarily, then opened, once again, but he said nothing.

Troubled and perplexed, the Ben-Drom stood mutely watching. Friend though he was, Ka had always been enigma. Faced with the certainty that Ka was internally disturbed, the Ben-Drom knew not consequences of his own any action upon the magus' psyche. And that could be dangerous to them both. Again, he had to quell a venom rush.

Though the Ben-Drom had, for turns, lived with Ka, both on Jenai at Rin and on Rhegar at Andromeda, and the magus had nursed him, bringing him through mania to health, he knew little more about the Ceoheician than he had when Ka had first discovered him in the crash of his ship on Ka's homeworld. But, through the eight full turns they had known each other, the Ben-Drom had never known the Ceoheician to be so utterly cold and unapproachable. The Ben-Drom drew a harsh breath, then tried again. "Ka?"

Slowly, the magus-warrior brought out his hand, the seven spindly, tapered fingers of it gradually uncurling from beneath.

Spooked, the Ben-Drom backed another step. He knew the magus-warrior's devastating powers and abilities. But, as Ka opened that pale hand, turning it palm up, the Ben-Drom calmed.

The Ceoheician inclined his head, indicating the small data-sphere cradled in that open palm.

The Ben-Drom reached for it.

LATER, ONCE KA HAD STABILIZED and finally spoken with him, the Ben-Drom audited the data-sphere. What it contained surprised him. More, it made the oddity of circumstances comprehensible. Despite the cost, the Legal Celac had been justified in her demand of the minor's memories. The Ben-Drom finally understood.

o   o   o

47

"THE XENTAURI LEGAL FOR THE MEGAN QUROC has filed a motion to compel disclosure of the Bjen Dvorkahn's minor's memories," Lurad said. "The Bjen Dvorkahn has agreed to comply."

It was rare for Lurad to initiate communication, especially via sublink. It took unusual circumstances. "She can't," Belamy stammered. "He wouldn't. The Ben-Drom would never destroy that minor. Any minor," Belamy amended. "He'd pull complaint first. There's got to be a mistake."

"There is no mistake," Lurad replied, its insides roiling and gurgling. "Upon failing to successfully counter Xentauri Celac's motion to compel, the Bjen Dvorkahn has agreed to release such memories."

From behind Belamy, Pryr chuckled. "It becomes a convoluted game, does it not?"

Belamy snapped a glance back. "You just concentrate on studying those conduct attitudes, Pryr. Your test with the Ben-Drom is just a decitar away. Get learning."

Another chuckle, quieter this time.

Belamy returned his attention to Lurad.

"We must intercept those memories before they become public domain," Lurad said once Belamy was again attentive. "The High Consul Quiloc's career and his value in negotiating with the Andromedans is jeopardized should their contents become common knowledge."

The last didn't make sense to Belamy. "But the Ben-Drom's bound to already have seen the memories," he said. "Quiloc is already ruined with the Andromedans."

"The Bjen Dvorkahn is not as strict in his codes as other Andromedans. If he were going to ruin Quiloc, he would have done so. He has not. Therefore, he is willing to forego such opportunity. He has much higher stakes, now: Exposing us. And, this is my plan to counter."

Belamy listened to Lurad elucidate its details to counter the Ben-Drom's any movement of discovery, amazed by the simple, yet confounded thinking. Yulandans just didn't think like Tellurians.

Referring back to the minor's memories, Belamy asked, "What about Quroc's defense?"

"The sire is more important than the son," Lurad replied. "Can you arrange intercept? The Bjen Dvorkahn will be submitting the memories through Fleet Judiciary as per Protocol. Fleet Judiciary will then submit to its Civilian counterpart. You must intercept from the intermediary."

"I don't think this is a good idea, Lurad," Belamy said.

Lurad turned black-purple.

Belamy hesitated, then said, "But I can do it."

"Do so," said Lurad, and terminated conversation.

"Lurad quickly becomes overlord, does he not?" Pryr said.

Belamy turned to face. He agreed with Pryr, but he didn't say so. Instead, he rationalized things according to his truth. "Lurad's the brains in this one, Pryr. If the Cadre is going to survive, we're going to have to play it out the Yulandan's way."

"And once the Cadre is secured?" Pryr countered. "Does Lurad continue to control us—it, with its lack of empathy for others?"

"No."

"Please ensure this," Pryr replied, his diamond foreridge swollen to a sharpened point. "I serve no master, save the regulus I choose to serve in my selected occupation." The Draco paused to cast his head in an action meant to be interpreted as threatening, the dragonet upon his shoulder rucks squawking and cackling as it began to pace back and forth, back and forth across the complete length of Pryr's shoulder width. "Be warned, Tellurian," Pryr said. "Never do or will I serve such a one as Lurad with its utter heartlessness. I have stayed thus far only because I believe our Cadre is the only avenue with which to salvage our cosmos as peaceful home for our various kind, but I will not remain should this continue."

In answer, Belamy signed in Omniversal, "understanding," and "be calm, at peace." But he *was* warned. The Draco had never before voiced objection. That he did now alerted Belamy. If Pryr had come to the point of giving ultimatum, so would many others. Belamy could lose the Cadre, anyway, even with Andromedan support. The binding tie of principle was the glue. It had to be maintained.

"Once this operation is over, Pryr, the Cadre will be as it was meant to be. I'll make sure of that. It's my baby, remember?"

"You are wrong, Tellurian. It belongs to all of us. Without us, you are nothing, and the Cadre is just a name."

The Draco's tri-faceted, rare eyes glittered dangerously. A cautious Belamy did not respond.

"I could be Quroc. I see that all too clearly," Pryr said. "I do not like it."

"Neither do I," Belamy agreed after a moment. "Lurad is boss for just a little longer. Until we have Andromedan support."

"Rocht."

o   o   o

48

STEPPING FROM HIS SHIP, THE BEN-DROM gave pause. He felt naked and vulnerable without Ka. For once, neither Sitad nor Ka had accompanied him, and the Ben-Drom felt their absence.

"Come, Erana," the Ben-Drom said to the Syrene entire who stood yet within the portal of the shierka. Come in Sitad's stead, to this bidding the pale yellow Syrene descended the shierka's central void, its movement cautious down the sloped curve as it followed the Ben-Drom from his ship to Fleet Academy's simulator facility.

Also trained to kathcom just as Sitad was, Erana was less forgiving of mistakes. As such, the Syrene was much more suitable for a navarch examination than was Sitad. It was more sensitive to other's callous treatments, and that was what the Ben-Drom really wished to test. He already knew Pryr capable. But he didn't know the megarch's disposition. Especially toward Syrene. It would be Pryr's disposition that was tested. It was that test that Pryr would fail with the help of, both, natural prejudice and Erana's unforgiving nature.

THE BATTLE BRIDGE SIMULATORS at Iban's Fleet Academy were empty, the formal testing sessions for cadets and for rising officers having long since been completed. It was between terms at the Academy, and the oval hallways echoed their deserted status, no dampers engaging to counter the sound of the Ben-Drom's heavy tread with its resounding click of heel-spike.

The Ben-Drom liked things empty. The less population and techtronics, the better. One could sense one's enemies' approach in emptiness.

Reaching a main command station, the Ben-Drom checked building security for others present. There was no one. Only the mechanicals moved about, their purpose cleanliness. So, excepting Erana, he was alone.

Settling to work, the Ben-Drom opened a small case he carried, pulling forth a special data-sphere. He dropped it into the maincom's input, then grunted his satisfaction moments later when the adjustments to his crews flashed on-screen. Within itar, his agents had successfully traced the whereabouts of many of his old crew. So the Ben-Drom decided to enlist them all, under special names and civilian titles, whether or not they had yet been found. He was that confident they would be. He even included Orcon Dra's name, though still no inkling of that being's whereabouts had yet been discovered, not even rumors. But it was a big cosmos to search. And the Ben-Drom still had time.

Of the Requisition Board's substitutions, the Ben-Drom did nothing. Let them stay. He needed them for his purpose, but he would also have his own among them, and none would be the wiser. Another half-a-thousand-plus would not be noticed now—not on record. He had ensured that. Nor would they be noticed on board fleet. His ships were large enough that none would ken. Easily done. His fleet would swallow them, as the Ben-Drom himself would swallow those who worked against him. Therefore had he let be conspiracy's crew exchanges. He would catch them all. Exactly in the middle of their game.

Impatient now that his main objective was accomplished, the Ben-Drom checked the external building monitors, watching for the arrival of the Draco, Megan Pryr. It was not yet time, for the Ben-Drom had given himself generous leeway, but, having finished, he wished to consummate this last charade.

To his left, upon another maincom, Erana's attention was rapt. Bored with his wait-watch, the Ben-Drom touched the board in front of him, requesting access to that which the Syrene was studying.

Reviewing tests—Erana was thus engaged in preparation—but the speed with which the Syrene scanned was much too fast for the Ben-Drom's slower senses. He dropped out, then placed another data-sphere into the maincom's input and began to load his own test.

Data loaded, again the Ben-Drom checked external monitors. Still, the Draco was not evident in approach. The Ben-Drom grumbled.

Moving back into the maincom's memories, the Ben-Drom placed fiat to retrieve the hardest test of the most recent kathon trials. Regulus Shattam's test came up, and the Ben-Drom smelled manipulation. Pryr was member of the Shattam's fleet. They—his enemies—tried too hard, but, nevertheless, the Ben-Drom opened the test and its result.

It was a Xentauri—a female by its body language and fields—who moved in miniature within the holomorphic re-enactment of her test. On the viewing stage, a cross-section of a translight's battle bridge was superimposed within one corner of an objective view of the combat field, the starless space of it littered with gilded wedges of Tornigan war cruisers that far outnumbered and out-positioned the fleet the Xenti commanded. Analyzing the situation, the Ben-Drom saw that it was hopeless for the Xenti.

Touching up the resolution, the Ben-Drom grunted, at once disturbed by what he now identified as no Xenti she, but the Megan Quroc. And, seeing his performance, the Ben-Drom was surprised to find himself agreeing with the Xenti's moves. Not all of them. But most.

Each decision the Megan Quroc made was excellent, despite the fact that the test that Shattam had contrived was arduous to the point of pushing the limits of Fleet's permissory standards for such trials.

The test was paradoxical and it had no possible successful resolution. No matter what was done, the consequences were yet the complete and utter loss of ships and crew. Yet the Xenti had done well.

Oddly, after the test, the Megan Quroc had thought he'd failed. And, despite his rancor toward the family,

Xentauri Q, first for Quiloc's termination of Raganth and, then, the subsequent incident with his minor, the Ben-Drom had to admire the Q Dynasty's young heir. He also had to chuckle. The Megan Quroc was like his sire in many ways, but not in some, it seemed. Unlike his sire, the Megan Quroc took everything very seriously—every little thing—a bad thing for a fleet lead.

"Regulus Primus Ben-Drom?"

Accustomed as he was to Ka's telepathic warnings of in-comers, the close presence of a stranger startled the Ben-Drom. His talons snapped out to full extrusion as he rose and spun. He fell back one step immediately, however—without striking—and let his talons sheath. "Megan Primus Pryr," the Ben-Drom said. "I apologize."

"None is needed, Sir. I am used to Shattam."

"Hmmr."

The Ben-Drom had not physically apprehended Pryr before, though he had reviewed the Draco's profile and records. Purposely, the Ben-Drom had also avoided viewing holomorphic images of the Draco prior to their meeting so that he could receive a clean judgement. And what the Ben-Drom apprehended did impress him: Outwardly, the Draco was tall, wiry, and of uncommon handsomeness for his species. A devoid Syrene stood at his side—not too far behind, the Ben-Drom noted—and a small, green dragonet stalked back and forth across the Draco's shoulders, uttering, alternately, small whirs and shrieks. Field-wise, the Draconian read clean, and that surprised the Ben-Drom. Honor he had not expected to find within the lackey of an unknown enemy.

Tipping his head to the Draco, the Ben-Drom said, "Well enough. You are here to test for navarch. Let us test."

The Draconian bowed. "Yes, Sir."

"Take your place at the auxiliary station, Simulator Fifteen, Megan. You will use this Syrene, not your own," the Ben-Drom said, motioning Erana forward.

"As you say, Sir," the Draconian lackadaisically replied as he dismissed his devoid.

Despite his seeming nonchalance, the Draco's fields now displayed a mild discomfort, and the Ben-Drom noted it. It was obvious that the Draco had prepared himself, and had probably programmed his Syrene. And the Megan Pryr was not just primed to test. Someone had taken time to school the Megan Pryr to all the Ben-Drom's random proclivities—to every sensitivity. It was obvious. And the Ben-Drom doubted that the teacher was the Shattam, Pryr's present Altan regulus. The Shattam would not have given time for such.

Inside himself, the Ben-Drom chuckled at the foolishness. No matter how well prepared was Megan Pryr, it would matter not—not with him, and not with this test. The Megan Pryr was about to fall into a trap.

o   o   o

49

PRYR HAD NEVER BEFORE WORKED with a Syrene entire. Nor had he wished to. Wary, he spent extra time pre-testing in the simulator, redundantly familiarizing himself with the Syrene and its responses to him. He only relaxed once he was assured it would follow orders.

That this entire seemed no different from one devoid startled Pryr, but then he supposed that was to be expected. Had it not, the Ben-Drom could not comfortably utilize it. The Drom would be arrested for breaking Omniversal covenant, the Syrene destroyed.

Waiting for the test to begin, Pryr wondered if his use of an entire in these circumstances, even under orders of a regulus, would be grounds for his own arrest should someone inadvertently discover it. He decided that it would, and that caused him shiver. He did know the Syrene was entire. Belamy, Lurad, and Quiloc had all warned him of the fact of the Ben-Drom's use of them. That meant he agreed to use it, thereby breaking Omniversal Law.

"Be you at-ready, Megan Pryr?"

It was the Ben-Drom's voice through intercom. "Yes, Sir," Pryr answered, realizing the question to be a nerve tightener. The Drom would try to fail him.

"Well enough."

The monitors within the simulator, a haze of neutral grey, instantly blinked to full screen. It was a nasty jolt to

Pryr's senses. It was a nastier jolt to realize that, contrary to standard, the test gave no background. But Pryr hadn't the time to complain, suffer, or recover. He had only time to act. Yet, he didn't act—not yet. Instead, his brain plunged into battle-high and began to analyze, Pryr's state becoming almost trance-like.

A planet to his left, two big fleets—Omniversal fleets—converging…. Pryr recognized the situation instantly. He didn't even need to check objective. He already knew. It was the battle of Donjon, and the battle was already joined. And a part of his fevered brain separated from its focus now to file complaint. This was too late a time frame in the battle for fair trial. This would have been disallowed within an Academy-sponsored test.

But this was not an Academy-sponsored test, another part of Pryr's hyper-functioning brain realized. This was a private war. This was a battle between himself and the Altan Drom.

Precious millitat had been wasted. Veerwings were now hazing past in closed formation about Pryr's small fleet. He had only twenty-five outmoded battle translights—this against two fleets of eighty ships apiece. And he was being warned to stand down by the larger fleets. But his duty, by his regulus' command, was to protect the planet against the incoming force—a force obedient to the same service that Pryr was sworn to…was *supposed* to be serving even now upon this battlelight of the Regulus Primus Omega Ben-Drom. However, the Ben-Drom's orders were very clear: Stop the incoming, regardless the force necessary to do accomplish. Protect the planet! Against the Omniverse! Against Fleet.

Pryr fell in, then. The test was test no longer. The situation was no longer simulation, but reality. It was a real battle bridge on a real battle translight that he stood upon, with real voices—the voices of the two regulus who commanded the incoming fleets—demanding him stand-off. And the Syrene at com kept querying for orders. It did so over and over as he stood there in confusion.

"What are your orders, Megan Pryr?" the Syrene again requested.

Pryr wanted to scream at the Syrene. He wanted to attack it. He did neither. He just stood there.

Those were Tornigans down below upon that blighted planet, just beneath and to his left. And he was supposed to be defending them against his own compatriots. But Tornigans were enemy. They were beyond enemy. Pryr hated Tornigans. Every fleet, every Omniversal citizen, despised the Tornigans. The hordes were ultimate terror. They were the scourging multitudes that sought to end all kind within the cosmos. And the Ben-Drom expected him to defend them against Omniversal forces?! He couldn't. He just couldn't, even though he knew upon what law the Ben-Drom based his logic.

Pryr could hear the Ben-Drom's reasoning inside his head. It came as clear to him as when, in shock, the

Omniverse had heard it two turns back, just after the Ben-Drom had successfully defeated two of the newest and largest Omniversal battle fleets ever launched— defeated them with a has-been bunch of rickety translights, outnumbered and of inferior ordinance. "Omniversal Lexus," the booming voice had said, "the right for all species to exist, the right to self-determination, and the right to non-interference. If these be our precepts, then, by definition, they include even those who are our natural enemies. We must honor that. To do less would jeopardize us all." The Ben-Drom had said that publicly, and the High Consul, much to its own chagrin (for it had been that body which had ordered the attack), had concluded that the Altan commander was correct.

"What are your orders, Megan Pryr?" the Syrene queried.

The reality had broken. Remembering that speech had snapped Pryr out of the delusion he had momentarily suffered. He wasn't on a real bridge any longer. This was just a simulation. It was his test. He had to pass it. And he remembered how the Ben-Drom had maneuvered in the real battle, knowledge which now he used, engaging the same tactics. "Mount machon, all fighters and battle cruisers—they are to haze and harry only. "Once mounted, full shields and deploy the fleet to I-Dash-C formation about the planet."

The Syrene at kathcom responded, translating his orders instantly to light for every other com within the phantom fleet to read. Moments later, as the commanders and the crews of each ship responded, Pryr's imaginary fleet began to move, each ship positioned and at-ready about the equatorial perimeter of the planet just beyond atmosphere.

"Tachon:" Pryr snapped, "Set an antimatter web to frequency zero-point-one, directional detonation outbound." This was a small deviation from the Ben-Drom's originally elected course. The Ben-Drom had set an Andromedan d'tazt web.

"We don't have time, Sir. It's too late," some simulated tachon ghost screamed. "We're taking fire." And, they were...because of the necessity of lowering shields to mount out the machon. It was one of the worst problems of a battle translight.

"Set the web," Pryr repeated calmly, even needlessly, knowing the Syrene had already set the order. He then turned to the panicked tachon ghost and remonstrated. "We may die," he said, "but the web will protect the planet."

"Do we return their fire, Sir?" some kath commander queried.

And, here, Pryr again deviated from the Ben-Drom's historic course of action. "No," he said. Even in simulation, Pryr would not attack his own to preserve his fleet. He had done his duty to his regulus. He had protected the covey of luckless, stranded Tornigans that populated the planet immediately abaft him. No enemy could touch them. Of course, neither could they escape to their own space or receive any aid to help them. Now, they would have to survive as they could—adapt if they could—in an environment hostile to their very being. But that was not Pryr's problem. He had followed orders. No force—not that of Omniverse, nor any—could now penetrate their nest...their tomb.

In himself, Pryr knew that he destroyed the Tornigans. He knew that he had actually defied the Ben-Drom's orders. His reaction was to chuckle. He hadn't meant to. His subconscious, he supposed, had worked his own will forward, despite his conscious plans. He would fail...he *had* failed this test.

"Fleets are closing on us, Sir," the tach advised. It was a request for orders.

The Syrene: "What are your orders, Megan Pryr?"

NOT ONCE DURING THE TRIAL did the Megan Pryr show temper, impatience, or recklessness—all tendencies typical to Draconians, this in a trial that measured, not only correctness of action, but, more importantly, quality and character in extremely adverse and trying conditions— conditions that pressed an archon to his mettle's edge. The Megan Pryr had done well, the Ben-Drom grudgingly admitted. While he obviously did not agree with Pryr's tactics, the Draco did much better than most. More, he had followed his own heart and conscience. Despite knowing the correct answers to the questions the trial had posed, the Megan Pryr had acted counter to them. That had placed his personnel in extreme jeopardy. But Pryr had managed, by some very heroic action and genius of strategy, to save them, anyway, though he had lost the fleet, the ships beyond salvage. So, despite his suspicions of the Megan Pryr, the Ben-Drom liked him.

"Sir."

The Ben-Drom turned his sight from the com analysis of the examination to the subject of it. "Megan Pryr," he acknowledged, then fell silent, studying the mein of the being, once more.

From the tiny dragonet upon the shoulder to the high fighter boots upon the slender legs that identified Pryr as once having been among the mach elite, confidence registered. It was an assuredness devoid of any insolence. Pryr wore the mantle of his ranking very well. He was, truly, one of Fleet's best. Of that, the Ben-Drom was most assured. He just wondered how a being of such caliber could come to be a part of some conspiracy. The Ben-Drom had expected much more criminal a personality.

"Sir," the Draco said, again. And the Ben-Drom realized that the Draco waited for some judgement.

"I will inform you of my decision when I make it," the Ben-Drom said. "First, I meet with Shattam."

"Sir," Pryr answered, bowing lightly. "I'll take my leave, then, Sir." And he strode off, after collecting his devoid Syrene, his dragonet bobbing and weaving as it strove to keep its balance atop the Draco's shoulder.   And, watching, the Ben-Drom found himself thinking that the Megan Pryr was a very peculiar entity.

o   o   o

50

"How did you fare on your test?"

The words came out of nowhere, but Pryr recognized the speaker instantly…because she allowed it. He turned and, isolating her shrouded form, grinned. "Rocht, Matac. You should not frighten a simple soldier."

"A simple soldier, is it?" she countered, walking up, then passing him, to turn around and beckon onward. "Let us walk together."

"The Ben-Drom has planted some extra 'specialists' in his crews," Matac said as they entered a pool garden adjacent the Academy's simulator facility. "Approximately five-hundred. Does that number carry significance to you?"

"No."

"Perhaps indeed you are a simple soldier, Pryr."

Ignoring the jibe for the moment, Pryr bent down to let his dragonet dismount, waiting patiently as the creature lifted a drink from one of only two gel pools available in the park. He laughed, then, as the creature dove in and began to splash about. Turning to Matac finally, he said, "I am not given to the contorted reasoning of the paranoid, that is true, Matac."

"Paranoiac?" she said, sarcasm dripping. "Then see this."

Humoring her, Pryr scanned the portacom she handed him, then gave it back. What he had seen disturbed him. "He has his rebels, then," Pryr said, scooping up his pet as it emerged, dripping, from the glycogel.

"I cannot be sure, but that is as it seems."

"I will need you, then," Pryr said. "Onboard his fleet when the time comes."

"My thoughts are the same, Megan Pryr. Unless I can manipulate another way, however, my presence will have to be as stowaway. Belamy is not pleased with me because of Quroc."

"Rocht," Pryr said. He did not add that, equally, he was not pleased with her choices in the matter of Quroc. Instead, he said: "If it cannot be arranged another way, I will secrete you."

"Provided you are chosen by the Altan, you mean," Matac reminded.

"Providing that," Pryr answered. And thinking of the test, Pryr said, "It may well be, Matac, that we both may join the ranks of stowaways. Technically, I failed the Ben-Drom's test."

"Currurr," she warbled sympathetically. "Until another time, my friend."

"Until another time," Pryr answered to the empty atmosphere. Matac was already gone, vanished in a fading camouflage of her peculiar, advanced form of transfer.

Deep in thought, Pryr didn't see the massive shierka rise. He didn't see it until the silent menace was just above the garden, tipping over in the sky, its silent atmospheric thrusters flaring to an iridescent red that filled the void amid its muted, double raoid hull. The Bjen Dvorkahn was leaving Iban. Pryr's rational brain recognized this. But, for just an instant, what his fancy saw was something else, and terror filled him.

o   o   o

.

51

A HUNDRED MILLION EYES—red eyes, chatoyant in their glimmer—flew at him. Out of darkness, coming through from nowhere, they were all around.

He recognized them, yet he couldn't name them—not quite. He couldn't grasp exactly what they were, yet somewhere far away inside, he knew them.

Their outer rims—the lids—were real. The eyes themselves were fathomless...untouchable, something from his deepest fears of a nameless hell. What were they?! He had to name them, identify them. He had to. To save himself. And all the others.

What others?!

He ignored that question and concentrated on first task. *Identify*, he commanded of his brain. But the flying eyes, their meaning, kept eluding him.

Then, suddenly, he knew. Those were Andromedan eyes that flew at him. His brain wrestled with the problem: eyes don't fly. *But shierka do*, his memories whispered. *The shierka fly and look like eyes when coming straight upon you.*

And, despite his medication, beneath his fur, beneath the skinsuit he wore even now in sleep, the translucent portions of his skin between the pigment-rich striping began to glow. Quroc was afraid.

o   o   o

52

THE BEN-DROM JERKED UPRIGHT, his blood high, poison pumping from his venom pores. It had been a dream, he realized, calming. That was all.

"Lord?"

It was Ka, the faintest rustle coming from the floor where the Ceoheician insisted upon sleeping—his kindway, hard and unforgiving.

"A dream, Ka," the Ben-Drom answered. "The K'har was taken, and the shierka flew, again, as in the old times. In this dream, however, it was in attack of Omniverse itself—a hopeless battle for all, upon every front. It woke me, this dream. That is all."

The magus-warrior rose to crouch beside. He was silent, but his eyes spoke.

"No," the Ben-Drom said. "It is not premonitory. It was but dream."

"Dream-seeing," Ka said softly. And the Ceoheician's crests rose. "Destiny sorts its futures."

"Your beliefs, my friend. Not mine," the Ben-Drom said. But Ka's words disturbed him. Despite that Regar's light still held the searing harshness of post-meridian that was his mid-sleep time, the Ben-Drom rose. He cleaned away the poison residue that clung to him—remnants from the dream. He did that in the old way with a venom wash, its sting astringent to his rough, unyielding hide. Then, he retreated to his office chamber, there to think.

IT COULD HAVE BEEN ONLY ITAN, or it could have been two decitar, the Ben-Drom wasn't sure how long he'd sat there smoldering in silence, angry at the dream and Ka's interpretation of it—but the maincom broke his brooding. It blinked on, the signet of judicial override request making the Ben-Drom move to watch.

The maincom allowed the override, and the Ben-Drom frowned. It was unusual for his security to approve any signal less its source be pre-authorized by him. And he had not authorized *any* communication excepting Rin, Andromeda, and those of the Andromedan engineers in charge of constructing his fleet. Those only, and, of course, the mandatory access Fleet Command enjoyed because he owed them his enforced allegiance.

Grumbling a little, the Ben-Drom flicked a talon out and touched the link open. A stern Oronian face appeared, the waxy skin of it shiny with the tenseness of impatience. "Omega Bjen Dvorkahn?" the interloper queried. It was a whiny voice that absolutely matched the mein of the pale humanoid.

"I am he," the Ben-Drom replied, holding propriety, despite the rudeness.

"I am the second chief magistrate, Civil Judiciary Council. You are charged with withholding evidence.

Unless you rectify this situation immediately to the satisfaction of this—"

The Ben-Drom bolted upright, bellowing. "CEASE THIS!" he commanded. "What evidence?!"

The magistrate's round eyes bulged out. "If you so interrupt again, Alta Andromedi Omega Bjen Dvorkahn, I will hold you in contempt. Is that understood?"

Again, all a whine, and the Ben-Drom's hatred for the Oronian Light Supremacists that were members of his own home universe rose to ancient peak. He checked it, answering, "Yes," but his answer was all snarl.

"To your question: The litigation pending is a conduct hearing, Fleet Judiciary: Fleet Academy verses Megan Primas Xentauri Quroc Su Verdan, Q Dynasty, First Family, ab Verdaje cum Nadejan, the first and only known of that naming, Xentauri citizen number…."

The Ben-Drom patiently listened to the rest, including the full, formal charges pending against the Ben-Drom and his specific misdemeanor. Only when the magistrate had finally exhausted himself of further declarations did the Ben-Drom respond again, performing the necessary acknowledgments and covenants of redress demanded by law. To do so, he utilized the magistrate himself as notary, much to that being's surprise and discomfiture. Then, when all was finally in order to the magistrate's startled satisfaction, the Ben-Drom politely excused himself of the unctuous bureaucrat and placed a call to the Xentauri Legal the

Oronian had named as having filed complaint against him.

The Legal herself appeared on-screen, her focus to some task upon her desk's computer maincom. "How may I help you, Omega Bjen Dvorkahn?" she queried, her voice clipped, her tone decidedly flippant, as she finally raised her sight to his.

The Ben-Drom growled, but bit back the sharp retort that automatically sprang to throat. "Did you not receive from me, via Fleet Judiciary, some two dectar past, a data-sphere of Syrene memories containing evidence clearly absolving the Megan Quroc of any misdeed beyond that of, perhaps, some procedural technicality owing to his attempt to protect his family?"

"No," the Xentauri said, all stiffness.

The Ben-Drom paused, quelling another rise in temper. Mastering himself again, even as he realized that, perhaps, Ka was right in diagnosis that he, once more, suffered his old stress illness, the Ben-Drom said: "It was sent immediately in response to your motion to compel. The fault is not mine that Fleet Judiciary did not forward as was mandated. All that is remedied, however. A copy of same has just been sent, once more, this time through the offices of Second Chief Magistrate Oronian Nu Pol. Fleet Judiciary cannot intercede upon behalf of Fleet Academy, again."

The Xentauri had dropped her sight down. Then, taking audible breath, she looked back to him. That she suffered a combination of worry and exhaustion was extremely evident. In the service, it was recognized as battle fatigue, and the Ben-Drom sympathized.

"A lot of good your delivery of the minor's memories to the magistrate does me this late," she said. "It should arrive here in about a dectar. Thanks *so* much for your cooperation!"

The Xentauri dropped her sight, again, but this time it was to attend whatever was displayed upon her comstage. She began to touch a light stylus to her input interface. "Now, if you please, and even if you don't, I have to finish my dossier on this case." She looked up, again. "Without benefit of your great majesty's presence."

She reached to touch out the link, but, with a touch to his own com, the Ben-Drom overrode her act. "A moment," he said.

"How did you do that?! How dare you?!!" And, fervently, her digits flew across her board, trying any, every, bypass to code out.

"A moment, She-Xentauri. Let me help you."

The Legal paused, her head canting insolently. "Oh?"

"Let us meet."

The Xentauri scowled. "Quroc's hearing is next itar, and I have an inordinate amount of work to do, yet— most of it thanks to your disregard of law, which is something only a regulus in Fleet could get away with, I have, by experience, now learned."

Irked by attitude and insolence, the Ben-Drom lowered his head belligerently. He stopped himself just short of transferring himself directly into her presence to confront her livetime. He had the means, and, much as K'har constrained use of such technology amidst civilizations of lesser advancement, the Ben-Drom was sorely tempted. Taking hold of his flaring temper one more time, the Ben-Drom asked, "May I meet with you?"

"No. I told you, I have too much work—"

"Xentauri, I cannot help you if you refuse me. Do as you please, but the offer has been made. I will personally deliver copy of the evidence you seek. I will even permit you license to place question to me, should that aid you."

The Ben-Drom paused.

The Xenti's fields did likewise.

"Dinner, then. If you're so willing to help, you can host, as well. I'm tired and I'm hungry, and I don't have time to waste. I like my meals a little on the raw side, please. And a real blood meal. Not synfabricated. You can arrange and afford that small bit of illegality, I'm sure."

She was pushing him, testing his word and his volition. The Ben-Drom pondered. To arrange such illicitness, he would be putting himself in a legal compromise that she could use to her advantage should she so chose. Yet, there were places that he knew. Best, there was one such place where he was known and liked. "I will dine with you in private suite at Regency Vul in point-two-five decitar."

She didn't even blink her eyes at his mention of the most prestigious of all establishments in Ita Centralis. "At the Regency in point-*one*-five decitar, then, Regulus. Endcom." And she touched him out.

"You push me, Sheeta," the Ben-Drom muttered irritably, then prepared his notes for the meeting, including a portacom and another copy of the data-sphere that contained the images from the Syrene minor's memories.

○　　○　　○

53

MEGAN PRIMUS QUROC STOOD in full dress formal, the long overrobing of his rank with its smooth, draping flare unfamiliar and cumbersome to him. This was only the second time he'd ever worn the dull brown robes, and he felt uncomfortably self-conscious to be dressed so before his fellow archon. That Celac stood next to him, Quroc was grateful.

The chamber was an amphitheater, exit-entrance ramps running between its large audience areas. To one end was a benched, raised dais where the five Peers-to-Review presided. The Chair of the Peer Review Board, a neutral-phase Dgorian commander of Quroc's ranking equal looked down from the center of this dais. "Do you understand the nature of the charges being brought against you?" it asked.

"Yes," Quroc said.

"Do you understand the consequences should you be judged unfit?"

"Yes."

The Dgorian turned its attention to Celac, and the center-body speech folds that protruded from its robe rifled a little as two of its three eye copkets rose to bend down toward her. Their pods opened and closed with soft popping sounds—agitation. After a studied perusal, the pods retreated, returning to the exposed hump at the top of the body where they slid into other creases from which safety the eyes could watch, protected and secure, if slightly furtive looking. "I see that you have legal counsel," the Dgorian said. It looked decidedly unhappy. In fact, all members of the Peer Review Board looked unhappy about Celac, save the elder female Xentauri commander—a white and orange tiger with alluring green eyes.

Ostensibly innocent as it seemed, the Dgorian's observation was a rudeness to the civilian. Quroc bristled. "Yes, I do have legal counsel, Peer-Chair," he replied. "…As this board was fully aware some dectar ago." And, with that, he formally introduced both Celac and himself for benefit of the record.

The Dgorian muttered something. Then, with an acknowledgment toward Fleet Director Belamy who sat inconspicuously in the back of the chamber, it turned to where the hearing's complainant representative stood. "You may present your case," it said to the Fleet Academy's Legal.

"Peer Chair," the blue sheathed Regellian replied in answer. She nodded in turn to each member of the board, then to Quroc and Celac, her willowy body graceful in its every gesture. Amenities complete, she said, "We will show the Megan Primus Xentauri Quroc Su Verdan, Q Dynasty, First Family, ab Verdaje cum Nadejan, to be guilty of conduct unbefitting an officer of the Omniversal High Fleet and, therefore, deserving of the review board's rendering of a dismissal from service under Disgrace. We will also show that the Megan Quroc has committed criminal acts that demand this board's condemnation and its recommendation for court-martial and subsequent trial in the civil quarter."

"Enter your evidence," the Peer Chair said.

AFTER THE INITIAL IDENTIFICATIONS of all litigants and of the minor in question—its ownership and other such technicalities and details—the prosecution began to present its evidence. As was typical, it did so, not in a chronological order of events, but in mounting order of alleged malfeasance.

The Regellian Legal began with a visual log of Quroc's reputed attempt to escape from Iban, and the images presented were vivid and powerfully convincing. The ship portrayed was Quroc's ship, just as the capturing interceptor was that of the Ghirran mach-lead. Some of the presentation was authentic; most was not. Whoever had made the log had known their job and done it well. For Quroc, it was discouraging to realize that the Fleet he had always held as unimpeachably high principled could resort to such deceit.

Other evidence against Quroc was equally convincing: There were images of him at the Academy Syrene Holding, showing him there at the same time as the minor's disappearance. There were notarized acknowledgments beside holomorphic reproductions of the scarred and maimed minor that the brand laid upon it was indeed that of Quroc and his sire. But the evidence that made Quroc gasp was the last the prosecution presented: an actual Xilarn blade—Quroc's own—the flattened curl of its crystalline double cutting edges shimmering. Alongside it was documentation identifying the weapon as the actual weapon used to cut out the Academy brands from the minor, the Xilarn blade's microscopic nicks and flaws matching perfectly the grooving in the minor's wounding scars. What made Quroc gasp was not the fact that the Xilarn blade was actually his own, registered to him. (Celac had warned him of that piece of evidence.) What unnerved him was the fact of the blade's physical existence in the courtroom. For the prosecution to have secured it meant that someone in his family had betrayed him. Image-evidence of the weapon was an easy thing for any to secure. The actual blade, however—that was different.

Quroc shook his head hard enough to make his ears snap in his distress. This action caught the Dgorian's attention. "What is your objection?" it asked.

Celac whispered to him, then nodded encouragingly. Quroc swallowed. "I haven't even seen that weapon...I haven't handled that weapon since before I left Verdaje for Academy...since I was nineteen turns, Peer Chair," he said.

"But it is your weapon?" another member of the Peers-to-Review asked—this one the squeaky-voiced Medagian.

Quroc felt his mouth go dry. "It…was."

"Did you transfer ownership?"

"No."

"Then it is still your weapon."

Quroc was silent. He couldn't tell them that he'd lost it. On a hunt. On Nadeja. Just before his father shipped him out to Fleet Academy at Iban. That his real mother had sent it back to household, but that his step-mother had never shipped it on, the blade becoming one of those objects of his youth he'd thought to be forever lost to him. He couldn't tell because no one was to know about his real mother—no one outside Dynasty.

"Megan Quroc?" It was the Xentauri peer.

"Yes?"

"Was the weapon lost to you?" she asked. Knowing kindway, she was probing. She had guessed, or she knew rumors.

"It was," he said.

"Is there any proof of this?"

Again, Quroc maintained silence. He couldn't speak of his real, his Nadejan, mother, and only she could verify.

The Xentauri queen cast an ear back, just slightly, acknowledging him, kind-to-kind, then said, "The evidence of the Xilarn is damning to your case, Megan Quroc."

Quroc dropped his head.

"Do you have any counter, Mega-Archon?" the Peer-Chair asked, and Quroc sensed the peers becoming more sympathetic to his cause, the Xentauri peer's questions having clued them.

"Do you have any counter, Archon?" the peer-chair asked, again.

Quroc looked up. "No."

The Dgorian slumped into itself. "Archon," it began, its manner chastening. "If you will not defend yourself, you condemn yourself. And your family," it added, indicating its grasp of situation. "We, as Peers-to-Review, are also bound by codes."

"I have a question for the expert who prepared the evidence of the Xilarn blade," Celac said, stepping forward.

The Peer-Chair extended palp, indicating the forensic. That creature, all stalks and hinges, moved from its position in the audience to fore. "Ask it," the Dgorian said.

"Since you had the actual blade to work with, Forensic," Celac said, "I want to know: Was there any residue upon the blade suggesting that the blade had been used recently by the Megan Quroc?"

The Forensic clicked.

Celac waited.

The Forensic clicked again. Then, with several stalks waving in agitation, it fiddled with something. "No," came a mechanically contrived voice from somewhere amid the creature's under. The speaking was formal Omniversal, but the voice was one that grated on many of the hearers in the room, including Celac.

"Thank you," Celac said, her ears flattened to muffle any answering response from it.

"However—" The Regellian Legal began, moving forward.

"Thank you," Celac interrupted. "That was my question."

"However," the prosecution's Legal said again.

"Peer-Chair," Celac said, stepping toward. "My question was directed for Forensic to answer, not the prosecuting Legal.

"Noted," the Dgorian said.

"Prosecution still presides," the Regellian threw back. "We still hold floor to present evidence."

"Also noted," said the Dgorian.

Nodding, the Regellian said, "Thank you," as she moved further to forefront. "Forensic: Was there any evidence to indicate that any other had utilized the Xilarn blade, recently or otherwise?"

"No."

"And there are methods available to remove traces of recent handling?"

"With skill."

The Regellian addressed the Peer Review Board entire. "We have established that the Xilarn blade entered into evidence is the tool used to remove the minor's Academy brand. Therefore, someone, whether that be the Megan Quroc or another, used that blade to so cut the minor's brand out, and then, perhaps, washed that blade clean of new residue?" This last the Regellian redirected as a question of the forensic.

"Yes," came the mechanical reply. "With the help of another skilled enough to do so."

The Regellian began to softly vibrate in her confidence. "Where was the Xilarn blade found?" she asked.

Several of Forensic's stalks snapped up. It seemed startled by the question. There was a moment's pause, then: "I was *told* by the head of the investigating department which I serve that the blade was discovered at the Iban apartments of the Megan Primus Xentauri Quroc ab Verdaje. But *I* was not present at that—"

"Thank you," the Regellian interrupted. "Now, between the time you calculate the blade to have been used upon the minor and the time of Megan Quroc's apprehension, was there time for him to secure skilled enough help to clean the blade of residue?"

"There was more than adequate time, though the cost would be enormous," the Forensic answered.

Again, the Regellian Legal addressed the Peers. "And, as we all know," she said, "the Megan Quroc, as member of the First Family, Xentauri Q Dynasty, has more than adequate means of securing the necessary credits-to-accomplish."

Calmly, Celac stepped forward. "Prosecution: Do you carry proof that the Megan Quroc did secure such expert help? Or even that he expended such enormous volume of credit alluded to in testimony?"

The Regellian, pale blue throughout, now turned slightly deeper blue. "No."

"Then I object, Peer-chair. On grounds—"

"I am familiar with the Legal grounding of your objection, Legal Celac," the Dgorian said. "I would not be chair of this assemblage were I not." It paused a moment as if considering, spoke with the Medagian next-to, then said, "Normally, I would sustain. However, since this is not a trial, but is, instead, a hearing, I will let stand Prosecution's suppositions."

Celac's fur rippled. "Then I submit that while the evidence suggests that the Xilarn blade was the tool employed upon the Syrene minor, any connection to my client is pure speculation. All evidence is circumstantial, and, therefore, inadmissible for use in judgement of this case."

"Noted. However, we cannot erase our memories, Legal Celac," the Dgorian Peer-Chair said. "And I will remind you that this is not a civil court of law. This is a Fleet hearing. Different rules apply, rules of which you should have become more familiar, it seems."

"By Prosecution's own injunction, this is a court of law," Celac argued.

But the Peer-Chair ignored her, asking Prosecution, "Any other?"

Smug smile to Celac, the Regellian stood fore and said, "The prosecution rests."

Tired-acting, the Dgorian looked to Celac. "Do you have any evidence to counter?"

"I do," she said.

"Present, then," the Dgorian said, slumping back. "We will listen."

And Quroc heard Celac whisper, "You bet you will." He flinched. Celac didn't understand that this was Fleet, not Legis. She didn't understand that she was fighting a losing battle, that his situation was already that of fighter-down-and-dead. He knew it, but a civilian couldn't, and Celac's ignorance embarrassed him.

Civilians didn't understand that Fleet ran by completely different rules. Fleet and Omniverse, though the former served the latter, were completely different universes. Watching, Quroc had to admire, though. Despite the obvious futility the Peer-Chair all but vocalized, Celac stood indomitable. She was warrior in the best modern rendering of a civilized Xentauri queen, and Quroc, who had never really found pride in his Verdajen heritage, found pride now. So, though he knew the battle to be already lost, he didn't stop the Legal Celac. And not just because, as male, he had no right to hazard a queen's hunting. He didn't stop her because it was his small way of honoring her.

Celac had finished her own formalities with the Peer-Review Board, presenting her aspects of case just as the Regellian had. Translating the legalese, Quroc realized that Celac was going to go chronologically point by point in her attempt to destroy the prosecution's case. Bored, he tuned her out, until he saw her stand foreground, turn to, and formally call forth.

"We call the Metan Rajan Tag Ajin ab Ghirran," Celac said.

Quroc blinked. Rajan? The Ghirran mach-lead? He would have no career left in Fleet if he testified. Quroc cringed inside himself. He didn't want to be responsible for the destruction of another. "Celac," Quroc whispered, touching her with a Xentauri "to-stop" sign.

Celac shook him off. "...Simultaneously, we enter the following: As Defense Exhibit A, this flight recording."

A holomorphic stage blinked on, still-formed Veerwing Quadstar Harriers hanging mid-flight, the glaring brilliance of Iban's Ring as clear and obvious as Quroc's own Harrier was in the image.

"...As Defense Exhibit B, the witness's deposed BT scan concerning the situation in question."

Another holomorphic stage blinked on, this one showing the typical haze associated with the beginnings of BT scans as the biocoms penetrated through the haze of drugs administered to the subject—in this case, as was notarized in the corner of the stage, the Metan Rajan.

"…As Defense Exhibit C, the deposition taken of the Megan Quroc, defendant in this case."

And still another holomorphic stage—the last available in the chamber—flared, another notary seal evident on this, the computer generated productions of Quroc's own descriptions.

At a word from Celac, a small mainframe computer she had portered in adjusted, then began to sequence and synchronize the images on the stages. "All is to be concurrently exhibited, while, simultaneously, the Metan Rajan Tag Ajin ab Ghirran testifies," Celac said.

During all of this, it was as if the room had gone into stasis. Now, it exploded: The prosecution stormed objection as the Peers-to-Review actually stood, each one babbling incomprehensibly to each other and the next in their own language. And, in the middle of this pandemonium, the Metan Rajan entered the chamber, his large, reptile-like saurischian body a muscled undulation as his powerful legs placed careful steps down the ramped aisle leading to the witness stand. And, to his surprise, Quroc saw Fleet Director Leon Belamy actually begin to laugh.

Stepping into the witness place, the Metan Rajan looked around, and Quroc saw humor playing in his eyes and around his mouth. That humor dissolved all Quroc's fears and objections. The Ghirran wanted to do this.

The bedlam finally ended, the Dgorian righting things with effort.

"Peer-Chair?" Celac asked, once quiet again prevailed. Her mouth was smug, her voice sweet ice. "Did I hear objection from Prosecution?"

"You did," the Regellian said.

Before Prosecution's Legal could again voice that objection, though, the Dgorian Chair extended and leaned down one eye pod, bringing the copket level to the Regellian. "I suggest that you also remember Fleet rules of conduct in these cases, Academy Legal," it warned. "What is true for you, is also true for Legal Celac. Fair is fair." Then, tilting the eye copket toward Celac, the Dgorian twitched it. "Let your evidence be entered, Legal Celac…though how you expect all of this…." It extended palps, spreading them inclusively toward Rajan and the three holomorphic displays. "…To be simultaneously absorbed and comprehended by this board, I do not know."

"I think my reasoning will become apparent, Peer-Chair," Celac replied, fang teeth faintly glinting. "Please swear the witness in."

And, to that, the grinning Ghirran's eyes began to glow.

o   o   o

54

IT BEGAN IN WHAT WAS KNOWN AS THE GAP—that space between Iban's phototransmission web and the artificial planets—light from The Ring adding backdrop glare, the planets with their intricate details of varied topography giving orientation. Three holomorphic stages simultaneously showed three different orientations of the same incident, all synchronized with one another. Thrusters flared, ships banked and dove and darted, their wings, useless out-atmosphere, veered back into a configuration designed to protect vulnerable fuselages. It made them seem evil. And all of it occurred within an eerie silence broken only by the chatter of mach-speak and the drone of Quroc's voiced-in deposition.

Quroc shivered. That—the silence—was the most unnerving thing about battles in void-space, and Veerwing Quadstar Harriers, specifically designed with elements meant to evoke fears common to many kind, seemed even more menacing and deadly when flying at you soundlessly. Harriers—closing, yet giving no warning of their presence—it was what was so unnerving about them even in-atmosphere. Their thrusters made no roar. Their flight was soundless. Only once weapons-fire began, did the sound of impact reverberate when contact was made with solid objects. But not in space. There was no sound, at all, in space. Only movement and light. And disintegration, of one form or another.

Celac had designed the presentation well. Quroc's computer generated version of the flight was displayed upon the center stage, while both other viewpoints—the one from Rajan's ship log and that from the Ghirran's BT scan—were flanked to either side of it around the chamber's arc perimeter. The chamber became vividly alive with darting forms of dull grey fighting ships while Rajan's lisping voice, amplified to overshadow any other sounds, including Quroc's deposition, described the incident as observers in the chamber watched it. But Rajan only described the battle from his perspective—his thoughts, decisions, actions. Yet, observers saw more. Observers gleaned an objective rarely available where all sides of a conflict can be comprehended simultaneously. And Quroc's perspective, launched from center-stage, couldn't help but draw one's sympathy. Out-numbered and alone, he was obviously vulnerable to the mach flight driving at him, darting in around him.

Only once Quroc broke and ran, diving into The Ring itself, then jumping to the planet, did the fight seem fairer. Still, psychologically, the chased—Quroc— unconsciously drew support. Rajan, as chaser, became the enemy to all who watched. One could feel it in the room. One could see it in the watchers' biofields.

It was the drive along Planet Iban's surface that brought strongest reaction, though. Watchers actually flinched and ducked as the war-birds vectored in, around, between each other and all the varied obstacles of city-scape—obstacles that seemed to jump at one. That was how it seemed in flight at-speed, and the watchers felt full brunt of it.

Now, the looming wall of FleetCom.... Even Quroc gripped his seat. His body had relived it all—every moment, every movement of the flight. He relived this, now—the looming wall and his decision to let the machon die. Even though he knew the ending, his clawtips still broke sheath.

Now, the tunnel. Then his move to give Rajan a chance. Their brake from speed—ships slowing, stopping—and the appearance of reporters from the NewsNet, Fleet M.P.'s...the Altan Drom.

It was over, then, all watchers spent and devastated from vicarious participation. Including Quroc.

CELAC HAD BEGUN THE DEMONSTRATION with short, pointed questions that were unmistakably choreographed to encourage Rajan to a natural spontaneity that displayed the saurischian's obvious mach-fever. That the Ghirran's descriptions of the flight matched exactly what was occurring on holomorphic reproduction, that all three holomorphic testimonials more or less agreed with one another, the only deviations being those occurring by perspective—this fact was impossible to avoid. Even the willowy Regellian prosecuting Legal's attention had been rapt.

To Quroc, the impact was incredible: To hear the mach elite's report of his flight—Rajan's thoughts, his analysis of Quroc, and his contingent strategies, all as over-audio to the displays surrounding—made Quroc realize that he was lucky to be alive. The Metan Rajan had played him every moment. Top flyer though he was, Quroc knew he was far out-classed. Rajan was a machon so much better-than, that Quroc wasn't sure the like had ever been seen or known. Metan Rajan was much more than mach elite. There could be no known name for what the Ghirran was, and Quroc felt a thrill rise up in him. He had flown against, flown with, the very best there was, and that was *Something.*

The Dgorian was the first required to speak. With effort, it emerged from encased, protective cover, its copkets easing out to peek around. "It is over?" it asked.

Though not exactly protocol, that comment was enough for Celac. She began her second formal call. "Defense dismisses the Metan Rajan and calls the Regulus Primus Alta Andromedi Omega Bjen Dvorkahn, u'd K'hor, Huur C'iri Rhegar, Mote'hb K'har, Klah d' K'hir'sh'an, Pharan az T'jeir."

Silence greeted the announcement. Celac looked around: Everyone was still and silent.

The Regellian Legal was the first to recover. "OBJECTION!" she screamed. She was totally dark blue. "You cannot call a regulus commander. It is completely beyond regulation for peer review!"

Bewildered, Quroc could only agree. Looking to Celac, wondering if she was utterly mad, he flicked both ears in alarmed question, the native kind-sign delivered as emphatic. Here was something of which she had told him nothing.

Celac stepped back to him and turned an ear down, warning him with her eyes. "I'm your Legal," she said, her lips clamped tight about her teeth. "This is better than the data from the Cyber-Sentries or any of the evidence I put together from all the other sources. This shows everything just the way it happened." Celac's eyes narrowed. "Now, you tame," she said. "…Trust me." And, turning back to face the Peers, she said: "There is no law nor precedence to substantiate Prosecution's objection to regulus as witness, Peer-Chair."

The Dgorian was very noticeably in shock. It neither stirred nor spoke for one full itan. In its stead, the Medagian engaged. "This is highly irregular," it squeaked.

"Irregularity does not preclude action under law— not by Omniversal Lexus, nor by Fleet Legis," Celac countered sharply.

The Dgorian dragged at the Medagian with a palp, then urged the other Peers to come around it. Together, the entire body of the panel conferred.

After some intense whispering and gesticulating, the Dgorian emerged, the others returning to their places. "It has been agreed," it said. "Let the witness come forth."

Once more, the Ben-Drom's formal name was read, and, with more than some trepidation, Quroc watched the giant Altan Drom enter, the heavily draped, gold-brown robing of the Drom's regulus status as ominous as the gilt badge that proclaimed the Bjen Dvorkahn to be exactly what he was: one of the most senior of the senior high commanders who ruled Fleet—one whose very presence commanded not just respect, but full submission; one whose awesome power, whose every word and sign and look in Fleet was Law.

Immediately and automatically, despite his own cumbersome robes, Quroc found himself downing, his head bowed away, his sight elsewhere. Silence descended on his hearing, and he became oblivious to everything around him except the now unseen presence of the regulus. He was unaware that the entire board had likewise dropped into similar attitudes of obeisance—that the only ones left standing were the Altan Drom himself, Leon Belamy, and a totally bewildered Celac, who looked around the hearing chamber in astonishment. Had Quroc in his haze of submissicity been aware, the only thing that would have surprised him was the fact that Belamy and Celac still had the audacity to stand. *This was regulus.*

"Keheirat! Cease this." The Altan's words broke against the silence with a crushing potency despite their being softly uttered, the native Alta Androm language mingling in odd contrast to the Formal Omniversal vernacular the Altan employed just after.

Multiple rustlings, and Quroc felt more that saw the others rise as he himself stood-to. "Regulus Primus Omega Bjen Dvorkahn," Celac said, speaking to the giant who stood midway down the entrance ramp. "Would you please take the witness stand?"

"Needs be I sworn in," he replied, looking toward the deputy clerk.

That official, however, shrunk back, mumbling, "I don't have the authority to swear you in, Sir."

Likewise, the members of the Peer-Review abstained, all of them shuffling, squirming, sighing or wheezing as they claimed that they didn't have the rank or right to so discharge.

"Oh, for the lives of Xenac," Celac swore, the first time in turns Quroc had heard the name of the ancient Verdajen goddess spoken aloud in public. Celac directed a stern gaze to the prosecutor, then spat derisively. "Is this your way of undermining the Defense?" she asked. "By some crippling farce of bureaucratic paradox and hierarchical paralysis?!"

The prosecutor looked away. The Regellian was hiding it, but she was snickering.

Celac surveyed the room, her eyes seeking some recourse, but there just wasn't one. "This isn't a court of law," she said finally. "You're right in that. This is a court of injustice—corrupt. A mockery."

Quroc felt a touch on him. It was a hominoid hand. He moved aside.

"I can swear him in," said Belamy, who had stepped up from behind.

"As can any here, were not all so craven," snarled the Drom. "Let us be done about it, then, Director."

Fleet Director Leon Belamy stepped up to where the deputy clerk should stand. The Drom stepped to the place-of-witness. "Do you swear that what you present before this board to be the truth?" Belamy intoned.

"By the honor of my house, the House of K'har, I so do swear," the Drom responded, his chisel teeth showing momentarily in vehemence.

Belamy bowed out, retreating to his chosen seat, and Celac, a look of triumph lavishing her features, stepped up, fanning her hands toward the Peers. "Now, if you would please, Omega Bjen Dvorkahn: Tell this 'prestigious' body what you so recently and generously shared with me."

The Drom specifically turned to face the Peer Review Board.   "Fleet   Officers-to-Review,"   he   said. "Two-point-three dectar past, I submitted evidence absolving the Megan Primus Quroc Xentauri ab Verdaje, who stands before you for your judgement, of any but the most technical of wrongdoing regarding the incident of my Syrene minor's theft and privation. Such evidence was submitted to Fleet Judiciary to be filed with the offices of prosecution, as well as those of the defense. Belatedly, I discovered that this evidence was, of convenience, lost."

Somewhere from his robes, the Bjen Dvorkahn pulled a small black globe. "Here, then, is the evidence to clear the Megan Quroc, brought forth of the memories of my Syrene minor which was stolen, then returned."

Quroc felt himself close to dropping. Darkness threatened to engulf him. After everything he'd done to save it, they had killed it for its memories. After everything, his family would be implicated anyway.

Desperately, Quroc fought the darkness that sought to drain his consciousness away. He fought it back, and stepped in front of Celac. "No," he said.

All sensorae within the room turned toward him, startled mein on every countenance and form. Including the Bjen Dvorkahn. Including the Regellian Prosecutor and the Peer Review Board.

"What are you doing!?" Celac hissed, trying to step around him.

Quroc stopped her, holding her behind him with a hand. And he warned her, flattening an ear, his mind awhirl and threatening still to plunge him into the darkness peculiar to him.

"What is your objection?" the Chair asked.

"This...this evidence," Quroc stammered, trying to keep himself conscious.

The Dgorian questioned him, again, but Quroc didn't hear. Frantically, he searched the Bjen Dvorkahn's mein— the Altan's body language, fields...his every expression.

Quroc rudely stared into the Drom as if trying to see the Altan's very soul.

"Archon?" the Dgorian warned. "I need your statement of objection."

Quroc shook his head. He couldn't think of how to say it. Anything he said would implicate his family. Ultimately, he just said, "No," again, his brain scraping at its bottom in a failure to raise some uncompromising rationale.

Slipping by him, Celac stepped around. "As defense council speaking for the accused, there is no objection, Peer Chair," she said.

"Archon?" The Dgorian had now risen.

Seething—scared of what would be divulged—Quroc nodded once abruptly to indicate he'd heard and would respond. A moment given, and his brain had found a way, though it meant addressing a regulus in a way no regulus could be addressed. One problem at a time, Quroc told himself, then spoke his answer. "I have no objection if the honorable Regulus Primus Omega Bjen Dvorkahn promises that what evidence he brings will not implicate another—*any* other."

There. He had locked the thing down. If the regulus refused, Quroc could stop the delivery of the evidence. If the regulus agreed, the evidence still could not be delivered. It was too damaging.

Quroc locked his sight on that of the Drom's. *You will NOT bring my family down*, he swore within himself. *No matter the consequences, you will NOT destroy the Q, Altan.*

The Drom's shield-eyes shifted, locking onto Quroc. The head reared slightly, then slipped sideways. "Agreed, Xentauri Q," the beast said, his emphasis upon the family symbol very pointed. And Quroc felt the words as if they had physically hit him.

"Begging your permission, Sir, you are, ah...out-of-order, Sir, Regulus Primus Omega Bjen Dvorkahn, the Dgorian minced. Then it turned to Celac. "...As were you to interrupt us earler, Legal Celac." All three of its eye pod copkets came out and strained forward toward Celac—strong censure to come from a neutral Dgorian.

Suddenly, it sat back and, with a glance toward the gold-and-white Xentauri peer, smacked its pods and said, "Nevertheless, you may proceed." One copket leveled on Quroc. "But, Defending Legal, I beg you to please constrain your client. Or he will have to be removed."

Celac slid a warning glance to Quroc, then said, "Thank you, Peer-Chair."

Walking toward, Celac lifted the data-sphere from the Altan's grasp. "Let it be entered, Defense Exhibit D, the following image deposition of the Syrene minor, identification number one-four-seven-xi-dash-eta-six, subtype not identified."

The Chair was licensing the admitting of that evidence, the Dgorian's voice hollow-sounding to Quroc's sensibilities. The darkness was so close, now. And a whispered voice—images of the minor.... It was too much. *"NO!"* Quroc screamed out. "He *promised*—"

"ARCHON XENTAURI QUROC, YOU WILL HONOR THE PROTOCOL OF THIS PROCEEDING." The Chair proclaimed this, shouting out at Quroc. But Quroc wasn't aware to hear it. He had collapsed.

∘   ∘   ∘

55

COMING TO, QUROC DISCOVERED HE'D BEEN MOVED to a holding cell, its confines square and small and beige, its light subdued. He'd been placed on a pallet. There was sign that a Medical had been and gone: A complex lifesign monitor clung high up on Quroc's arm, someone having rolled his robe back, then stripped back the underlying fabric of his skinsuit. The device's beaded lights blinked various rhythmic color sequences that Quroc supposed corresponded to his body processes. He plucked it off, then rose to pace.

He was angry; he was scared. He felt powerless, and was.

A long while later, Celac appeared. "What happened?" Quroc demanded.

"Nothing happened," said another.

Quroc felt humiliation spread to try to color him.

"Have you been taking your medication?"

"Yes, Father," Quroc said, finally looking to where his sire stood, his blacker-than-black body framed by the access.

"I'll send for the family physician," Quiloc said. "Perhaps an adjustment is needed."

The black, male Xentauri looked to the brown-striped female. "Celac, would you leave us?"

The queen dutifully removed herself, looking very grateful to do so, and Quiloc sat down on the empty pallet. "I won't ask you why you did what you did," he said. "I don't condemn you for it, either. The fault lies wholly with me."

HIs father's words made Quroc's insides wither. It was his fault, not his sire's. "If I'd listened," Quroc said. "If I'd let the minor…."

"Currur," Quiloc agreed. "But you didn't." The senior Q looked away. After awhile, he said, "Conscience is an interesting phenomenon, Quroc. So is an individual's perspective of what is right and necessary."

"I have brought dishonor to the Q," Quroc said.

"No, you haven't. The Ben-Drom did not expose anything except that you removed the minor from somewhere on Xentauri's Verdaje and were returning it to Fleet Director Belamy. Everything else, everything incriminating, he removed from the datasphere."

Relief flooded Quroc, and he sank, robes binding around him, to the floor of the small cell. Darkness threatened, once again, but, this time, with it came the keening—both Metaxi's and the minor's. Of its own volition, Quroc's body shuddered. Quroc cursed, fighting all of it—the sensations, the gathering darkness, the keening. He beat it back.

His father rose and came to stand by him. A hand grasped Quroc's shoulder, kneading. "Quroc, I don't know what will happen. The board is deliberating, now. But, whatever comes, you are my son and heir."

"It's time," Celac said, poking her face around the access's edge.

Guards entered. Quroc tried to rise...found that he was caught in his robing. The guards pulled him up, the robe swirling free its bind as they lifted him.

Quroc nodded his thanks, then followed Celac out of the holding cell, his father and the guards shadowing.

THE PEER REVIEW BOARD ENTERED to settle at the high bench of the hearing amphitheater, the gilt Fleet insignia on their brown robes boring into Quroc's brain. Their mein—even that of the Dgorian's non-face—was stern.

The Chair called the hearing back in session, then addressed him: "Megan Primus Xentauri Quroc su Verdan, Q Dyansty, First Family, ab Verdaje cum Nadejan, Kathon: Please stand forward."

Quroc did as told, his knees threatening to buckle again as his body flushed with heat.

"You have been cleared of any potential criminal complaint."

Quroc closed his eyes—relief.

"You have been cleared of the onus of Disgrace."

Quroc opened his eyes, elation mingling with incredulity. He looked around for his father, but failed to catch the elder's sight. He looked to Celac, but she ignored him, her eyes remaining locked upon the Peer-Chair, her face set and hard.

Quroc shrugged inside himself, then also returned his attention to the Dgorian. He found eye copkets watching him, waiting.

"...But it is the judgement of this body that you be declared persona non grata, and you are hereby given mandate to voluntarily resign your commission to this service."

The heady thrill he'd felt just moments before plunged to heavy. Stunned, Quroc could only stare at the Peer-Chair. And, now, when he wanted darkness, when he would have welcomed it, embraced it, it did not, would not, come.

"OBJECTION!" It was the Ben-Drom's bellow, the Altan bolting upright, his shout almost deafening Quroc. Even Celac recoiled. The board—everyone—flinched as one.

"Regulus?" the Medagian squeaked, the Dgorian having completely shelled itself.

"By the power vested in me by right of rank and office, what reason give you for this behest?!"

There was a buzzing among the available board members. The demand of a regulus was no small thing.

And the Ben-Drom was challenging their opinion, calling them to give full substantiation. If they didn't, and even if they did, he could call them before a review board of the regulus command...if he didn't discharge all of them himself right here and now...which was also his right.

Finally, the Xentauri archon stood, and it was obvious that, though respectful, she was not afraid. ...But then she was old enough not to be. And it was obvious that she knew the Ben-Drom. "Regulus," she said, speaking strictest Formal Omniversal. "We mandate this of Megan Quroc by reason that no command within Fleet will now offer this archon a posting, as is evidenced by this...." She held forth a datasphere. "...By this our poll of regulus." The Xentauri stopped to set the datasphere aside before continuing. "And, by the statutes, no officer within this Fleet may continue to serve without assignment, but must voluntarily resign."

The Xentauri commander's eyes met Quroc's. Those eyes were hard and soft—sensitive to his predicament, but decided in conviction. Quroc dropped his gaze away. He had not anticipated this particular turn of events. To him, it had always seemed to be an all or nothing proposition.

The Medagian spoke up, "During recess," it squeaked, "we did re-canvas all regulus presently seeking high archon. All, including you, Regulus Primus Omega Ben-Drom, declined offering assignment to this archon, either actually or by their silence." The Medagian paused.

"Forgive my liberty, Sir, but you did receive the query, did you not?"

The Drom grumbled, then slipped head to the affirmative. "Yes," he said.

A flash of shields; a low, vibrating growl. "Quroc ab Verdaje," the Ben-Drom said, spitting out the name.

Quroc looked up, straight into the now snarling mouth.

"Do you accept the judgement of this board and tender resignation, or do you accept such temporary command as I may offer until permanent command can be found?"

A shiver rode down Quroc's spine. Enmity was the standing condition between the Ben-Drom and the Q Dynasty, yet the Drom was offering to save him. For honor's sake, Quroc realized.

He sucked breath. But he didn't like Dromedans of any ilk and kind. He especially didn't like this one in particular, not from what he remembered of him when they had both served under his father's last command.

The Drom stood rigidly upright, openly challenging the Peer Review Board to voice objection to his offer. The board, in turn, was, as a body, squirming. It was painfully apparent that most were *not* pleased. But the Xentauri was. And so it seemed was the Dgorian.

Quroc turned and sighted his father. His father shook head, then dropped his eyes away. Quroc's insides knotted. His father was against this.

But Quroc wanted his career. He wanted his life—his chosen life.

"Take it. The Ben-Drom's offering a way." It was Celac who said that. "If you want your career, then never mind your father or anyone else," she said. "Make your own choices. I did, and I've never regretted going against Dynasty expectations of me."

Dilemma. All the 'but's, they kept rolling around like stinking scat inside his brain pan. If he accepted, Quroc knew he'd be spurned by every archon of his rank in Fleet, as well as every other officer. If he declined…. Well, it wouldn't matter, then. And he wanted his career.

"Megan Quroc?" It was Belamy.

Quroc looked toward the civilian Director of the Fleet he served.

"You do have a commission waiting for you in the Xentauri Fleet. Your father has already sanctioned it."

Arranged it, Quroc thought with disgust. It was his father's way with him, much as he had always fought against it. And in the Xentauri Fleet!

Quroc lowered his face. Then, just as suddenly, he raised it and sighted the Drom. Even if he was despised, he'd take his chance. He'd had to prove himself before— at the Academy, in the machon ranks, and, most recently, among the kathon candidates. That had been hard, and he knew this would be harder. But he had always had to prove himself, just because he was always seen as son-of-privilege. Well, damn them all.

"I will accept such posting as you offer, Regulus Primus Omega Bjen Dvorkahn," Quroc said. He said it stiffly, hating himself and the board for the necessity, hating the Drom for giving him the option, hating most the minor that had caused it all. "I will accept."

o   o   o

END PART I

Read the conclusion in *A Gathering of Rebels, Volume 2.*

If you enjoyed Part I, would you honor me with a review on Amazon.com?

To sign up to receive notification of new releases and special offers from D. L. Keur, Aeros, and E. J. Ruek, you can enter your email address on the website www.TheDeepening.com.

A Sneak Peek at *Seeming Eidolon* by Aeros.

SEEMING EIDOLON:

BOOK I: THE COMING

SPACE FICTION

BY AEROS

"Cut a blade of grass and the universe quakes."
--Unknown

Part I
Catalyst

"The Beginning was a Question …."

AEROS

1

EDGE SPACE, MU UNIVERSE

DEEP SPACE, MU UNIVERSE—THE VERGE OF THAT COSMIC BODY: Nothing exists there except the nebulae—massive, swirling mists of green and gold, lavender and pink, blue and charan ...every color known within the cosmos. They are thick mists—almost impenetrable—and somewhere in their depths the quarry waits. ...So does Edge.

CALCULATING THE ODDS, the hunter chose the gold—the one that held the most rare subtype—then wondered if his luck would hold as he guided his specialized cheliform transport into the shrouded eeriness of that giant nebula. Syrene emulsion nebulae were notorious for catching even the wary, then dooming them to endless wandering within their vastness. But this hunter had a formula. It worked. It always worked. Provided that the elders didn't notice.

But the elders hadn't noticed yet, and Hunter Vegas Devon had been penetrating the strange and lustrous foaming denseness that was Syrene space for over three ita now, three ita of successful and profitable hunting of Syrene minors and significants within this his favorite hunting territory. In that span, he'd not had much more than a couple of close calls with the much feared and deadly elders.

That's what Vegas liked about Mu habitats. For all their heavy distortions that decimated ship navigational systems and sensors, the Mu, though rich in quarry, were almost devoid of elders, and nebulae lacking those omnipotent Syrene meant less chance of being shattered to a billion bits of nothingness by their soundings.

The hunter's ship reached full penetration of the nebula, sensor readouts first faltering, then spiking wide in all directions, technology gone useless as was usual in the thickly cloying mist. In the habit of experience, Vegas switched to manual scan, his filigreed blue tendrils dancing on his touchboard con. He hoped to catch an audio, any variety of visual being nil.

Shuddering a little, the transport's panels suddenly went dim— just a little. That was it. That was what the hunter had been hoping for. And it was a strong one. He hoped it wasn't too strong.

His crescent-shaped ship shuddered again—an attack by Syrene harmonics— and the hunter seriously considered abandoning his effort. This one felt too strong. Must be an old significant. Or an elder.

Couldn't be an elder, though. Not so soon. Not in this nebula. …Unless his luck had quit him.

Static erupted across the ship console, and the concussive boom that followed was both tangible and audible to the hunter's senses. Out the old viewshield, the hunter caught the suggestion of something huge. He blanched. It passed.

But the biocom went out. So did the engines integrated with it. Not thinking, just reacting, the hunter went to backup, coming hard about on residual motion.

He cursed his luck.

Dropping tendrils to mechanical, he touched a brand new vector series into the old manual con, then hit the drives and hoped. That had been an elder. It had barely missed him. Somehow, someway, it had not sensed him. But Vegus doubted that such luck would stand him twice. He had to vacate. Now.

The drives caught, then flared. Vegus shaped them a Terminate Three, then them blow, the force momentarily flattening him to thin. Then he saw it. A minor came into view just dead ahead on his trajectory.

Reflex action, and Vegus sideslipped the big ship to avoid collision, hitting the compression stun just as another shudder racked his transport.

Greed made the hunter ignore the threat of elder, and, swinging the cheliform over on itself, he retraced his flightpath. He was, after all, Devon.

The mist, now turned to warping ribbons of thick and thin, snapped and splayed around him. The nebulae was nothing but a seething, boiling storm that swirled around his ship. But Vegus focused. He felt riches tickling his waning credit reservoir. It would only take him moments.

He had to have just that much luck. He was, after all, Devon.

Easing forward, he peered through, every sensor useless, his only tools strictly his own visuals. But there was nothing there. Not anywhere. And then there was. Then he spotted it …just barely.

It was a smallish minor that hung inert just dectametron off his port. He angle-glided toward it, hoping.

From what he could discern, its color was good. But Vegus juices slowed even as he brought the ship to forward null. It was very small— too small to have stood the force of the compression stun, too small for profit.

He saw it move. It lived. He must not have hit it square. So his luck was holding. Half holding. He'd wanted an old minor or a young significant.

Nervous now, the mist around him finally settling, the hunter scanned as best he could, listening for, feeling for, any sign of the elder's imminent return. There was stillness. There was silence. Only. The elder was still gone elsewhere. Temporarily, he was safe.

Doing quick calculations as he maneuvered the remotes, the hunter figured maybe fifty, sixty credits at auction—not good. Maybe a couple thousand though if he could get a fast and needy buyer on the underground. Much, much more if he could find that Drom that liked them young-entire and knew the value of this rarest subtype. No sense selling it to some Oronian for sport if he could find his favorite client. Make good profit that way. And he needed that. Didn't make enough in Fleet to feed his lifestyle. Even auction prices would, at least, pay for the trip and pod. So no sense leaving it to terminate. He hated wasting them for nothing.

Again an echoed booming, this time with no preliminary warning shudder and powerful enough to instantaneously churn the glowing foam into vortices and strings of molten. The cheliform chattered as it shook, and the mechanicals went out for one long moment that stopped the hunter's circulating blues until they re-engaged. And Vegus prayed, petitioning his mother's gods for mercy even as he thanked his own foresight for refitting the mechanicals. Antiquated or not, he was alive because of them. But he knew he wouldn't be for long if he didn't get out now. The elder was closing on him. By the sonics, it was aimed directly for him, and the hunter knew it wouldn't miss. One more sounding, and he'd be torn apart.

Fighting panic, yet careful that the inner field didn't touch the minor's tiny, transmutable mass, the hunter finished easing the containment pod around the stunned form. Tractoring it in, he secured the cargo hatch and hit both drives and generators, arcing out of the forbidding space just as he felt the elder's sound consolidate.

...And the elder smiled.

DEEP INSIDE THE NEBULA with his com gone dead, the hunter couldn't sense them—long, darkened cylinders that seemed, each, more an obliteration of light than objects of mass containing entities of intent. They did not show, not even on long-range scan as Vegus spun his short-term arc. What the hunter never knew was that those huge cylinders held his death were it not for the act of one much alike but older than his captured quarry. It, a Syrene who acted on the snarled orders of a lone Xentauri weapons specialist who had discovered the true content of ordinance he was commanded to deliver into the nebula, was all that saved the hunter from oblivion. Its act alone spared time enough for the hunter's ship to complete its journey through the arc and out of the emulsion nebula before the specialist's order was countermanded, the insubordinate and his Syrene helper taken into custody.

What the hunter did see when his com engaged as his ship came out of arc a scant few terametron beyond the nebula's perimeter transformed him to the blackened blue of fear that was the rarest color his kind turned: That which had been his favorite hunting territory had erupted with a weird red-orange glow that was unnatural to it. As he watched, his hunting territory seemed to crystallize, then begin to systematically eat itself from outside in, the silhouetted forms of High Fleet translights floating before that brilliant backdrop.

That the ships were translights, the hunter was sure; that they were High Fleet registered, he couldn't really tell. Were they High Fleet ships, they were masked and silent runners, no insignia apparent, no beacon resonating signature—an illegal thing, except in war. But High Fleet ships were the only vessels which the hunter knew that could withstand, for even moments, the magnitude of shattering emissions that were now beginning to emanate from the nebula. No evidence confirmed the hunter's suspicion on sensor, though. The only things that registered to the hunter's automated scans were the fact of ships and the total annihilation of the nebula, punctuated by the distortions the hunter knew were death soundings of the millions of natural Syrene that dwelled there. And those soundings began to shake the hunter's tiny ship, threatening to disintegrate it.

Panicked, the hunter struck emergency arc once more into the drives and generators, not caring that it would decimate his batteries and his fuel. He didn't care how much energy he wasted or where the arc would take him. He needed gone before the soundings shattered him or the translights saw him and made him null and void as well. What Vegus needed was in fact the obliterating effect that only the interspace Betweens gave to erase all trace of him. But the Betweens he couldn't reach. He carried no Syrene significant that could take him through. In desperation, the hunter chose to arc, knowing that he needed all his mother's luck (and his father's) to avoid detection by the elite fleet's optimum technology.

So the hunter prayed again as his generated arc warped the matrix into a vortex that would swallow him. He prayed that some fluke would stopped the translights' sensor arrays from spotting him, unlikely as that was. But the prayers were futile effort. Necessity, instead, protected Vegus, the necessity that was survival, for even translights couldn't bear the brunt of Syrene sounding for more than itat. And closed sensors were part of that necessity. So was shifting.

The fleet never saw the hunter. They never knew him there. Even before the hunter's arc had taken him beyond the quadrant, the translights had shifted the Betweens themselves, fleeing from the intensity of destructive harmonics their seeding of the nebula had wrought.

IT IS SAID BY SOME THAT THE VOID between the galaxies is silent—that you cannot hear the screaming of the dying. Unheard by them who cannot hear, unfelt by them who cannot feel, the screams send ripples through the void. The sound is real—it exists and can be measured. Even Syrene Hunter Vegus Devon's antiquated ship scanners recorded them before he arced: the last emissions of Syrene Emulsion Nebulae Number One-Seven-Four-Four-

Zero, Mu Universe.

Vegus' scanners intercepted and recorded something else before the arc completed, that arc's warping vortex sweeping up every vestige of a broad-band subspace message secretly transmitted from the annihilating fleet. The arc compressed that message inside itself to pour it into the unknowing hunter's com. And the message was a warning.

END EXCERPT

To sign up to receive notification of new releases and special offers from D. L. Keur, Aeros, and E. J. Ruek, you can enter your email address on the website www.TheDeepening.com.

AEROS